MW00913194

Jane looked up at Mr. Fotheringay and thought that he did not look like a fool or a poseur or a mere scribbler, or any of those things she had been so sure he was. He was overpoweringly handsome and commanding, and there was nothing she wanted more in the world than to have him kiss her.

She looked down st her feet. Suddenly all the fight went out of her and she thought that she loved this man since his first twinkling look at her.

"Please say yes," he whispered.

They looked at each other, besotted. And then Jane felt the strength of the man she loved pressing urgently against her and felt herself softening against him as though she were water embracing rock. She lifted her face to his and they kissed in a long, passionate embrace.

"You know," Jane said, reaching up and laying a hand on his cheek, "I think I am meant to be happy."

THE BEST OF REGENCY ROMANCES

AN IMPROPER COMPANION   (2691, $3.95)
by Karla Hocker
At the closing of Miss Venable's Seminary for Young
Ladies school, mistress Kate Elliott welcomed the invitation to be Liza Ashcroft's chaperone for the Season at
Bath. Little did she know that Miss Ashcroft's father, the
handsome widower Damien Ashcroft would also enter her
life. And not as a passive bystander or dutiful dad.

WAGER ON LOVE   (2693, $2.95)
by Prudence Martin
Only a rogue like Nicholas Ruxart would choose a bride on
the basis of a careless wager. And only a rakehell like Nicholas would then fall in love with his betrothed's grey-eyed
sister! The cynical viscount had always thought one blushing miss would suit as well as another, but the unattainable
Jane Sommers soon proved him wrong.

LOVE AND FOLLY   (2715, $3.95)
by Sheila Simonson
To the dismay of her more sensible twin Margaret, Lady
Jean proceeded to fall hopelessly in love with the silver-
tongued, seditious poet, Owen Davies—and catapult her
entire family into social ruin . . . Margaret was used to
gentlemen falling in love with vivacious Jean rather than
with her—even the handsome Johnny Dyott whom she se-
cretly adored. And when Jean's foolishness led her into the
arms of the notorious Owen Davies, Margaret knew she
could count on Dyott to avert scandal. What she didn't
know, however was that her sweet sensibility was exerting a
charm all its own.

*Available wherever paperbacks are sold, or order direct from the
Publisher. Send cover price plus 50¢ per copy for mailing and
handling to Zebra Books, Dept. 2879, 475 Park Avenue South,
New York, N.Y. 10016. Residents of New York, New Jersey and
Pennsylvania must include sales tax. DO NOT SEND CASH.*

My Lady's Deception

LINDA WALKER

ZEBRA BOOKS
KENSINGTON PUBLISHING CORP.

To Ralph Aldus Robinson and
Nadine Yates LaMar Robinson
with love and gratitude

ZEBRA BOOKS

are published by

Kensington Publishing Corp.
475 Park Avenue South
New York, NY 10016

Copyright © 1990 by Linda Walker

All rights reserved. No part of this book may be reproduced in any form or by any means without the prior written consent of the Publisher, excepting brief quotes used in reviews.

First printing: January, 1990

Printed in the United States of America

Chapter One

"Must we admit him?" the young woman asked.

"We could pretend not to be here," said the young man, one year her junior.

"Oh, yes!" cried the girl, "Let's hide. We could take food up to the attics! They would never find us, we could hide for months and months. Just like Lady Glorianna in *The Escape from Deathhall Castle,* when the evil duke . . ."

Lady Jane Marlingforthe managed a smile for her young sister, but it faded from her face as she looked again through the window at the approaching carriage.

Her brother, Sir Edgar, pulled at the faded damask that draped the window. "Look at this," he said in disgust, lifting the cloth toward his sister, "it's rotting and threadbare, it stinks of must and dirt." He shook it angrily and a small cloud of dust billowed out. "What a midden this house is. There's nothing that is not about to rot, collapse, or disintegrate."

He looked about him at the great hall of Thrate House, the seat of the Marlingforthe family since

Queen Elizabeth had bestowed the land upon the first earl. "It's a hovel—the chimneys smoke, the window panes are so small the rooms require candles at midday, the halls are draughty. I can't walk through a single doorway without cracking my head . . ."

Jane looked with sympathy upon his bluster. She knew that for all that he might decry its condition, he loved their home with all his heart. The man arriving in the carriage was here to tell them it was no longer theirs and that they must leave.

As the three continued to watch the coach, now drawn up before the front entrance, one of the coachmen jumped down to lower the steps and open the door. They watched their father's solicitor, Mr. Hasbrook, lean forward and hand out his satchel before emerging from the carriage.

It was only then that Sir Edgar Marlingforthe said, "I suppose I should go down and play footman."

He took a long look around the hall, then turned, and left the room.

Mr. Hasbrook looked at the drawn faces across the wide table and wished himself back in his comfortable home in London. This was not a task he welcomed, but it had to be got through, and then he would retire to his inn and the fine bottle of port he had had the foresight to bring with him. He adjusted his spectacles and looked over them at the young people facing him.

Lady Jane Marlingforthe had grown even more beautiful. She had always been so, even as a nine-year-old romping with her brother near the cliffs of Cornwall, from which Thrate House overlooked the

6

Atlantic in lordly splendor. He doubted that she had ever had an awkward phase. She had the kind of beauty he most admired. It was so restful. Demure. Her long black hair was worn severely back in a bun, and the line of it on her cheek made a frame for the most remarkable blue eyes. Or were they green? Or violet? Odd, how they seemed to change. And those lashes!

He cleared his throat and shuffled the papers. Sir Edgar, her younger brother, was dark, but with russet tones to his hair, and his eyes were a dark hazel. He was furious beneath his quiet demeanor, and it was that taut rage which Mr. Hasbrook wished to avoid.

The young chick, Livia, was staring dreamily out the window at the brilliance of the fiery sunset.

In the corner sat the governess, Pridwell. A non-entity.

"I am afraid you know as well as I the sorry business that brings me here today."

Silence greeted him. Now Lady Jane as well was staring out the window. Only young Ned attended him, and he glowered at him from under lowered brows. Mr. Hasbrook sighed.

"Your father tried unceasingly to hold on to Thrate House. It drained his energies and taxed his health. Whatever you do, you must never be tempted to blame him for what has now come to pass."

"I can assure you that we do not blame our father," Ned said icily.

Jane glanced at him, wishing he could feel less pain, but knowing there was nothing she could do to comfort him.

"It was the war. You were victims of it as much as if you had been wounded in battle." Mr. Hasbrook liked

7

that idea. He thought of elaborating upon it, but the look in Sir Edgar's eyes stopped him. "When the mines flooded, he tried to recoup his fortune by investing in woolen mills in the north. He could not have known they would be practically valueless when there was no more need for uniforms. But it was the collapse of the Darlington and Grenville Bank which undid him. These investments, wise during the war, bankrupted him when it was over.

"Perhaps if your father had lived, he might have been able to regain his losses, but he was not given that chance. For two years now, since his death in the summer of 1817, we have had Thrate House and its contents on the market.

"You know that I come today because there has been a buyer. I have agreed to the purchase as your trustee, Sir Edgar," he said, nodding to a remote and blank-looking Ned, "since of course you are still a year from your majority.

"A Mr. Francis Coggelshall of London has bought the property, and I am afraid that I must tell you that he wishes you to vacate Thrate House at once."

Lady Jane's eyes flew to his, then she looked down at her hands. Ned's face was immobile except for the line of his jaw which grew suddenly taut. The young girl was staring up at the ceiling, slumped in her chair, seemingly inattentive. The governess knitted in the corner.

"You are not completely destitute, as you know. You still own the three tin mines here in Cornwall," he nodded to Ned. "And your father was able to settle £500 on you, which he arranged to be held in trust by me until you reach the age of twenty-five. In ad-

8

dition, Lady Jane has her grandmother's inheritance of £1000 and Lady Livia £250, most of the principal of which has not been touched. Miss Pridwell has her salary of £35 per annum, which will continue until her death as arranged.

"Have you any questions?" he asked, finally unnerved by the lack of response.

"What of the contents of the house?" the governess asked from her corner. "I recall that when they were inventoried in 1817, the contents of the attic and the bookroom were not included."

Mr. Hasbrook revised his opinion of Miss Pridwell. "You are correct, ma'am, those possessions were never inventoried. However, an agent of Mr. Coggelshall will be arriving at the end of the week to complete the task, and to compare the present list against the original one."

"Then we shall have to speedily remove the contents of the attic and bookroom and put them into storage, won't we?" said Lady Jane.

Mr. Hasbrook gaped at her. Had she said that? He studied her serene face and folded hands.

"As your solicitor, of course, I cannot recommend that you . . ."

"We understand, Mr. Hasbrook, please don't trouble yourself. Personal effects . . . ?" Miss Pridwell continued.

"Clothes, the contents of dressing tables . . ."

"Jewels?"

"Are there any jewels left?" Mr. Hasbrook asked in surprise.

"Only the garnets and pearls," Miss Pridwell replied.

"Well, I think you could keep them. I shall tell you to

take what you need in the way of bedding, pots, dishes, to set up household, but of course no furniture, and none, I'm afraid, of the Marlingforthe Oriental collection."

Ned looked over at the mantle were a Sung vase his grandfather had brought back from his travels had graced the room since he was a boy. He shrugged. He would gladly smash the vase in the grate if it would enable him to keep Thrate House.

"I don't understand," said Livvy, speaking suddenly, "where are we going to live?"

"Essex," Jane said thoughtfully, staring at a map spread out before her on the round table before the fire in the great hall.

It was night. Mr. Hasbrook had gone, and the four of them had prepared and desultorily eaten a meal and were now seated as near to the hearth as they could while the wind from the Atlantic battered at their house, seeping in through closed and draped windows, down the chimneys, along the floor, under doors which no longer hung straight.

"Why Essex?" asked Ned, standing next to her, tugging the map over to see it better.

"Because it is as far from Cornwall as we can get," she said, pulling it back.

"Well, if that's what you want, why not Scotland? Greenland?"

"And freeze to death, never to be seen again, our frozen remains found on peaks of cruel mountains . . ." said Livvy from the sofa where, curled up under three blankets she had brought down from her bed, she was reading one of her inevitable gothic novels.

"Essex doesn't make sense," said Ned, pulling the map back. "We should go to London. God knows, Jenny, you and Livvy have seen little enough of the world, stuck in this godforsaken part of the country. You deserve to go to London."

Jane snorted quite undemurely. "When you stayed in London those two months last year after you came down from Cambridge, could you afford to gamble at Brooks? Or attend the theater? Or purchase horses at Tattersalls? It takes money to live in London. But if we move to a part of England less dear, we would be able to live comfortably."

"Who wants to live comfortably?" Ned said scornfully.

"I'm talking about shelter, food, clothing. Have you found a way to do without those?"

"Children!" Miss Pridwell said warningly.

They subsided. Jane continued to study the map. She glanced up at Ned and found his eyes on the Marlingforthe shield and banners over the mantel. She made a mental note to have them put away with the books and contents of the attic and anything else they could steal from themselves to store until more secure times.

Jane tried to understand what Ned was feeling. She minded being poor. She minded having lived alone with Livvy and Priddy through the years she should have been having her Seasons in London, meeting a man to share her life and marrying. But she did not at all mind losing Thrate House. She hated it. Standing on a remote spit of land in a remote county facing the implacable Atlantic, it had always seemed an exile to

11

her, the remotest outpost of Britain, hanging onto it only by the tenacious grasp of its claws on the cliffs.

She could not wait to leave it behind, to leave her waiting behind, and to move out and meet a new life, no matter what its risks or dangers.

"I for one will be glad to be quit of this place."

Ned looked at her with shock.

"Oh, Jenny, how can you say that," wailed Livvy, "to be homeless, bereft, tossed on the stormy seas of life. But then," she said, brightening, "it could turn out that there we are in an inn on our way to new lives, and we find, hidden in a casket under a floorboard, a cache of jewels, ancient jewels, left there by a lady making her escape . . ."

"Yes, Livvy. I suggest we contact an agent in Harwich or some other town on the sea, and ask that inquiries be begun for a small house."

"Harwich!" Ned exclaimed in disgust. He flung himself onto the sofa with Livvy, reaching for her novel and guffawing as he read the title. "What is *The Woes of Lady Alianora* about? Ancient jewels under floorboards?"

"Yes! How did you know! And the heroine, Alianora—isn't that the most beautiful name—has alabaster skin. What is alabaster skin? Do you think I have it?"

She raised her earnest gaze to Jane who smiled. "Alabaster is very white, like marble. And no, you don't have alabaster skin. You have the skin of a very healthy girl."

"But don't you think alabaster skin would be better than mine? Perhaps I should stay out of the sun."

"You need more sun, Puss," Ned said, reaching over

to run his fingers over her hair. "You are pale from being indoors so much. I can't blame you with weather like this." He paused and they listened to the wind roar around the house, a wind which had begun in the ocean and blown unimpeded until it reached Thrate, and blew with such fury that it seemed the stones would be blown from the earth.

Livvy smiled complacently. "Then it *is* like alabaster."

"But Jenny," Ned said, "what would we do in Harwich? While away our lives until we die from boredom? We should take the money we have, and live in London and have a good time."

"You know that would be shortsighted, Ned."

"But is it any worse than spending our lives moldering away in some tiny cottage somewhere in the swamps of Essex?"

"I don't think there are swamps in Essex. But listen, you haven't let me finish. I have a plan!"

"A plan." Ned rolled his eyes.

"A plan!" Livvy clapped, delighted, ceasing her careful scrutiny of her arms and running to Jane and hugging her. "Oh, a plan. How I love plans! Yes, oh, I shall become sick, I know, an invalid, pallid, a delicate beauty. A great, handsome doctor will come . . ."

"I plan to marry a very wealthy man and support you all," Jane said.

"I prefer Livvy's plan."

"It *is* a good one, isn't it?" Livvy said, excited.

"It's the only way I can think of to establish ourselves, my marrying a wealthy man."

"Jenny, I have long since learned that those looks of yours disguise the most disagreeably managing woman ever born. But I will not accept fantastic schemes from you. Those are Livvy's department."

"But Ned, Jenny could marry an earl or a duke, with a palace!"

Miss Pridwell broke in. "This has been a long and trying day. I think the hour has come to retire to bed. There is much to do in the next week, packing up things to store and to take with us. And we must be ready early if we are to ride with the Alvenleighs to services."

"Oh stuff the Alvenleighs!"

"Edgar!"

"Young man!"

"Neddy, oh yes, they are stuffed. They're like those dead animals in Papa's study." Livvy laughed. They all had to smile, for the Alvenleighs had patronized them in the haughtiest way throughout their years of penury. Every ride to church or any other favor they bestowed upon the Marlingforthes was accompanied by advice and criticism which Jane and Livia, their chief recipients, had to endure in silence, and worse, with the appearance of gratitude.

"Oh, Priddy, do let us stay up a bit longer. We have hardly had time to discuss what we're about. An hour?"

Sophia Pridwell spoke little and seemed to those who knew her only slightly to be a dessicated shell of a woman, so thin, plain, and retiring she looked. Probably only the Marlingforthe children knew her humor and good sense, and understood the love which had supported them since the death of their mother from childbed fever when Livvy was two. She was devoted to them: they were her family, her comfort. She indulged them as much as she could in line with the strict deportment she required of them.

14

Of them all, however, she especially could not deny Jane, her darling girl. She had watched her beautiful charge grow into womanhood with no money, no lovely gowns, no dances at the assemblies in Camborne, no parents to put her forward, living a life little changed from that which she had led before she left the schoolroom. Livvy, too, suffered from the isolation, and sought refuge in her world of books and dreams.

Miss Pridwell sighed and settled herself back in her rocking chair.

Jane smiled gratefully. "We have some assets, as Mr. Hasbrook noted," Jane said, standing before the fire, her hands clasped before her, looking across at a portrait of her grandmother. "We have enough to establish ourselves creditably, for me to appear well-dowered and wealthy. We would need a place where no one who knows of our reversal of fortune would be, of course.

"One of us must marry someone of wealth to support the rest of us. That is the only long-range solution that makes sense to me. It can't be Ned, for he would have to have wealth enough to support a family, or some occupation, such as the church, the law, or perhaps business in the City." She saw Ned's look of dismay, and added drily, "I thought not.

"It can't be Livvy, for she is too young. No," she said, holding up a hand to stop what she knew would be a spate of highly colored attempts to justify a twelve-year-old's marrying to save her family's fortunes, "you are too young.

"So it shall have to be I."

"Why do you think you will find it so easy to marry?"

"Because I am beautiful."

15

"Oh, right. I forgot. That takes care of everything." Ned leaned back in elaborate nonchalance.

Jane shrugged. Even removed from society as she had been, she knew that there was something special about her appearance which affected everyone she met. It was not always to her advantage, for indeed although some might treat her with a special indulgence, like Priddy, others were as likely to treat her with envy or the censure some found it necessary to direct at what they assumed was an accompanying vanity. Her beauty was simply a fact to her, and she knew it to be a valuable commodity in seeking a husband. Since her heart had never been touched, her beauty was not a source of gratitude or pleasure to her.

Ned studied her, thinking how modest she looked. Who would ever guess that the delicate, composed woman standing serenely before the fire was evolving the most harebrained scheme he had ever heard of? Given her bossy and managerial ways, she would run them all ragged.

"We shall go to some place where we are not known and pose as persons of wealth, which a hired carriage, new clothes from London, and a well-chosen house will allow us to do. Priddy shall act as my mother who has come to the sea for her health. We shall say we came from Yorkshire or Northumberland."

"What about me and Livvy in this plan of yours?" Ned asked, fascinated in spite of himself. "And what about servants to run this elegant household?"

"Ah, you are bright, Ned. You have answered your own question."

"What do you mean?"

"Jenny, I know. I understand. Ned, Jenny wants us

to be her servants, don't you?"

"Precisely. Livvy, you are a great deal smarter than your brother!"

"Well, children, it is definitely time for bed," said Miss Pridwell, rising, not bothering to respond to this freak of Jane's.

"No, Priddy, you are not to leave, you must sit down and listen." Jane went to the rocking chair and held it while her governess sat back down.

"You must admit that I am the only marriageable one among us. My marrying a man of substance will further Ned's chances of marrying. We would not be able to afford servants: we shall act as our own. We have already done so for all intents and purposes, since Mrs. Parrish can so seldom be relied on, and since Finch left," she added bitterly, remembering the economies forced on them.

"This is the stupidest start you have made yet. I—be your servant! That would help me a long way toward marrying!"

"Yes it would, Ned. Consider it. How else can we hope to rise unless I marry, and how can I marry unless we appear to be wealthy, and how can we appear to be wealthy unless you play servants, and we all actually run the house without them?"

"And after you marry, do I remain your servant?"

"You goosecap, what do you think?"

Ned was sullen. It was not just the outlandishness of the plan which irritated him, but his own small and unheroic part to play in it. "I suppose you plan a wedding-night disclosure, and I can be magically transformed from a butler to your brother again."

"I was thinking footman. You are too young to be a

butler. Coachman, groom, gardener . . ."

"Anything else?" he asked sarcastically.

"I shall be the scullery maid. I shall never see the light of day except for one hour on Sundays, once a month. I shall peel onions and carrots and potatoes until my hands bleed. I shall grow pale from lack of sunshine . . . alabaster!"

"Maid, Livvy. You shall be my dresser, too."

"I shall bob curtseys."

"Of course, and call me and Priddy 'Ma'am' and back out of the room."

"Yes, I shall never turn my back on you, or I shall be impaled on a sword."

"Children, I am going to bed. This is enough fustian for one night, and I am quite worn out."

"Priddy," Jane came over and took her hand. "Don't leave. Don't reject this plan out of hand. Think it over. What is wrong with it?"

"We would be lying to all whom we should meet. I am not your mother, and I could never presume to be. I would not engage in such a deceit, nor could I allow your sister and brother or you to engage in it either. We should never fool anyone, for we haven't the money to sustain an elegant life. And there is no guarantee even if all that were not true that you would be able first to fool a gentleman into marrying you, and then keep him after he had learned of your dishonesty."

It was a categorical condemnation of her plan, to put it mildly, Jane thought. A silence grew up about them, interrupted only by the angry rocking of Miss Pridwell's chair, the howl of the wind, and the crackling and sputtering of the fire.

"Well, what do you suggest for our future, then,

Priddy? That we hire some horrible cottage here in St. Agnes which will be even colder and damper and darker than this, that we all wear linsey-woolsey to economize and knit shawls and mufflers to sell to strangers, and keep chickens to sell their eggs? And that we do this for the rest of our lives?"

"Lady Jane . . ."

Jane grew passionate. "I have seen nothing of the world. I have lived in this desolate moor all my life. I have been to Falmouth once, when I was seven. I have never been to London, and will probably never see London in my life. I have not had a new dress for five years. Livvy has never had a new dress. She has nothing but her books, and we will have to steal them from Mr. Coggelshall or she shan't even have those. I realize that this is a plan with risks and based on deceit, but the world if full of fainthearted people who roll over and die when adversity befalls them. I am not going to do that, and I am not going to allow Ned or Livvy to do so either."

"Miss! Mind how you speak to me!"

"Oh, Priddy, please forgive me. But please listen, it isn't so eccentric a plan. We are Marlingforthes! My father and his father back for centuries have been lords of the realm. It isn't that we are going to put ourselves above our station, but only that we are going to appear to have money which, unfortunately, is more important than titles for securing comfort in life.

"Perhaps we might spend three or four hundred pounds on this pretense," she continued. "For the hire of a house, a carriage, the purchase of clothes. Please say we could give it a try for a year, and if nothing comes of it, we shall still have enough to live on. Ned

19

could find employment, I could go out as a governess, you could live with Livvy somewhere near us."

Jane saw tears spring to Miss Pridwell's eyes. She knew that that would be more than Priddy could bear. She felt guilty playing on Priddy's pride and love for her, but knew that desperate measures were called for.

Miss Pridwell was defeated. She could never allow her darling girl to act as a menial in someone else's home. Where she herself had had the good fortune to be loved and valued, such was not the case for most women forced to work in the homes of others. She thought, *why not?* One year. Her Jenny deserved one year.

Jane saw the expression on that dearly loved face change from one of pain and disapproval to softness and hope. Finally she smiled. "Jenny, I will approve, but I am warning you, that I must be in charge of how we go on. If I am to play your mother, then you shall obey me as a mother."

Jane clapped her hands, delighted, and ran over to hug her governess. She glanced up at Ned who suddenly lifted his gaze from the flames and looked at her with bright eyes and the beginning of a smile. Livvy was lost in some world which required of her that she have a very long neck and hold her head with stiff, queenly grace.

Long after everyone else had gone to bed, Jane left her room, wrapped in her thickest cloak, let herself out the door in the morning room, and made her way along a path through the front garden to the cliffs above the sea.

"Jenny?"

She turned. Ned was standing behind her, silhouetted against a full moon and the dark mansion.

He came toward her and they clasped hands and remained silent, standing with their faces turned toward the sea and the wind.

Chapter Two

Charles Ralph Henry de la Marre, Earl of Leith, flung down his quill and ground his teeth.

The knock at the door sounded again. He counted to ten, pushed the papers he had been working on under the ledger he should have been attending to, and called, "Enter!"

His butler, Follett, stood in the hall, knowing full well what that impatient bellow meant. His silence required Lord Charles to call again, "Come in, come in, Follett."

Follett took a hesitant step forward, slowly turned the handle, pushed the broad door open and waited, not daring to enter, making an equivocal noise in his throat.

Leith wanted to throttle him. Summoning patience, he merely said, "Is it about the bridge, Follett? Come in. Was Albertson able to arrange for the work to begin?"

"No, sir. There is a gentleman to see you."

"What gentleman, Follett?" asked Lord Charles, a

veritable model of good breeding.

"His card, sir," and Follett stepped further into the room holding before him the salver on which lay a card and a letter. Lord Charles lifted the card and read, "Symonds. Isn't he the solicitor for my uncle?"

"I believe so, sir."

"What can be the matter now?"

"And the letter, milord."

Lord Charles took the heavy letter and noted the familiar hand of his all-but-announced betrothed, Susan Avery. He turned his back on Follett, tore the seal, and began to read. Susan hadn't spared expense, since she was writing under his frank, and had filled three pages with, as far as he could see from his impatient perusal, nothing but gossip from London and complaints that he had been at Windmere for entirely too long.

Follett, watching him, could see that the earl was in one of his moods; he sighed. The earl was in every way a model master: considerate, attentive, and diligent in carrying out the responsibilities of his considerable obligations. But his heart was not in it, and never had been.

He was a soldier and a diplomat. Follett suspected—in fact he had once deigned to share this opinion with Mrs. Trammell, the housekeeper—that Lord Charles would never be happy with such a tame life as Windmere required of him. It was a shame, he thought, watching his master, that such a splendid physique, such handsome looks, and so much intelligence should be put to the service of something their possessor so detested. Annoyance was clear in every lineament of the earl's body.

23

Had he always found Susan so boring? Perhaps, Lord Charles thought, he had been too long absent from her inviting smiles and promising touches. He threw the letter down, half-unread, thrust his chair back, and strode toward the door.

"And, oh, about Wilson, did you not wish to be reminded that he would be here today to see to the draining of the marsh?"

"Where did you put Symonds, Follett?"

"In the green room, if it pleases you, and if I might remind you, your mother, the Countess, wished expressly for you to meet with the vicar this afternoon at three, about the subscription for the repairs to the poorhouse roof in Kirkbury."

Lord Charles stood with his hand on the doorjamb, forcing his thoughts back from the exchange between Lord Castlereagh and Talleyrand which he had been trying to reconstruct from his notes, and brought himself back to the present.

"And, milord, you remember that Lord Randolph will be dining with you tonight to discuss the magistracy . . ."

With a grim set to his mouth, Lord Charles marched down the hall to do battle with responsibility, routine, and boredom.

Late that night, over a bottle of port after his guest had retired, the daily accounts entered in and gone over with Albertson, his bailiff, and his mother given an appointment for the morrow, Lord Charles knew that something had to be done or he would soon start shooting one by one, all guests, bailiffs, and mothers who dared to cross his path.

The thought made him happy, and he leaned back and put his feet up on the Chinese table which his grandfather had not brought back from his travels to have a grandson put his feet on. He leaned back against the damask-covered chair and stared up at the elaborate plaster work on the ceiling of the ornate blue room where he sat before a fading fire.

Immediately his thoughts travelled back to Vienna, to the Congress. How he missed those days! He shook himself at the unworthy thought. He knew better than to repine over what was past and done. But in spite of good intentions, his thoughts roamed back to the intrigue and tension, the excitement and gaiety of that time in Vienna, when he had been young and thought that the whole of his life would hold the same heights of excitement.

After coming down from Oxford, Lord Charles had gone immediately into the army to fight in Spain. His parents were appalled, but nothing would dissuade him. After that he had caught the notice of the Duke of Wellington, then Wellesley, and given the opportunity to serve at Waterloo. He was thirty now, and now there was nothing but Windmere.

He had never understood exactly what it was to run an estate such as Windmere, or the affairs of a family as wealthy and notable as the de la Marres. His family's fortunes were centered in Kent, but their interests ran from local farms and villages to investments in mills in the north, mines in the north and Cornwall, plantations in the West Indies, shares in the East India Company, and homes in Scotland, London, Paris, even a small villa in Italy—every one a burden.

His heart lay in the world of diplomacy he had tasted in Vienna while on Wellington's staff. His taste for excitement was satisfied, as he knew, in travel and the knowledge of the world that travelling imparted.

Well, that was behind him now. Now all he was trying to do was write his memoirs of the war and its diplomatic consequences.

He downed the port, put his glass on the table, and walked to the fire which refused to flame despite vigorous stirring. He strode to the windows and then made a useless circuit of the room. His tall, well-muscled torso seemed out of place even in so emphatically masculine a room, and his air of suppressed energy and vitality was better fitted to fields of hunting or battle.

In truth he was blue-deviled. He found the interruptions to his writing almost unbearable, and knew that he had been just passably civil today. He had to do something, or he would not be able to tolerate the frustration of not being able to complete the memoirs while the events were still fresh in his mind, and while his views on the changing balance of power in Europe so urgently demanded to be made known.

Perhaps he should give them up. He slammed his fist down on the mantel.

"No!" Again he paced the room.

How odd it was. Here he was stuck at Windmere with so many responsibilities that he hadn't even the time to do a little scribbling. Above him, weary no doubt from a late trip back from London, was his younger brother, Stephen, who was as fascinated by the running of Windmere as Lord Charles was ennervated. He made a face at the thought of such mismanagement, that he whose duty it was to run it hated the running of it, and Stephen, who enjoyed the challenges it posed, was kept by the accident of birth from doing so.

Leith threw himself back into the chair and stared into the embers. Suddenly he sat up straight, pushed the oriental table from him, and threw his body out the room and up the tall staircase to his brother's room to waken him from his sleep with a startling proposition.

Three weeks later Lord Charles, traveling in a carriage which bore no trace of the Leith arms, riding only with Cheever, his former batman from the wars now his jack-of-all-trades—groom, coachman and valet—left the environs of London and headed due east to the edge of England.

Windmere was behind him, left in Stephen's capable hands. Broad outlines of policy had been established for his agents to carry out in his absence, and everyone had been sworn to a sober if puzzling vow of secrecy. Almost as an afterthought, and yet what seemed the most satisfying act of all, Lord Charles had broken with Susan Avery. A trip to London and two days of the most bitter attacks had freed him from a woman he now knew he had never loved, and moreover he had learned while there, one who had been borrowing heavily against the possibility of her marriage to the wealthy Earl of Leith. This last had dispelled whatever compunctions he may have had. He had paid her bills, endured her spite, and disappeared.

Night was beginning to fall. He had decided to push on as far as possible since the moon was full and he was in haste to complete the journey. It was well after nine when he felt the carriage turn off the road.

He stepped out into the uncobbled, rutted yard of an inn whose air of neglect and antiquity suited his purposes admirably. There would be no one who would recognize him here. He walked to the inn disregarding the muck underneath, pulled open the door, and dragging his greatcoat from his shoulders, thrust it at the innkeeper, requesting a private parlor and bedchamber. The host was astonished by such an unlikely guest, for in spite of the rough buckskins which Lord Charles had affected as his disguise, every inch of him proclaimed wealth and rank.

"I . . . I'm sorry, sir, but we have only the one parlor and it is bespoken."

"Then unbespeak it. I wish a private parlor."

"But—"

Leith lifted his eyebrows. He was seldom challenged.

The innkeeper faced the intimidating stare from the intimidating height and said, "You see, sir, there's a miss and her mother, well the truth be they are regular watering pots, crying into their tea . . ."

Two weeping women presented a serious obstacle, indeed. But Lord Charles was unused either to partaking of his meal in his bedchamber or of deferring to anyone—weeping women or apologetic innkeepers —so he repeated, "If you would show me to the parlor."

"But, sir, I couldn't."

"But you will."

"Yes, of course." Slipping the coin into the pocket of his apron, the innkeeper nodded toward Lord Charles to follow him.

Leith swept through the open door and turned to close it in the face of the innkeeper. Then he turned sharply and said in his iciest accents to two startled women, "You are occupying the private parlor which has been reserved for myself. Allow me to assist you abovestairs."

The two women stared with all the shock that people who have thought themselves entirely private evince when suddenly broken in upon. They rose from the table; in this case, however, their rising did not alter anything consequential, so slight of stature were they. The older woman, the mother, spoke calmly in spite of obvious distress. "We will excuse your rude intrusion into our privacy, sir, if you will leave on the instant."

The younger woman didn't speak, but lowered her head as she also waited for Lord Charles to leave.

Lord Charles felt like a fool. He doubted that the women together would equal him in either height or weight, but even so neither seemed at all intimidated by his presence or authority.

He tried another tack. "Please forgive my unannounced presence. I have had a taxing journey and was expecting to have a room waiting for me."

The older woman regarded him levelly. "How unobliging of so fine an establishment."

Lord Charles flushed. "Be that as it may, ma'am, the fact remains that I have no place in which to partake of a meal I am quite eager for. So, if you will excuse me, ladies," and he turned to open the door to usher them out.

The contretemps was resolved by the appearance of a young country maid bearing what was obviously not only his own supper but one for the ladies as well. She laid it out on the table, clearing away the dishes of tea which the women had been drinking, while Lord Charles and the women stood awkwardly, staring at the food.

Lord Charles, used to command as he was, found himself unsure how to proceed without behaving like a churl. That he should sacrifice his comfort by retreating did not occur to him.

"Ladies, may I suggest that however awkward the circumstances, we proceed to enjoy this . . . meal before its becoming cold robs it of what small appeal it may have."

He held out a chair for the mother who hesitated, her eyes on her daughter. She touched her hand to the young woman and said, "Let us eat, Sylvie, we can talk later."

Leith seated the two, feeling overlarge and overbearing, and then gave himself over to the stringy mutton and watery potatoes with a concentration they did not merit.

As he ate, he appraised the women. They seemed equally genteel and poor. Their manners, demeanor, and conversation bespoke education and respectability, but their clothes were not only out of fashion, but shabby as well. The mother had been a beauty, she was delicately featured with pale blond hair covered by a cap of the strictest utility. Her features were grave, and Lord Charles could not help but be curious about the circumstances which had led them to this out-of-the-way inn.

Of the daughter he could see little, so resolutely did she keep her face averted or bent over the plate from which she seemed to eat nothing. Her hair was brightly golden, a veritable torrent of curls, and her features had her mother's delicacy. But it was not until she lifted her face inadvertently, startled by a sudden noise at the door which signaled the innkeeper returning with ale, that Lord Charles saw her face.

Her eyes were green and bright, and the vividness of her coloring made her seem as fresh as a flower. But all the brightness was dimmed by a shy air that he instinctively found disappointing. All that bright beauty should be accompanied by merriment and high spirits. But then he reminded himself that he had interrupted them in the midst of a crisis which might have been the agent for quenching the light in those lovely eyes.

There was no conversation. Lord Charles was acutely aware of the distress these obvious gentlewomen felt on having to dine with an unknown man. Tact finally asserted itself, and with the briefest civilities he took himself and a tankard of ale away to his room to the obvious relief of both women. Within an hour he had thrown himself into a lumpy bed whose linens could have benefited from airing and disinfestation, and fell into a deep sleep.

He was awakened abruptly by sounds he was too groggy to identify. The sun had risen but the light was still muddy in his room. It couldn't be much past daybreak. The noises were repeated. He realized someone was softly knocking on the door, and he cursed the quality of the establishment while he drew on his pantaloons and pulled a shirt over his chest.

He flung the door open abruptly and the two women, faces ashen, clutching their possessions, with dresses incompletely buttoned and boots inadequately

31

fastened, tumbled into the room. What might have been a moment of delicious comedy was made fraught by the look of absolute terror in their eyes.

The older of the two threw herself against the door and pushed the bolt into place while the younger one ran to the window and carefully moved aside the curtain to look down into the courtyard. Her mother joined her and Lord Charles, fastening his shirt, inquired with what he felt was heroic restraint, "Is there some way I might be of service?"

All he got for his pains was, "Ssssst."

He strode across the room and stood behind the women to look over their heads at the scene below. There in the courtyard was a carriage, and beside it, expostulating with flailing arms and purple cheeks to the innkeeper, was a man who was familiar to de la Marre, but because they were looking almost directly down upon his bald pate, he could not recognize.

Suddenly the man stopped and lifted his face to the upper floor of the inn and swept it with his glance. The women drew back with gasps and let the curtain fall, but not before Leith had recognized Reginald Flood, a man notorious in London for his womanizing, a jumped-up Cit who had married well and had been received by the ton for the sake of his wife until her death, and whose reputation lay just this side of the law. Not many years ago, if he remembered correctly, Flood had been acquitted of theft in a case where he had mysteriously lost funds he had taken to invest for an old woman from the country. The case had aroused considerable contempt for the man, and even though he had not been found guilty, he had not been welcomed by the ton since.

What his connection could be with these women—who were clearly terrified and hiding from him—was a mystery it was now the moment to unravel.

The older woman saw his eyes on her and his apparent expectation of an explanation and held out her hand. "Sir, I implore you, please do not give our presence away. We have reason to be afraid, to be running from that . . . gentleman. Would it be possible for us to remain here until he leaves?"

Lord Charles glanced from her face to her daughter's.

"But of course, ma'am."

"You see—"

He had no time to see, because at that moment there was the unmistakable sound of heavy feet on the uncarpeted stairs, and not a moment later fierce banging on the ladies' door across the hall.

The women clutched each other.

"Oh, Mother, where . . ." The older woman cast her eyes about the room looking for a place to hide.

Lord Charles gestured to them to stand behind the door, and they all waited frozen, listening for sounds from the hallway.

Within seconds the hammering started on his door.

He called, "What the devil!" and other imprecations of an honest fellow roused from his slumbers at an ungodly hour, and thumped and stumbled and then finally threw open the door and startled both Flood and Cheever who was expostulating with him.

Closing the door firmly behind him, he turned toward Flood and raised his eyebrows.

"I'm sorry, I couldn't get him away . . ." Cheever said, panting.

33

"What is the meaning of this?" he asked, not deigning to acknowledge that he recognized the man or had met him years before in London.

"Leith!"

Lord Charles pierced him with a gaze which had caused greater men to experience fear.

"Ah. Lord Leith." Flood subsided, obviously taken aback by discovering such a majestic figure in such a run-down hostlery.

"Well, what is it?"

"Ah. Ha-ha. Oh, nothing. Well, that is. You see, it's my affianced wife and her daughter. They're missing. I thought perhaps they might have been abducted, that they might have been brought here. The landlord looks none too honest to me."

"Are you suggesting that *I* have abducted them?"

"Oh, my lord, of course not, how absurd. Ha-ha. What a quiz. No. Well, if you will excuse me. Sorry, Leith, and all that." A gasping and uncomfortable Flood backed away.

Cheever scowled as he watched him leave, unhappy to see him go so easily, and then looked at his master.

Lord Charles motioned him into the room, closed the door, and bolted it.

"Now ladies," he said to the women who cowered before him, "it is not my custom to go about embroiling myself in the domestic relationships of London gentlemen. But then Reginald Flood is no gentleman, and I would be reluctant to commit a spavined mongrel to his care."

"Do you know him?"

"By reputation only."

"We shall have to allow you into our confidence, I

am afraid. It is too obvious that we shall have to continue to rely on your aid." The older woman put her arm around her daughter, but before she could speak, Lord Charles interrupted.

"Ladies, I suggest that I remove myself while you finish your toilette. I will arrange for a pot of coffee to be brought to us, so that we might discuss this matter in comfort."

"No," cried the older woman. "No, we must leave immediately, he was deterred only by your presence, he will return to track us down. But," she added bitterly, "we have no conveyance."

The women stood before him, holding hands, pressed against each other, but even that could not still their trembling. Lord Charles felt inevitability descend upon him.

"How can we get you away? Very well. Cheever, go bring the carriage round, then distract Flood while I bundle the ladies in. We shall leave instantly.

"Ladies, I am on my way to Wixton. If you wish conveyance in that direction, I am happy to extend an invitation."

In both women warred a battle between the exigency of the moment and the training of a lifetime's admonitions against impropriety. Exigency won. "We are grateful, sir," the mother finally said.

Leith leaned back against the squabs and regarded the two women. The younger was staring out the window, her face a mask. The older woman, once the fear of pursuit had passed, was studying her hands. Lord Charles bided his time. He was sure that she was

35

delaying so as to choose her words to explain how this ramshakle flight had come about.

"I know that we owe you an explanation—"

Lord Charles raised an elegant hand. He knew it was required of him, a show of uninterest.

"No, no, we owe it to you. And perhaps, also, you might advise us. You appear to know Mr. Flood?" She spoke as though it were an offense to pronounce his name.

"As I said, I know him only by his reputation, which is unsavory."

"In what way, if I may ask?"

"Well." Lord Charles considered. Finally he decided only honesty could help. "He is said to have taken for investment the fortunes of retired ladies and then absconded with them. Several years ago, he was brought to trial but acquitted. However the belief that he succeeded on other occasions has made him unwelcome among his peers in London."

He held the riveted attention of both women.

"And then there is the problem of women. Young women, to be exact."

The women exchanged a look and both turned pale. "I think there have been cases, one that I know of personally, where he debauched a young servant of friends with whom he had been staying."

The older woman's jaw set. "So it is true. I'm glad you have been honest with us, sir. It makes it easier." She paused and then began her recitation.

She and her daughter had lived out of the way in Shropshire in a small cottage after the death of their father and husband, a vicar. They had a small competence and lived comfortably in the society of a small out-of-the-way village. Mr. Flood had come into their lives while staying with a friend, and he had immediately sought out the widow with particular attention. He had courted her and had actually gone so far as to speak of marriage, although he never actually proposed it.

She had been gratified. Although not in love with Mr. Flood, she had been comfortable with his manners and pleased that his wealth might make it possible for Sylvie, her daughter, to lead a wider life, including even, perhaps, a Season in London.

The younger woman clasped her mother's hand. "But you know a Season is not important to me, Mama."

Her mother smiled. "I know that you think that, dear, but I know, too, that you have led a sheltered life and find interest in it only because you don't know the delights of a more varied one."

Sylvie looked doubtful. Her mother continued.

"I can't pretend to say that I wasn't flattered. But after our friendship lengthened, I began to have doubts. And the night before last those doubts were realized, but not, alas, before he had talked me into investing in some enterprise which he had undertaken. It was foolish, and I doubt I'll ever see that money again. But there was worse to follow. We were visiting him in Kelvedon . . ."

Sylvie flushed. Her mother continued. "He made unwelcome advances to Sylvie. Yesterday I came upon her struggling in his embrace. He struck me and locked us in a downstairs study. We escaped and came across the inn. You know the rest."

Lord Charles finally broke the silence. "You have

37

been ill used."

"It is so shaming," Sylvie spoke. Her voice was low and melodious.

"Hush, child. There is no shame on your part."

"No, indeed." Lord Charles added his comfort. "It is no doubt his way to prey on his victims through gaining their trust and rendering them reluctant to believe in his perfidy. He counts on shame and embarrassment to protect him from prosecution. That does not mean, however, that he is not dangerous. If he's bothering to pursue you, it must be to intimidate you into silence."

"He will pay," the older woman spoke grimly.

"Mother, you can't think of prosecuting. We must just stay away from him, hope he will give up pursuit and forget us."

"Where could we go, Sylvie?"

"There is Uncle Joe."

"Joe has eleven children bursting the walls of his cottage."

"I could become a governess. I'm educated. I know Latin and Greek, as well as French and Italian. I could . . ."

Lord Charles' eyebrows flew up. "Latin? Greek? French? Italian?"

Sylvie lifted her small chin. "My father taught me."

"You are to be congratulated," Lord Charles said placatingly, glad to have roused a spark.

"Thank you."

"Well, ladies, it would seem that neither of you has a suggestion where I can deliver you. So, if I might make a suggestion . . . First, let me introduce myself: I am Florian Fotheringay," he said with the blandest air of innocence.

38

Sylvie's mother introduced them in turn as Mrs. Mary and Miss Sylvia Churchill.

Lord Charles made a shameless half-bow unperturbed by his deception, and put forth his suggestion. "Would it afford you ladies any comfort to accompany me to Wixton and stay there until you have sorted out your affairs? Of course, to protect our reputations, it would, regrettably, be necessary for you to assume the name of Fotheringay as you would have to become my sister and, ma'am, my honored mother."

Chapter Three

"Three shops! No assembly room! Not one . . . how do you do?" Jane interrupted her hissing complaints to Ned to smile at a woman passing on the narrow path that took the place of a pavement in the godforsaken village Ned had landed them in. "Why couldn't you find accommodation in Harwich? We shall meet no one here."

Conversation was awkward. Custom required that Ned, posing as her footman, walk behind. He was accompanying her to carry packages on this, their first excursion into the village, and their first public appearance on the streets—if that is what they might be called—of Wixton, Essex.

"I told you," he hissed back, "Harwich was by no means out-of-the way enough for us—well, for me. You forget it is the major port for Holland."

"Yes, all the more reason for us to . . . Good morning."

"You shouldn't be greeting people. You haven't been introduced."

"Oh, nonsense, in a village like this, manners aren't the same as in stuffy Cambridge."

"It's worse in a tiny place, Jen. You have to mind your manners."

"My manners are fine enough for this ... this ... oh!"

Fury silenced Jane and she strove to swallow her rage at what she was seeing this first morning in their new home. She was appalled to think that Edgar had already paid the lease of this house for a year rather than just a quarter, and that their fortunes were tied to a village where it was clear nothing had happened in the last two hundred years, since the wool trade had collapsed, and nothing would probably happen for another two hundred more.

But here was the shop, the kind of country shop Jane detested, where food jostled with bolts of fabric on the shelf, where the smell of overripe turnips took the pleasure from what might be a small moment of enjoyment, such as the purchase of a pair of riding gloves.

She managed a quelling glare at Ned before she assumed a pleasant smile and entered the shop.

She stood regally in the center of the large room amid tables and counters laden with a dismaying assortment of items—chiefly having to do with the rural pursuits of her new neighbors—and waited to be greeted, carrying her head in an elegant way she was sure Livvy would approve.

She made an attractive picture. Their ten-day stay in London had been bliss, and expensive as well, the results of which were displayed on her comely person. She wore a delft blue walking dress with a bonnet

41

banded in the same blue, and she knew that the exquisite cut and deep color flattered her as nothing else could. She had chosen it this morning purposely, for no matter how small the village might be, they were here, and from this appearance would radiate out the rumors of her arrival and assessments of her standing in the world.

For a moment the weariness of the long road of deception which lay ahead weighed on her, but it was balanced by the excitement the anonymity of charade allowed her, and the hope, however remote, of success. But the die was cast and she spoke her first words as Ariadne Montcrief, lately of Northumberland.

"Is anyone here?"

"Madame!" A man appeared from behind a distant counter. He bowed and looked at her with not a little awe.

Jane was pleased with the awe. She had never before awed anyone in her life.

"How do you do," she said, nodding graciously to him. "I am new to the village and require some items for our home."

"Oh, yes, you must be the party who moved into the High Street."

"Indeed. We arrived yesterday."

"May I welcome you to Wixton? I hope you will find our village a pleasant place to live."

"Thank you. I am sure I shall."

"Are you planning to settle here . . . ?"

Jane knew she must depress such curiosity in keeping with her lofty position, but it was also necessary to suggest a long enough stay that they must be reckoned with by the local populace. "It is a charming village, so restful after the rigors of London. We shall be remaining here for some time. My mother . . ."

Jane left the sentence incomplete, ending in a sigh which expressed sadness.

"Your mother, is she an invalid?"

She smiled at his quickness. "You have fathomed our situation, Mr. . . . ?"

"Gregg."

"Mr. Gregg," Jane nodded, and turned toward a table to study what turned out to be an assortment of pens, bags of flour from the local mill, a couple of pillows, some desperate-looking cabbages, and a very large pile (which looked as if it hadn't been disturbed for a decade) of rough greyish washing soaps.

Jane bit back a smile and glanced up at Ned whose eyes expressed a shared amusement. It was her plan to dally long enough in the village to meet some of its residents, or at least to be seen by them, and so she began a slow circuit of the shop, carefully keeping her skirts from the dust of the floors and the contents of the shelves, and directed the eager Mr. Gregg to select items for her to be bundled up and carried back to her home by the dazzlingly liveried (in a lovely purple and gold selected by Livvy) and respectfully silent footman who attended her.

As Jane had hoped, within fifteen minutes of arriving at the shop a number of matrons began to appear. Jane was well acquainted with the communication patterns of small villages, and understood just how long it would take for word to get around that the new family was making an appearance, and for the hurried

43

gathering up of pelisses and reticules and the rapid walk to the shop by the ladies of the village.

Jane kept her attention on her purchases, choosing carefully among some faded embroidery silks with great care. From time to time she would casually glance up and discovered a face being quickly averted or a glance continue to slide away toward a spot a couple of feet from her head. Ned, standing in a corner taking in the whole scene with amusement, lifted his eyebrows at her.

She hid a smile and noticed that none of the others were speaking. Clearly they were waiting for her so that they might overhear whatever she said.

"Mr. Gregg, I have discovered that the fireplace in the main saloon has no andirons. Would you be able to help me remedy this lack?"

All eyes were on her.

"Oh, yes, ma'am. I have quite a nice selection. Well, I think I might have one in the back . . ." he nodded deferentially as he backed himself out under a hanging cloth to the nether reaches of the shop.

"How shocking! No andirons in the main saloon!"

Jane looked into the eyes of a lady all in black who had a cheerful face, plump, wreathed in wrinkles.

"Yes, it is inconvenient."

"I'm sure. You've taken the Yates place I understand."

"Yes," Jane smiled to offset the reticence of her speech, a reticence she assumed she should employ.

"Well, it has been vacant for some time . . ."

"Indeed. But it has been maintained quite well. We are pleased with it. It has such a lovely prospect of the village, especially the church."

44

The lady was gratified. "Yes, we have a lovely church here in Wixton. Are you from Essex?"

Jane studied a green silk against the light of the small bowed window. "A lovely color, don't you think?"

"Ah, yes," the woman said, her manner cooler. Jane hesitated a moment and then added, "No, we come from Northumberland. But we find it so lovely here."

"Northumberland! That is very far!"

"Indeed, Northumberland is very far."

"I have your andirons," Mr. Gregg interrupted, as though envious that anyone else should have conversation with a woman he considered his own discovery.

"They will do. Thank you, Mr. Gregg. That will be all, I think. Can you please send the andirons to us separately? My footman will carry the rest. My mother will no doubt be wishing to open an account here. You have such an . . . interesting selection of goods."

"It would be an honor, ma'am. And the name?"

This was the moment they had all waited for. A silence fell in the shop.

"Mrs. Montcrief."

It was a name they had chosen in accordance with a principle Livvy had devised, that they should use names that began with the same letter as their real ones, so that any false starts in naming each other might be overcome. Montcrief was a fine-sounding name, they had decided, and one which had the added advantage of having belonged to a noble Cornish family which had died out in the last generation. In saying it, she was satisfied with the way it sounded.

As Jane was bestowing a patronizing smile on the indeterminate distance before her, she caught sight of a tall, fierce woman dressed as an upper servant, and was

45

shocked at the pure malevolence of her expression.

As they strolled back home, Ned buried under a pile of packages, Jane was dispirited. The unpleasant woman in Gregg's shop had unsettled her, but it was the meager offerings of the village which most discouraged her. All that she had seen that morning confirmed her first impression: everything was small and undistinguished.

She did have to admit to herself, however, that it was lovely. Unlike the wildness of the shore she had known all her life, pummeled by storms and wind, where the hardiest trees, shrubs, and flowers were twisted or killed by the onslaught of even a few winters, this village by the sea was the very picture of tranquility. The sea gently hugged the shore, as though they were long-time friends.

At home everyone gathered around as they unloaded both their packages and their impressions of their first foray into their new world.

Priddy, now in her disguise as the ill—but not too ill—Mrs. Montcrief, was dressed in a pale grey cashmere gown of such an excellent cut, and so flattering to her silvering hair, that she seemed changed. Her very gestures and movements, her voice and intonation were more confident and direct. Jane had noticed the change even in London. Priddy was indeed still their governess, but no one would guess that now. Her doubts about the wisdom of the undertaking had not abated, but she had committed herself to it and addressed her formidable will to making a success of it.

Ned ripped at the buttons of his livery, which was hot even on this cool spring day, and let loose a howl of relief when he had taken the coat off.

"I'll never get used to this! All that standing around. Not being allowed to say a word. I'll go mad before this is over."

"Madame, may I relieve you of your pelisse?"

Well, Jane thought, at least there was one person who was enjoying her new life.

Although Livvy was twelve and looked it, after they had put her hair up, and in her new uniform, with the elaborate formal manners she had adopted, she would pass for a maid of sixteen years. They had decided to explain that she had been taken in as a favor to a dying housekeeper whose last child she was.

Jane removed the pelisse, untied her bonnet, stripped off her gloves, and handed them over, careful not to smile. Livvy took them gravely, executed a magnificent curtsey, and turned to put them away.

Jane laughed, relieved to have the morning behind her, and went upstairs immediately to change her dress. Although she was the one allowed to play the role of a leisured, useless lady, behind the scenes she had a great deal to do, and this afternoon they were to make up a supply of breads, scones, and cakes to offer guests who might come once Jane had managed formal introductions.

It was Sunday and no one had yet paid a call. Jane wasn't too surprised, and the interval had allowed them to polish the silver they had hired in London, to lay in adequate provision, and put the finishing touches on

47

the house which would make it unmistakably theirs.

Although they had not been entitled to the furnishings of Thrate House, and had found it prudent to store the better part of the books and attic stores, they had culled a selection of luxuries and necessities for their life in Wixton. These consisted for the most part of trimmings: laces, feathers, old gowns—the makings and ornamentations of clothes for Priddy and Jane— and, of course, books for them all, but especially for Livvy.

They had left telltale Marlingforthe possessions: arms, portraits, and the oldest family records in storage in London. They had brought some sentimental favorites with them, including a portrait of their mother with a brother who had died when he was eight, and the Sung vase which had stood on the mantel of their father's bookroom. It was probably foolish that they had chanced being prosecuted for theft by taking such a noticeable piece from their grandfather's collection, but at the last moment, none of them had been able to leave it behind. It was a vase perhaps two feet in height, of exquisite delicacy, pale green, almost white, and translucent, with patterns of leaves that could be detected only when held up to the light. It had been their father's pride and joy.

What they had felt about the necessity to abandon their home and its possessions, and the small pilferings from that which they had grown up believing to be theirs forever, they felt according to their ages. Livvy had wanted to steal wholesale from the loathed Mr. Coggelshall. Priddy had urged them to take nothing. Finally Jane acted as mediator, allowing everyone to take one favorite thing. It had been Ned's decision to take the vase.

The attic trunks had not only yielded up riches for their gowns, but also for decorating the public rooms. They had found oriental brocades and silks which Priddy and Jane—working with the skill at needlework poverty had imposed on them—had fashioned into cushions and draped on the backs of chairs and over tables, lending a rich, rakish air to the drawing room.

The house was ready for visitors. Jane saw their attendance at church as the beginning of what she hoped would be an expanding network of friends and acquaintances. Not only was such a network necessary to her plan, but she was genuinely hungry for company, eager to make new friends and be a part of society.

They walked to church together and separated at the door, Jane and Priddy to seat themselves in a pew in the middle of the church, Livvy and Ned to sit in back on the benches. For the first few moments, Jane was caught up in the comfort of the familiar service, reassured, obscurely, that even here across the breadth of England, they celebrated holy services exactly as they had at home.

Once she had become accustomed to the lovely flintwork church, she sat back and undertook to study the men and women of the congregation. The majority of those present were without particular interest to her, being composed of the shopkeepers and farmers who made up the chief population of the village and its environs. She identified the vicar's wife as a stout woman in brown whose head turned with every entrance, as though she were taking attendance, and who had greeted Jane's inquisitive glance with a polite nod.

There were two parties who particularly held Jane's interest. The first occupied the enclosed pew of the family which held the living of the church. The party was made up of three persons, one of whom was the malevolent-looking woman Jane had encountered in the shop, an apparent housekeeper or companion. The gentleman was in his fifties, a cheerful-looking man with a portly figure, who peered up at the vicar over wire spectacles and seemed prepared to smile at everyone who caught his eye.

But it was the third person in the party who held Jane spellbound. She was a dazzling creature, the likes of whom Jane had never before seen. She was tall, statuesque, and blessed with a luxurious head of russet hair. Her profile, which was all Jane could see of her face, was distinguished by almost perfect proportions, and her gown, of teal silk, molded an almost perfect figure. Unlike Jane herself, her attention seemed completely held by her prayer book.

It was not only shame at her inattentiveness which made Jane's head drop to stare blankly at her own prayer book. It was the awareness that with such a splendid woman in the neighborhood, whatever charms she might have, and most of them counterfeit at that, would be little esteemed. She thought that the hopes she had nourished to capitalize on her modest store of beauty had just received the dashing that such vanity deserved. For five minutes she paid the strictest attention to the service.

But then her eyes strayed to the other party in the church which had caught her notice. They were sitting across the aisle, and included one of the handsomest men Jane had ever seen. In fact, she thought, it was a miracle that the church held such startling specimens of both masculine and feminine good looks, apparently unrelated by birth or marriage. The gentleman had hair almost as black as her own, and from a quick glimpse he made of her side of the church, eyes of deep, wild gypsy brown—Jane enjoyed the Livvy-like thought— and the most magnificently muscled masculine body she had seen at such close range. She glanced back to where Ned sat with Livvy and saw that her own brother—whom she had always thought of as a paragon of masculine good looks—seemed almost stunted by comparison.

There was an amusing anomaly in the trio which caught her fancy. The man, large and commanding, was married to one of the most petite creatures Jane had ever measured herself against. Really, she would certainly not come to her own shoulder, and Jane was of average height for a woman. But the young woman was lovely, with curly blond hair and bright green eyes. It must have been her mother with them from the similarity of stature and delicate beauty. The man was richly but conservatively dressed in a dove grey coat of superfine, but the women's clothes were surprisingly plain. Both wore muslin gowns which would have been more appropriate for morning wear at home. Jane found herself speculating about such a mismatched trio, where the man displayed sartorial distinction, and the women were apparently either unwilling or unable to dress above the common run.

But that concluded the interesting company. There were no other young men, except those whose clothes or manners proclaimed them to be anything but the rich husband she was seeking. There were no men in regimentals. There did not even seem to be a curate who might turn out to be the very rich younger son of a very rich duke.

She managed to turn her thoughts back to the service, but as she rose for the benediction she found herself thinking, "Whatever else happens, I have at least lived ten days in London."

At the door of the church the vicar greeted them and they introduced themselves. Jane curtseyed and smiled and held out her hand which the vicar warmly took. His name was Mr. Woods and he introduced them to his wife who was as welcoming as they could wish.

As they spoke with the vicar at the door, their attention was caught by the magnificently beautiful woman who came up behind them and claimed the vicar's attention. Mrs. Woods walked with them out into the churchyard, and Jane was pleased that she did not abandon them to pay respects to the squire. Instead she satisfied their curiosity by saying, "That is Lord William Sneed and his daughter Arabella. They live in the great house on the Bourne Mill road, you may have seen it when you drove into Wixton."

Jane gazed at the lovely Arabella as Priddy and Mrs. Woods conversed, and she found in this closer inspection all the perfection she had feared. Livvy and Ned joined her, standing slightly apart as they had been coached to do.

And then from the church ushered forth the tall man and his petite wife and mother-in-law; and Mrs. Woods beckoned them over for introductions.

"You must allow me, Mrs. Montcrief, to present you to our other newcomers. Indeed Wixton becomes quite fashionable, it would seem.

"Mrs. Montcrief, may I present Mrs. Fotheringay, her daughter, Miss Georgianna Fotheringay and son, Mr. Florian Fotheringay. Miss Montcrief."

Jane and Priddy extended their hands and were greeted in turn. Jane felt herself quite delighted to discover that this man, whose good looks at the distance of their extended arms were completely riveting, was apparently not married after all.

"So, you are sister and brother," she found herself exclaiming, and tried to make up for the gaffe with an artless smile.

The gentleman's stern, almost harsh features relaxed into a charming smile. "My stepsister, actually."

Livvy, who *should* have been standing much farther off, under too much self-restraint to dare to utter a word, and with too much sense even to think of doing so, had been instead creeping ever closer and suddenly spoke.

"Of course," she burst out excitedly, "she is your stepsister because she must stand on a step even to talk to you. But it would have been better if she were your halfsister, she's half your size and so—don't you see how much better that would be?"

Chapter Four

"Liv—Lizzy!" Ned lunged and caught his sister by the elbow and yanked her back.

"Ow! Let me go, Ned—Nettles! Ma'am, make him let me go!"

Jane and Priddy exchanged tortured looks, and while Priddy strove to calm the querulous brother and sister, Jane turned back to the astonished group before her. "Lizzy, our maid, is quite young, you must forgive her."

She held her head as though the incident were the merest trifle and was pleased to see that although Miss Fotheringay blushed, no one seemed to be unduly outraged. She could have sworn that there was even a twinkle in Mr. Fotheringay's eye. "We have taken her on as a boon to our former housekeeper who recently died. It was her parting wish before she succumbed . . . " She drew herself up and changed the subject.

"So you are also new to the village," she said, directing her queries carefully to the ladies of the party, so as not to betray her interest in the tall gentleman with the pleasing twinkle.

"Yes," replied Mrs. Fotheringay.

Jane set her sights on making the younger woman, whom she had already deemed to be shy, speak. "And whence do you come, Miss Fotheringay?"

"Northumberland," Sylvie murmured low.

"Oh dear. I mean . . . what a happy coincidence. We come from Northumberland as well."

"Oh," said Sylvie, dismayed. "It is . . . far, isn't it?"

"Yes," said Jane, "it is far."

"It was quite a journey here, it was so very far," said Sylvie, desperately.

"Yes, it was the same for us . . . a long journey."

Lord Charles rescued them. "From what part do you come?"

"Oh, from a part which is much colder than this lovely village here," said Jane with noisy gaiety, "isn't it a welcome change, though, to have such an early spring?"

"We are pleased with the climate," he responded, "as it is for my mother's health that we sought it out."

"Oh, but another charming coincidence. My mother also," she said, taking Miss Pridwell's arm, "is here for her health."

She looked from Priddy to Mrs. Fotheringay, and thought idly that she had never seen two such fine examples of matronly health.

"How fortunate, then, that you should have come to the same village, for in fact, we have been finding the company a bit thin." Mrs. Fotheringay spoke. "It will be a pleasure to further our acquaintance."

"Yes, indeed," Miss Pridwell responded, "my daughter would be grateful of a friend in Miss Fotheringay."

"Oh, you must call me . . ." Sylvie blushed, stammering, stepped back a pace, and resumed, "You must call on me at our home, it lies just beyond the village, to the east. And, you must call me Georgianna," she hastened on, finally remembering the name they had agreed on. Her mother, Mary, was to be called Emma.

"And you must call me Ariadne! Let us walk together now," Jane exclaimed, taking Sylvie's arm. The two older woman paired off and Lord Charles, after hesitating a moment to throw a bemused look at the two Montcrief servants—red-faced and bickering behind their mistresses' backs—fell in at the end of the procession.

At the lych-gate, Jane stopped in apparent fascination to study its design. This necessitated a small shuffling in the order of march and the older women continued on while Sylvie and Jane stood together. When they resumed their slow promenade through the village, Lord Charles found himself with a young lady on each arm.

Jane, pleased with her strategem, set herself to be charming. "Don't you adore these small out-of-the-way villages after the rush of London, Mr. Fotheringay?"

"I should have thought Northumberland as far out of the rush of London as one would ever need to be."

"Yes, true. Isn't that a charming house, just there? Why it looks as though it hasn't been touched for centuries. Don't you dote on architecture, Georgianna?"

Sylvie peered around Lord Charles's arm. "Oh, yes. Yes. I do like architecture."

"I thought so, I thought I detected in you a fine

intelligence and a warm appreciation of art."

"Oh, no, I didn't mean . . ."

"I myself find nothing more challenging than an hour's conversation with one who is versed in the arts, in history, in the more elevated pursuits of the mind."

"Then you must speak to my brother. He is a writer," Sylvia said, glancing up at the face of her companion who seemed amused by this conversation.

A writer. It was her punishment for prosing on about intellectual pursuits that he should turn out to be a pedant, a writer, a mere scribbler. Still, she lifted a fascinated gaze and said, "A writer! How absolutely enthralling! What do you write about, if I may inquire?"

"I am writing a memoir of my experiences in the war."

The war! That was much better. Jane stopped in her tracks to look at him with genuine appreciation. "You fought in the wars against Napoleon?"

"Yes."

"Where?"

"In the Peninsula. In Belgium."

"At Waterloo!"

He inclined his head.

"Then you have seen the world, indeed. I can think of nothing I would more like to hear about than others' travels unless," she added with an unfeigned air of sadness, "it would be to travel myself."

"So you are a traveler, Miss Montcrief?"

Jane looked up at him. My heavens he was a handsome man, she thought. His face was weathered and she suddenly saw him standing at the prow of a ship making its way through rough seas, his eyes, dark

57

brown and warm, but hard at the same time . . . she smiled vacantly.

"I asked if you were a traveler, Miss Montcrief?" he repeated with a sudden hauteur. He was used to that sudden fatuousness in women and bored by it.

"Oh, no. Yes. Well, only in England. I've been to . . . Northumberland, of course. And I've visited in Cornwall . . ."

"How interesting."

"Oh, dear, here we are. It has been so pleasant to make your acquaintance, Georgianna. Perhaps you would be so kind as to come for tea tomorrow?"

"I . . . I would love to," Sylvie answered, throwing an inquiring glance at Lord Charles who nodded.

Jane caught the exchange and wondered what kind of martinet this brother was that his sister was fearful to accept an invitation to tea without his permission.

"How kind of you to allow her," she said.

Lord Charles frowned at the impertinence. "I try to be the kindest of brothers."

Sylvie flushed furiously and Jane wondered at the source of the awkwardness between brother and sister. She suddenly thought that perhaps this sweet and pretty young woman had been sent into Essex to be got away from some ineligible *parti*, or perhaps she had embroiled herself in a scandal. She studied Sylvie. More likely her overbearing brother had taken it into his head to separate her from some perfectly satisfactory young man who wasn't plump enough in the pocket for his taste. Jane decided to dislike him.

The party made its farewells and Jane and Miss Pridwell entered their home, stripping off their gloves and bonnets.

"Well, I think we made a favorable come-out. What do you think, Priddy?"

"You certainly did find much to praise in intellectual discourse," Miss Pridwell lifted her eyebrow.

Jane laughed. "Didn't I just. I thought Georgianna, for all her shyness, must be something of a bluestocking, and I wasn't too far wrong. Her brother is some sort of scribbler. I wonder if he really was a soldier—he has the bearing. But in him it is unpleasant, an arrogance; I fancy he's a poseur and an officious one at that. I wonder where he acquired that cocksureness—I'll bet he's never left England. He appears to be one of those men who are forever prosing on about great hunts they have been on or storms at sea they have endured—all straight from someone else's memoirs."

"That seems like a remarkably firm opinion for such a short acquaintance."

"Oh Priddy. It's so discouraging. There's no one but him, and he's a puffed-up autocrat. Handsome, I'll grant, but nothing in his head but his own image. And, if you can deduce anything from the clothes of his womenfolk, ungenerous to boot."

Ned and Livvy came into the house at that moment. Both Priddy and Jane turned on them.

"That was the most disgraceful display! What were you thinking of? I hoped for better from you. You did everything but brawl in the streets."

Livvy's eyes blazed at Jane. "You didn't tell me maids aren't ever allowed to speak."

"Well, you aren't, ever. Do you hear? And to have said such a thing! You shouldn't remark on the disparity of their sizes under *any* circumstances, even if you were allowed to speak."

"They look ridiculous."

"Ridiculous!" Ned stormed. "What do you know about ridiculous? She's so far above you, above Jane, you couldn't appreciate her. She's an angel."

"Who's an angel?" asked Livvy.

"I think he means Miss Fotheringay," Jane said, dismayed.

Sylvie didn't feel like an angel. She felt as stupid and slow as she usually did in company. Miss Montcrief—Ariadne—had been so assured and lively. She sighed deeply. She was grateful for Mr. Fotheringay's having rescued them, but the past three weeks had been wearying. Her nineteen years had been spent as the daughter of a beloved vicar, so she had never mixed well in lively company, and now she was required to do so under the difficult circumstance of deceit. She was shy and accustomed, in the past couple of years, to finding company in her books.

Moreover, there was something intimidating about Mr. Fotheringay, which no amount of familiarity could erase. She tried to be at ease with him but could not succeed. The difficulty lay in the insecurity of their future, how to regain their home and money without encountering Mr. Flood. She and her mother talked about it during the long days while Mr. Fotheringay worked in the bookroom, but they had come to no agreement. She sighed again.

Lord Charles heard the sigh. He was trailing the two ladies, who were walking arm in arm as they slowly followed the road that led another mile to their hired home.

He sighed as well. He was finding the ladies' presence a burden. Indeed, they were kind and attentive, he found the smooth running of his household comfortable, and he was grateful for their thoughtfulness toward him. But that was just the trouble. They were abashed with gratitude. He couldn't turn around in his own home without encountering a grateful smile or a blush of warmth for some kindness, or discovering one of them leaping up to see to his comfort. Since it had been necessary for him to outfit them with new apparel they keenly felt in his debt, so much so that they insisted on purchasing only the barest necessities.

He found them excellent company, otherwise. They were both intelligent women, especially Sylvie, who was eager to put her knowledge and time to his service, helped him with translations, and offered to help him with editing—an offer he refused as he chose to do it himself.

He'd had servants all his life and was used to being waited on, but not with such eagerness to please and anxious attentiveness. It had made him think a great deal about the power and privilege of rank. He was actually enjoying his incognito and freedom from the responsibilities, not only from Windmere, but from being an earl. But the obsequiousness of the women made him feel uncomfortable in a way quite new to him.

Their company limited his freedom. He was strictly bound by the needs and expectations of two isolated, frightened women, who looked to him for their entertainment and, it seemed, for permission to say or do anything.

He sighed again and thought about the silly woman he had just met. A featherhead, but if he had seen her across a room, he would have thought her one of the most lovely women he had ever seen. It was something about the hair, the eyes. Yet as shallow and tedious as she was, she had, by the end of their conversation, taken him in dislike. He was not used to being disliked by women.

Lady Arabella Sneed regarded the party departing the churchyard and peremptorily interrupted Mrs. Woods's conversation to ask, "Who are those people?"

Mrs. Woods was well used to Arabella's commanding ways. The young woman had grown up in a small village with too much money, too much attention, too much social power. Mrs. Woods answered her with unruffled calm. "They are two new families, the Fotheringays and the Montcriefs."

"Which is which?"

"I believe the one with the gentleman is the Fotheringay party."

Arabella pursed her lips. "What do you know about them?"

"Very little. They seem both to hail from Northumberland, with invalid mothers in tow." She watched Arabella with amusement.

Arabella had been used to being watched all her life. Even now as she thoughtfully regarded the retreating forms she lifted her head just ever so slightly so that her jaw line would show to advantage. She knew just how beautiful she was, although she seldom wasted the effect on the wives of dependent vicars.

Her father approached, having quitted the vicar. "Are you ready to go, my dear?"

"It is about time you tore yourself away, Papa. I am freezing to death. Where is the carriage?"

"You would wear that silk," said Miss Bingley, who joined them from where she had been waiting, eavesdropping on the squire and the vicar, in fact, until Arabella should decide to leave.

"It is spring, Bingley."

"It is also cold, Miss."

The squire rubbed his hands together and laughed overheartily. "Well, we can't deny either of those assertions, can we, Mr. Woods? It's spring and it's cold. Now, ladies, let's go home where a nice fire and dinner await us."

"Mrs. Woods," Arabella said, ignoring her father, "will you be entertaining either of those parties for tea?"

"I have not even called on them, Lady Arabella."

"You will be doing so, of course, tomorrow."

Mrs. Woods inclined her head more inquiringly than affirmatively.

"And you could certainly ask them to call on you for tea by, say, Thursday. Yes, Thursday will do very well. I will be there as well."

She turned on her heel and departed without farewells, to put a word in the ear of the coachman that he should be so lax.

"Good-bye, then, Mr. Woods, Mrs. Woods," Sir William Sneed looked apologetically at the good couple, but, after a quarter century of training, didn't

63

say a word to suggest that Arabella's manners were remiss. Miss Bingley, a distant cousin of the family, now companion and chaperone to Lady Arabella, condescended to nod as she swept off in Arabella's wake.

"Well, Mr. Woods," his wife said, tucking her hand in the crook of his arm as they began a comfortable stroll to the vicarage behind the churchyard. "What do you think? Do you think we shall see something interesting?"

"It is possible, Mrs. Woods. It is just possible. The young man is fine, indeed, but the interesting part will be the ladies. Lady Arabella has not had such ladies living in the village before."

"No, she hasn't, Mr. Woods. And I strongly suspect she won't like it, either."

"Well, will you have them for tea on Thursday?"

"I wouldn't miss it for the world."

Chapter Five

The following Wednesday Jane found him, the man she had been seeking, and it was as though everything she wished for had come true. He was tall and handsome and as fair as the writer fellow had been dark. The stranger was standing before the Dancing Tides Inn, speaking with another man whom Jane had not seen in the village before. She pressed her new friend's arm while her heart quickened, "Georgianna, do you see those two gentlemen? Have you any idea who they might be?"

She was walking with Georgianna Fotheringay toward the home of Mrs. Penworthy, who—the vicar's wife had told them each in separate calls on Monday—ran a small lending library in her home on the High Street. When Jane had called on her friend this afternoon, they found it so mild and inviting that they had decided to stroll into the village to call on her.

Sylvie had noticed and had realized that whereas her companion's interest had quickened, she herself had experienced exactly the opposite reaction, wishing to shrink to the other side of the street, and wishing she had the courage to suggest it. "No, I've not seen them before."

"Hmmm." Jane took in the splendor of the blond man. He was in his thirties, she guessed as she grew nearer, older than she had first thought. He was splendid from top to toe. His hair was long and curling and brushed forward in casual disarray. His clothes were the height of fashion, as colorful as hers. In fact, more colorful. Whereas she was wearing a peach dress trimmed with blond lace, he wore yellow and green and brown and a very elegant crimson waistcoat. She saw the sparkle of a ring on his finger, but it hadn't taken that to inform her that he was wealthy, and the very man her hopes for their adventure depended on.

His companion was also fashionably dressed, in less bold colors, and his visage was also less striking. He was cursed with only ordinary brown hair and ordinary hazel eyes and clothes of the ordinary hues of brown and tan. His hair was not cut into wild curls, and his hands were bare of rings. Jane dismissed him.

The ladies passed the gentlemen and demurely averted their gazes.

"I wonder who they can be?" Jane asked.

"I couldn't say."

Jane realized her friend was going to be a trial to her. It would be harder to discover the identity of the handsome stranger with an unimaginative and incurious partner. She sighed and reminded herself of Georgianna's real virtues and her gratitude in having found congenial company in a village remarkably thin of it.

They arrived at Mrs. Penworthy's and entered into a

drawing room which had been converted to a library filled with book-laden tables. Mrs. Penworthy, the plump friendly woman Jane had met that first day at Gregg's shop, welcomed them with effusive delight.

"How wonderful to have two young ladies who read! Sometimes it is only I and Mrs. Woods. The ladies at the big house don't read, such a pity—but how it warms my heart to think that we might sit for a moment or two and discuss books. Now, what is it that interests you ladies? Would you like novels? I have a lovely one that I bought when I was in Colchester, by a lady, it's the most droll story—but perhaps you prefer sermons," she added doubtfully, looking over the modest clothes of the small woman and the absentminded gaze of the taller one. "I have Fordyce's sermons . . ."

Jane could see that her friend's eyes had begun to roam over the titles as soon as she had entered the room and that she was lost in them, so she took it upon herself to provide the conversation Mrs. Penworthy obviously hungered for, and soon turned it to her own interests.

"Tell me, Mrs. Penworthy, this is such a small village, and I had quite made the mistake of thinking I had met everyone of interest, and then it appears that there are two gentlemen who live here whom I have not yet met. I wonder if you could enlighten me as to their identities."

"Now whom could you mean?"

"They were standing in front of the Dancing Tides just a moment ago as we passed. I have not seen them before, surely."

Mrs. Penworthy was a woman after Jane's heart. She went to the bay window, drew back the lace curtain, and frankly looked out. "Oh, yes, those two men. I don't know their names, but they are visiting Sir William. I heard it this morning from the butcher, who said that Miss Bingley had ordered some quails from him, as if he would have quails at this time of year. That Miss Bingley. But she said it was because they were having guests from London. So that must be who they are," she added, dropping the curtain and turning with undisguised curiosity toward Jane.

Jane asked, "Do the Sneeds often entertain guests from London?"

"Oh yes, when they are not in London or at their hunting lodge in Northumberland."

"Ah, Northumberland!"

"Yes. So far to go hunting, I've always thought."

"Indeed, it is far."

Jane picked up a book, drawn to its blue cover, and then remembered that she was charged by Livvy with securing the lastest romance and she engaged Mrs. Penworthy's aid. Together they found a novel in four volumes which promised all the love and danger Livvy looked for in her reading. Jane noted that Georgianna, meanwhile, was picking up, studying, and discarding almost every volume in the room. At this rate, their visit would last hours.

As she settled herself to wait, Jane was addressed by Mrs. Penworthy. "You have not commented on my name."

Jane looked puzzled.

"Most people comment on my name when they discover that I keep a circulating library."

"Oh, Penworthy! I had not thought of it."

"Your own name, Ariadne—now, you must understand that this is a small village, in truth, Mrs. Woods told me—is a lovely name."

"Yes, I have always wanted to be called Ariadne."

"Well certainly you have been?"

"Been what?"

"Been called Ariadne?" Now Mrs. Penworthy was puzzled.

"Oh, yes, certainly. Well, you know how it is. It seems such a very formal name for my family, that I'm often called something plain and boring, something like, well, Jenny."

"Ah, well, my name is Frances. I always wanted to be called Cassandra."

"And you," Jane said, smiling at her studious friend. "what did you always wish to be called?"

Sylvie continued reading.

"She must love books indeed. Come," Jane said teasingly, "come out of that book long enough to pay attention."

"Oh, I'm so sorry. What did you say?"

"We were wondering what name you have always wanted to be called."

Sylvie blushed furiously. "Actually, Georgianna."

Jane paused a moment. "Well, then, isn't it lucky that you are?"

Sylvie murmured, "Yes," and dropped the book she had been perusing.

Jane strolled to the window and discovered that the gentlemen were still deep in conversation before the inn. She turned to Sylvie and said brightly, "Well, I think I have made my selection, how are you doing, Georgianna?"

"I don't think I would like anything, today."

"Nothing! I would have thought that you wanted everything!"

"No. Nothing today." Sylvie lifted a brave face to her friend.

"Georgianna, what is it? I saw you looking at the books, there was no want of interest."

"Do you mean my poor selection did not attract you?" Mrs. Penworthy asked.

"Oh, no, indeed, you have a wonderful selection, but it is just that I . . . It is the cost," poor Sylvie ended miserably.

"The cost! Of hiring books!" Jane said aghast.

"Please, Ariadne." Sylvie said quietly.

Jane was outraged but managed to hold her tongue. Surely the Fotheringays could afford such an expenditure. The son did nothing but indulge his vanity in writing memoirs, so there must be income from somewhere. Then Jane remembered his elegant clothes and the women's plain garments. The gown Georgianna was wearing today Jane had seen twice before, and it was an uninspired garment to begin with. Jane thought it another mark against the brother. A writer with a bluestocking sister and he begrudged her the money for books!

Controlling herself with an effort, Jane asked, "Would you allow me to borrow the books, Georgianna?"

"Oh, no, please, Ariadne."

"I shall lend them to you at no charge. Why I have never heard anything like. Have you no pin money of your own? I hear of such cases, but would never have thought it of that handsome brother of yours," Mrs. Penworthy said.

"Oh, this, please, I can't . . ."

But Mrs. Penworthy grabbed up the novel she had newly purchased in Colchester and placed it firmly in Sylvie's arms. "Now, Miss, I don't want to hear a protest from you. If you think you must pay me something, then do me the honor to visit me to discuss it. It would be my pleasure."

There was nothing Sylvie could do but accept the humiliating offer with as much grace as possible, but her heart ached that they should judge Mr. Fotheringay so meanly. She wished she could explain, and also wished with all her heart that she had not come here today.

Jane exchanged a glance with Mrs. Penworthy, and thought that no autocratic brother deserved such a sweet sister.

Holding their books to them, the young women emerged into the bright sunshine of the spring day and unconsciously lifted their faces to the sun.

The gesture was not lost on the fashionable man who stood before the inn watching them out of the corner of his eye. He hoped that they would return the way they had come and wondered how it might be possible to make their acquaintance. They were lovely women, less obvious in their charms than the statuesque Arabella, who might respond to some competition. One of the two was as exquisite as a doll, with unruly yellow curls and, yes, green eyes. The other less immediately striking and certainly not the kind of woman who would attract a man's eye with her severe hair and demure . . . but then, just as the women passed, her eyes lifted and she looked directly into his eyes.

He was startled into making a half-bow.

71

Jane was glad Miss Pridwell and Ned weren't with her. They would have been horrified at such brazenness. Jane was satisfied; she had won his notice.

The tea party was not going well. Jane and Sylvie had arrived together at Mrs. Woods's Thursday gathering and had chatted with that kind woman until Arabella had made her dramatic, late entrance. Since then neither Jane nor Sylvie had been able to utter more than a monosyllable against the full spate of Arabella's self-absorbed conversation.

"Neither of you has made a come-out! But that is past believing. I would have that thought it was *de rigueur* for all young women nowadays; my own come-out was two years ago," she lied smoothly. "And such a success, my presentation gown was unrivaled. But you have seen it, haven't you, Mrs. Woods? It was a pretty idea, I think, that I invited you and Mr. Woods to Wrabness to view my gown when we returned from London. It must have been such a pleasure for you. I must wonder, why you have come to Wixton instead of London. Soon the Season will begin, and we will be going there shortly ourselves, but it would be dishonest for me to say—and Mrs. Woods will vouch for my honesty—that either of you would take, for it is the rule that a young woman should have a certain *presence,* but then of course it is of the greatest utility to have the backing of a family which has been heard of beyond one's own county, but we shan't talk of that, although I do think that both of you might learn to go to the trouble of putting yourselves forward a little more from common courtesy, which is so lacking these days.

Miss Fotheringay, you have not said a word all afternoon, and I should think with such a brother as yours—who seems to have faultless manners—that you might emulate him. What is his name and what is he doing here?"

Sylvie stared at Arabella as she might a rather horrible spider. No words came to her, and her mouth was too dry for utterance at any rate.

Jane, who had been itching to speak, took the opportunity. "Mr. Fotheringay is a writer, Lady Arabella, and since it would seem to me you are no bluestocking, his occupation must render him beneath your notice."

"Of course I am not a bluestocking," Arabella said, indignant at the slander. "As to whether he is beneath my notice, certainly that is my decision to make."

"Of course, for I don't know how high you aspire, do I?"

Lady Arabella frowned. "I don't aspire. I am Lady Arabella Sneed."

"How do you do?" Jane responded. "Although I do believe we have already been introduced."

Mrs. Woods hid a smile as she reached for the teapot. "More tea, Miss Montcrief?"

Jane exchanged a glance with her as she replied sedately, "Yes, Mrs. Woods, if you would be so kind."

She plunged into a theme central to her thoughts since the previous day, taking advantage of the silence Lady Arabella created by a haughty perusal of Mrs. Woods's cakes.

"Yesterday, when Miss Fotheringay and I were on our way to Mrs. Penworthy's, we espied two gentlemen who were new to us. I wonder if either of you might enlighten us as to their identities."

Mrs. Woods considered, but admitted she knew of no men new to the village.

Jane could tell from Lady Arabella's smile that she was determining whether to satisfy her curiosity.

"It is such an out-of-the-way place for gentlemen to visit. I was surprised to find them at the Dancing Tides. Two such gentlemen you might think would be making a private visit if any at all."

"I can assure you," said Lady Arabella, unwittingly rising to the bait, "that that is precisely what they are doing, Miss Montcrief. You need not worry that they are staying at the inn." She laughed. "It would be quite beneath them. They are staying at Wrabness, of course."

"Ah, then, Lady Arabella, you know which gentlemen I mean!"

"Of course I cannot be sure which men you might mistake for gentlemen; there are many tradesmen who come to the village, farmers as well. But the gentlemen we have staying with us I am sure even *you* would recognize as such."

Jane almost laughed and she caught Sylvie's eye. The latter looked positively astounded, indeed, her mouth was open and she literally gaped at Lady Arabella.

It was just the expression that most gratified Lady Arabella. She was quite used to being gaped at, and considered it her due.

"Actually," she said as though conferring a signal honor in divulging what she was about to divulge, "one of the gentlemen was saying only last evening that it might be amusing to have a ball—or what might pass for a ball in our village—while he is visiting here. I assured him that there would not be enough families to support one, but he was so amused at the idea of a rustic gathering for dancing that of course I thought, wouldn't that be something to laugh about, a village ball." She interrupted herself to titter. "So I must ask you, ladies, all of you and your families to come to Wrabness on Saturday evening. Now please don't say that you would be overwhelmed. It will be just a simple affair, and I'm sure that your gowns will do admirably. No one will be expecting London standards of fashion."

Jane checked her laughter until she had accepted by nods and gestures and obtained the acceptance of Georgianna, too, although that young lady was singularly reluctant to speak for her brother. Jane rolled her eyes at this new evidence of his cruelty. Did he expect her to subsist on the company of her mother and himself? She vowed that Georgianna would attend.

Mrs. Woods accepted for herself and her husband and with that Lady Arabella swept out, her mission accomplished. None of the ladies knew how irritated she had been to have to perform such an invitation. Sharing the tall blond gentleman with other women had not been her idea.

"But how fascinating, Mr. Corydon!"

"I am so glad you find it so, Miss Montcrief. I took you for a woman of understanding."

Jane felt her heart soar with the music.

The ball was as small as Arabella had said it would be. Miss Bingley played the piano, a man from the village played the violin, and there were only four couples standing up for the country dance.

Jane had spent the better part of the day preparing for the evening, a fact that had set her household on its ear. Livvy had felt aggrieved having to press Jane's gown, and had been so careless that Ned had had to intervene and do it himself. His and Miss Pridwell's moods were barely tolerable. Jane had dismissed their complaints from her mind and indulged in preparations for her first dance in her first gown, that if not a ball gown exactly, came closer to such a thing than any garment she had ever worn in her life.

She had washed her hair and dried it by the fire, while buffing her nails until they gleamed. She had experimented with rouge and powder, and rejected both. She had perfumed her hair and her wrists, and had compared two pairs of slippers trying to decide which was the better to wear with a simple white gown with an overlay of blue, embroidered with silver butterflies. She decided on the silver slippers.

She had observed the final effect in the pier glass, and the whole household had gathered to give her their estimation as well, since their fortunes were tied to her success. Livvy had thought Jane looked plain and urged that she wear the garnets and the pearls and that she weave flowers in her hair and drape lace over her bosom and even add the ostrich feather to her hair. Miss Pridwell took off the pearls Jane had tried, and after studying her said, "Yes, that will do."

Ned had protested. "She should wear some jewelry, or she will appear poor."

"No, if she doesn't have a wide variety of jewels, then she should wear none, as though it were by choice.

Besides, Jane has the kind of beauty that is best unadorned."

"You don't think I look too dull?"

"No," Priddy had answered firmly. "You will do."

With such praise had Jane set forth, but it developed that after one glance at her, the newcomer had materialized, introducing himself as Mr. Hector Corydon, that he had been awaiting her arrival which Lady Arabella had told him he was so fortunate as to be able to anticipate, and that he wished to claim the first dance if that would be agreeable with Miss Montcrief.

It had been, and Jane was as happy as she had ever hoped to be. She had not been blind to Arabella's irritated glance, and that could not but add to the pleasures of being with a man who turned out to be a charming conversationalist, and as charming a dancer as he was a conversationalist.

"But you have all my admiration," she said with eyes shining. "It is such a bold plan."

"Not too foolish, you think?"

"Oh, not foolish at all, Mr. Corydon. Bold! Farseeing! Almost heroic!"

"I had not dared to hope for such encomiums."

"But have you met with opposition? That surprises me."

"It is not everyone who has your daring, Miss Montcrief. A plan to turn such a sleepy village as this into one of the most popular and important resorts on the coast of England is daunting to some."

"Oh, but not to me, Mr. Corydon."

"Nothing ventured, nothing gained. Is that not so, Miss Montcrief?"

Jane could only smile foolishly. She wished she could tell him how much they truly had in common, that they were meant for each other, two gamblers, two adventurers, two who dared! What a shame she could not tell him of her impersonation. How he would applaud!

Mr. Corydon looked down at the demure beauty in his arms and thought she might be well advised to keep the secrets of her heart more secret. He had not found it difficult in the least to fix her admiration. But then, he was not inexperienced in fixing the admiration of young women.

"You would be surprised at the opposition I have encountered in other villages for similar plans. If it were not for the leadership of Sir William and his daughter, why I would despair of Wixton, as well."

Jane looked doubtingly across the floor where Arabella, the object of his gaze, was dancing with Georgianna's stuffy brother. She was surprised to see him here at all, much less in a very presentable, if not altogether fashionable, black frock coat. But, she thought, looking up at her partner admiringly, Mr. Corydon's elegance could not be matched. Tonight he wore a coat of a green, the very color of some ribbons Livvy had wanted in London but Priddy had vetoed. Foolish Priddy, how well that color looked on Mr. Corydon. . . .

Who was staring at her with an amused expression. Jane came to herself and said somewhat stiffly, "It would seem that Lady Arabella is a farsighted woman."

Mr. Corydon smiled an intimate smile at Jane. "Between us, Miss Montcrief, it is not that Lady

Arabella is so farsighted, as it is that she wanted to be at the center of things. It appeals to her vanity that Wixton should become a fashionable spa. I believe that is the basis for her interest in my plan. She has none of the broader appreciation that characterizes *your* understanding."

Jane smiled, and saw that she and Mr. Corydon understood each other. Mr. Corydon lifted her hand as though to kiss it, but of course did not in such a public place.

Hector Corydon had aspirations to become a very wealthy man, and his favorite method of doing so was through the use of other people's money. With two associates he had hit upon the idea of trying to develop a watering place on the eastern coast of England to rival those in the south, and had been seeking not only a likely place, but people of substance whom he could interest in his plan.

The Sneeds, whom he had met the previous Christmas at the home of acquaintances, had turned out to be the very people he had been seeking. Together they would turn this stagnant village into a spa that would be the envy of all Europe. That he would become very rich in the process was the goal, and not a fortuitous by-product of the scheme.

He had outlined the barest details of his plan to Jane, and she had responded with an enthusiasm he found gratifying. Her face was radiant with pleasure, and she danced with an animation and liveliness at odds with the modesty of her appearance and the serenity of her expression. He was captivated. But then he had been captivated when dancing with Lady Arabella, and he intended to be just as captivated when dancing with

79

the young thing with the mop of gold curls.

The dance ended, and as he stood chatting with Jane, Mr. Corydon invited her to walk with him along the beach sometime in the next week, to understand the plan of the buildings, promenade, and other improvements he intended for the waterfront.

Jane accepted with becoming restraint.

Her eyes were alive with excitement and triumph as Lord Charles approached her for a dance. He felt chagrin watching the lively expression fade to one of coolest disdain. It was not something he was used to beholding in the faces of women he chose to partner in dance.

"Miss Montcrief, may I have this dance?"

"I am not engaged, Mr. Fotheringay."

He had to be satisfied with that as an acceptance. He took her hand and waited with her while Miss Bingley shuffled through her music looking for a suitable piece.

Jane withdrew her hand and thought how commonplace Mr. Fotheringay looked. Now that she knew what kind of person he was, prosy and selfish, she wondered how she had ever found him handsome. Oh, he was well featured, and his build was splendid, but he lacked the dash and excitement that marked Mr. Corydon as a superior example of his sex. His affected black dress made him look like a crow.

Lord Charles, as he waited, had the unwelcome and unusual experience of being examined by a woman and found wanting. He tried to find refuge in hauteur but it was too small a gathering and it was too late. He had asked her to dance and must be pleasant and civil.

"I think Miss Bingley has found her music," he said, leading Jane out to the center of the large second-story room which served as the Sneed's ballroom.

"Mr. Fotheringay. I am pleased that you have asked me to dance, for I have been wishing to speak to you."

Lord Charles displayed a certain smug gratification. "Yes, Miss Montcrief, and I, you. I have been wishing to thank you for your attentions to, ah, Georgianna. It has made her visit here all the more pleasant to have such a charming companion as you."

Jane snorted, "'Charming!'"

"Have I said something wrong? Most ladies do not object to the use of the word 'charming'."

"I am not most ladies," Jane said, with all the confidence of one whose interest is directed and returned elsewhere.

"Of course not," Lord Charles said, nettled by her immunity to his gallantry, but amused in spite of himself. "Please do forgive me if I so much as intimated that you were merely ordinary."

Jane frowned. "I wish to talk to you."

"Then please do."

The dance separated them and Lord Charles watched her as she danced away from him. Jane forgot her posture of disapproval and danced with relish. She had only danced with Ned and Livvy before this; they had passed the cold winter afternoons of their childhoods dancing strenuously, both to learn the dances and to manufacture sufficient warmth to see them through until evening. It was everything she hoped dancing in company to be, and she had to admit that for a bookworm, Lord Charles was a very accomplished dancer, and that his body, for all its size and strength, moved quite gracefully.

When she returned to him she recalled her duty, and

despite the pleasure she was enjoying and the breathlessness it created, she would not be deterred from the object of her conversation.

"It is about your sister that I wished to speak."

"Georgianna?"

"That is her name," Jane said sarcastically.

"To be sure."

The figure again separated them and Jane was finding it increasingly difficult to give him the setdown she intended while the dance required that they come together and part and come together and part, all the while hopping and twirling and leaping about as though there were enough breath in her body for both activities.

"Your sister, sir, is miserable."

"I beg your pardon."

"I said," she said, panting, "that your sister is miserable."

"I heard you, Miss Montcrief. I was just questioning your perception."

"Well, I beg that you not question my perception until I have had a chance to explain myself."

"Indeed, Miss Montcrief, I suspect that you are not accustomed to having your perceptions questioned."

"No."

"I thought not," he said, a smile competing with a superior lift of his eyebrows. "But I do question your choice of occasions. I wonder if I might suggest that we enjoy this dance, and that afterward we go out onto the balcony where it will be cool and quiet, and you can give me the setdown you wish. That way, you can enjoy both activities fully."

Jane danced on and then drew up, realizing that she

had been insulted. But then, Mr. Fotheringay's face looked so bland she decided that if she had been insulted, he was too stupid to realize he had achieved such a thing, so she simply nodded and threw herself into the dance.

She had the pleasure of catching, in one of the more lively parts of the dance, an appreciative expression on her partner's face. She was glad, thinking it no great thing to fix his interest, but knowing that it would mean that he would pay more attention to what she had to say about poor Georgianna.

So she made herself as charming as she knew how, laughing and leaping, and knew that she had drawn more than her share of attention, when out of the corner of her eye she saw Lady Arabella scowling at her over the arm of Mr. Corydon's friend. Ah, but this was the life she was meant to lead!

She closed her eyes momentarily and imagined herself in London, at Almacks, with dozens of young, eligible, rich men looking on as she danced the night away, having to diplomatically choose among all those who wanted her with wild passion and . . . she opened her eyes and blinked. Lord Charles didn't scruple to contain his laughter, and Jane felt appalled that she should have succumbed to daydreams and given this dullard the occasion to laugh at her. She glared at him, drew herself together, and finished the dance.

She was, then, in a fine frame of mind to give him the dressing down of his life when he took her arm to lead her from the floor. As she stepped into the golden light of dusk from the long doors onto the balcony, Jane sensed a disturbance nearby and glanced over to find Livvy and Ned pulling guiltily away from the windows.

83

They turned to face her, not more than five feet away. There was no avoiding them. She scowled, pinching her face into its most horrible glare, and stared at them before she lifted her shoulders, drew a breath, and spoke.

"Lizzy, Nettles, is there something you wished to see me about?"

Ned was flushed and glanced from her to Lord Charles who stood behind her and whose expression she couldn't see. Finally, tugging at his collar, he said, "No."

Jane wanted to grind her teeth. He was supposed to say "No, *ma'am*." They had been over it a thousand times.

"We just wanted to see the dancing, ma'am," said Livvy with a pathetic look on her face. "I know it was outrageous and not at all what we should be doing. I know we have incurred your greatest wrath and deserve whatever punishment you might set for us, ma'am, but pity," she cried, throwing herself to her knees before Jane and clasping her hands together in entreaty. "Please don't send us away. I promise you we shall never do anything like this again, but you see, we just wanted to see what dancing looked like." The beginnings of tears were present in her liquid blue eyes.

Jane opened and closed her mouth and stood staring helplessly. Behind her she heard what could only be the smothered laughter of Mr. Florian Fotheringay.

Ned, embarrassed to be associated with Livvy, nudged at her with his knee, "Come on, Lizzy, get up, for heaven's sake. Come on." He avoided Jane's eye and frowned at Livvy.

Jane found her voice. "Nettles, this is inexcusable.

84

However, I cannot fault you for wishing to let little Lizzy," she said through clenched teeth, "have the chance to see a dance. It was kindly meant on your part, I'm sure. But now, if you would be so good, you must both return to the servants' hall. I understand that they have some refreshments for you. But don't you drink too much, I mean, of course you will not drink too much, and you, Lizzy, will not drink at all."

Livvy, being half-dragged from the balcony by Ned, reached toward Jane with her free hand and cried, "Oh, thank you, good lady, thank you. You are generous and good, and it is only the greatest good fortune that has allowed me the honor of being your servant."

Jane stared up at the sky and thought, if I don't say anything, they will leave all the faster.

Finally Ned pulled Livvy around the corner and Jane breathed a sigh of relief. She stood overlooking the grounds of Wrabness, unable to face Mr. Fotheringay, but she didn't have to face him to know that he was laughing.

"Where did you ever find such a maid?" he asked. "One could almost believe she stepped from a novel."

If he only knew.

Jane waited until her own face was composed before turning to Mr. Fotheringay, who was wiping tears from his eyes. She stared at him coldly.

"Excuse me, Miss Montcrief. I do not mean to be laughing at you. It was the maid. She is certainly an unusual maid."

Jane chewed the inside of her lip. Livvy would land them all in the soup if she weren't more careful. Really that girl had no guard on her tongue at all. And then suddenly Jane smiled. Dear Livvy.

"Well, I'm glad you find it amusing, too. I would be shocked to think that you employ such an original young thing only to abuse her."

"I do not abuse my maids, Mr. Fotheringay." Jane was glad to find that her wrath had returned. "If you will remember, it was about your sister that I wished to speak."

"Ah, yes. I suspect that I am about to have it pointed out to me that I do abuse my sister."

"Well, yes, in a manner of speaking."

"Yes?" Mr. Fotheringay suddenly looked so cold and fierce that Jane experienced a moment of uncertainty. He looked quite . . . commanding. But then she remembered Georgianna's plight and plunged in to what she must say.

"I find Miss Fotheringay—Georgianna—quite subdued for one of her years and interests. She is obviously a woman of clear intelligence and curiosity, yet she hasn't the confidence of a wigeon. The merest thing sends her into retreat. But mostly, I suspect, she is intimidated by you. I saw at once that she has been dragged off to this part of the country as punishment inflicted by you for some no doubt mild indiscretion on her part. Indeed, Mr. Fotheringay, the only indiscretion I can imagine Georgianna having the courage to perpetrate would be to read past the time you wished her to douse her candle. She is quite biddable and extraordinarily reticent about her own opinions.

"But it is chiefly about money that I wished to speak. You must have noticed that tonight she is wearing the same dress she has worn at least three times in my company. She ought, at her age, to have the benefit of

86

gowns appropriate to her station. Her clothes would disgrace my maid. I have found it shocking that not only has she not been allowed to outfit herself as a young lady—and a beautiful one at that—should, but that she also has not the sufficiency to borrow books from Mrs. Penworthy. She wished to take them, but her courage failed her; I believe she is afraid of you. In short, Mr. Fotheringay, you are wounding her pride and spirit, and denying her the comfort and pleasures she is due by your arrogant, penny-pinching ways."

Lord Charles stood absolutely still, looking down into the earnest, self-righteous face of the woman who dared address him thus. He longed to slap her.

Jane knew it instantly. "You would like to dismiss me as you are used to dismissing Georgianna, wouldn't you? Well, you can't. And you can't dismiss the ideas I have placed in your mind. Remember, Mr. Fotheringay, I shall be watching to see how you treat your sister, and I guarantee you that I will make it miserable for you in Wixton unless I see an amelioration in her circumstances."

"Miss Montcrief," Lord Charles said finally, "I wonder if anyone has ever, in the whole of your pampered life, told you that not only are you impertinent, but that you are also quite stupid."

Jane smiled. "Ah, Mr. Fotheringay, just the man to take my measure! Thank you."

Lord Charles fumed. "Beware, my dear Miss Montcrief. You would not wish to make an enemy of me."

Jane burst out laughing. Throwing him a look of pure disdain she returned to the ballroom and, she hoped, to the arms of Mr. Corydon.

Chapter Six

Sylvie was up early one morning the next week and was surprised to find herself walking toward the Montcriefs', but she knew that Jane kept country hours as well and that she was assured of a welcome. Indeed, Jane was everything that she had always dreamed of in a friend, but had never had due to the isolated circumstances of her life. She sensed a fierce protectiveness in Jane and believed that it was no accident that after every time Mr. Corydon had danced with Jane, he had then danced with her. She couldn't have known that Mr. Corydon had needed no urging and that, anyway, Jane hadn't thought to give it.

Sylvie was growing more comfortable in her new circumstances. It seemed that just in the last few days she was more at ease with Mr. Fotheringay, that he seemed less distant and imperious. Not imperious exactly, she couldn't put her finger on it, but there was something about the man which intimidated her, even though there was nothing in his actual behavior she could name. He always behaved with exact and punctilious courtesy.

Perhaps that was it, perhaps in the last days he had been more natural, treating her and her mother with humor and directness, where before he had always been rigidly if not intimidatingly polite. He had even quite spontaneously suggested that she and her mother ought to have some additional gowns and insisted that they must allow him to outfit them as became their position. He had insisted, and had borne away every objection that it was by his kindness they were fed and sheltered already. He had pointed out that he was well tended by them, that they rendered him service as well, and that he was uncomfortable to be put in a position of indebtedness to them which they were not permitting him to discharge. They had been doubtful, but he insisted that he would be more comfortable if they would only allow him to make them less conspicuous by their limited number of gowns, and if they would take a modest allowance every month which they could use at their discretion.

That was kindness indeed. It meant that she might borrow as many books as she wished from Mrs. Penworthy's establishment, without worrying that she was spending more money than she ought.

It did cause her to wonder about the source of Mr. Fotheringay's income. Certainly he wrote a good deal—most days, in fact—allowing time only for rides early every morning and an increasing number of social engagements. But she could see no evidence that he had ever sold anything he had written, and doubted that even if he had, that he could live off such an income. So he must have another source of money which he had not told them of. Every week he received a large bundle of papers which he retired to his bookroom to peruse and would send off again in a few days.

Sylvie found herself speculating a great deal about Mr. Fotheringay. It made her feel guilty, but sometimes she found it hard to believe she knew everything about him, no, rather, she felt that he was concealing things from them. Well, of course, she had no right to know any of his private affairs, but the fact remained, she knew nothing about him.

That and her mother's absorption in their problems, her anxious worries about their course of action—whether to return to their home or not, whether to visit their solicitor in London or not—all these things made Sylvie feel very lonely at times. That was why Jane's liveliness and, lately, her clear indications of friendship were so particularly welcome.

She approached the house from a footpath which cut through a woods behind the High Street on which the Montcriefs' home stood and consequently approached the house from behind. She stood stock-still when she grew close enough to the garden to discover that she wasn't alone. There was a young man sitting in the garden enjoying the sun and reading. She didn't recognize him, but she saw the sun gleaming on dark brown curls tinged with copper, and she saw the head resting in the hand, the complete absorption in the book.

She studied the young man, wondering who he might be, and thought that Ariadne might be entertaining a guest, even though she had seen her just yesterday and she had said nothing about expecting anyone.

She stepped forward and cleared her throat.

The young man jerked his head and stood up

quickly, knocking the book to the ground.

Heavens! It was the Montcriefs' footman. Sylvie stared at him.

Ned stared at Sylvie and could have cried out, so beautiful was she. She was wrapped in a crimson cloak and wore black slippers which were wet with dew. Beneath the cloak she wore a white gown which brushed the grass. She was startled, her mouth was open just the slightest bit in a wordless *O,* and he wanted to gather her up in his arms.

Then he remembered who he was.

He bowed. "Excuse me."

"Oh, that is all right. I was just coming . . ." Sylvie raised her arm vaguely to indicate the footpath. "The lane is so much shorter . . . to see Miss Montcrief."

"Of course."

"But your book." Sylvie nodded at the book fallen in the long dewy grass.

"Oh, it was nothing." Ned flushed. Jane would have his head for this.

"But you can't leave it lying there . . ." Sylvie approached him, bent down, and picked it up. She thought he might be embarrassed to be caught reading one of the books that belonged to his mistress, but she was sure that Jane would not mind if her footman borrowed books from her.

She looked at the cover. "Addison!"

"Yes."

"You read Addison!" She marveled at him.

"Yes." Ned did not trust himself to say more.

"I love Addison. Do you read Dr. Johnson?"

Ned smiled his enthusiasm. "Yes."

"Oh, so do I. He is most entertaining. So few people

read him nowadays."

"Yes."

"Well, I didn't mean to intrude." Sylvie looked up into that bright, handsome, intelligent face—the poor young man was so embarrassed, but he was so unusual—he was not much older than herself. Impulsively she reached out and touched his arm. "I'm sure Miss Montcrief could not mind your reading her books."

"I'm not so sure." Ned said bitterly.

"No, indeed. I shall tell her, and you'll see."

"No, no. Don't tell her. Please."

"But I'm sure you are mistaken in her. She wouldn't mind if you read. I'm sure you do your tasks."

"No, I must entreat you. Please do not tell her."

"You make her sound like an ogre. She is not. I can assure you."

"Miss Fotheringay," Ned took a deep breath, pleased to have the chance to say her name. "I must ask you not to tell my . . . Miss Montcrief. Let it be between the two of us."

Sylvie looked into his eyes. They were such gentle eyes. "Yes," she said simply. "Yes, it will just be between us."

"Thank you."

"You're welcome."

They stood staring at each other for a wordless moment.

Then suddenly Ned came to himself and turned and gestured toward the door, and as a footman should, preceded her to the house, pausing to open the door to her and bow her inside.

As soon as he was inside he donned his livery and

combed his hair, and then suddenly stood still and thought how beautiful she was.

As the young maid showed Sylvie into the back parlor where Ariadne was stitching a new gown, Sylvie suddenly stopped and thought, "How extraordinary. Her footman can read!"

And then she blushed.

Jane looked up to find Sylvie entering with a blush on her face. Misreading the cause, she said, "But Georgianna, how lovely for you to come so early, this way we can have a comfortable coze, for my mother is still in her bedchamber attending to household affairs." Leaning over she confided, "Actually, she doesn't come down until ten or so, she enjoys having her chocolate all by herself."

"I wasn't sure about coming so early but . . . I came upon your footman outside. He's quite . . . There's something unusual about him."

"Did he offend you in some way?" Jane held her breath, her needle frozen in mid-stitch.

"Oh, no, not at all. We just chatted a moment. He's quite pleasant. No, he's intelligent. No, that's not what I mean either . . ."

Heaven help us, Jane thought, she sounds as besotted as Ned.

"Yes, he is intelligent for a footman," she dismissed him airily. "But tell me, what was your opinion of Mr. Corydon and Mr. Rankin?" They had not had a chance to talk about the ball properly since their previous meeting had been with their mothers in attendance.

"Oh, they were very presentable."

Jane was disappointed. "Did you think them elegant? Unusually well spoken?"

"No, did you?"

"Oh, no. What did you think of Mr. Corydon's plan for Wixton?"

"I didn't have a chance to speak with him a great deal. It does sound a bit radical. This is such a charming, small village. It seems a shame to alter it."

"But think of the excitement! I'm sure it would be very good for the village to bring in new people, new ideas. That's what these tiny coastal villages need. They get so set in their ways. They can be really horrible."

"Do you find Wixton horrible?"

"Oh, no. I was just speaking in a general way."

"Well, I find it comfortable. I'm enjoying my stay here."

"Are you?" Jane said, remembering to ring for Livvy to fetch them tea. "I wonder how your life goes on, sometimes. Your brother seems so wrapped up in his books. Do you . . ." She suddenly realized how improper her line of questioning was. "I'm sure he must have fascinating stories to tell."

"Yes."

"He has seen so much of the world during the war. Have you ever traveled with him?"

"Oh no. I don't . . . don't like traveling."

Livvy came into the room. She was completely grave. "You rang, ma'am."

"Yes, Lizzy, could you get us some tea? Or would you prefer chocolate, Georgianna?"

"Chocolate would be wonderful, if it's not too much trouble."

"It's no trouble, I'm good at making it," Livvy responded.

94

Sylvie smiled kindly. "I'm sure you are."

"I make it often now," Livvy confided. "I can make syllabub, too."

"Can you?"

"That is all wonderful, Lizzy, how much you have learned since you entered service with us, but then, it's no more than we would expect from a maid, is it?"

"No, ma'am. Everyone takes the accomplishments of a maid for granted."

Jane felt that sinking feeling come over her. "Well," she said briskly, "no one takes your accomplishments for granted, we all know with what difficulty you have attained them. Now," she said quickly, holding up her hand, "please do bring us the chocolate, thank you, Lizzy."

A mutinous look flashed across Livvy's face, but she spun obediently on her heel and went off to the kitchen.

Jane breathed a sigh of relief.

"You have such extraordinary servants," Sylvie said. "They're so well spoken."

"Too often spoken, I think."

Jane changed the subject and the morning passed with no more impertinent remarks from Livvy, and in face her "servants" performed faultlessly, except, perhaps, that Ned hovered more over Georgianna helping her with her cape and giving her his arm as she descended the front steps, than was entirely necessary.

Every graceful, elegant arrangement with which Jane had hoped to greet Mr. Corydon when he arrived the next day (to escort her on an expedition to the site of the resort) had most unaccountably slipped from her grasp. She had meant to be negligently but charmingly disposed on one of the silk-draped sofas, caught in the most beguiling domesticity.

It was not to be. Priddy, who had an appointment with the ladies Woods and Penworthy for tea, insisted in delaying her departure until Mr. Corydon had arrived. Then, realizing that with Ned away on errands and herself engaged, Jane would have no chaperone, decided to forbid the outing altogether. Jane protested, arguing that it was broad daylight, a matter of a few miles' walk, and that country habits permitted such an excursion.

Priddy was adamant. No escort, no excursion. Jane retreated to her room near tears, kept from shedding them more from the ravages they would create than from pride.

She dressed for the excursion anyway, wondering if she would have the courage to face Priddy down and accompany Mr. Corydon alone, knowing that if she were dressed and waiting when Mr. Corydon arrived, it would be very hard for Priddy to deny her.

But she was late, struggling alone to button the long gloves she had chosen to wear, unassisted by Livvy who had unaccountably disappeared. One half of a very long row of buttons remained when she heard the sounds of Mr. Corydon's arrival.

There was no hurrying buttons, Jane found to her intense frustration. Her fingers in her gloved hand were clumsy and stiff, unequal to the task. But she had more buttons buttoned than unbuttoned and feverishly worked on, listening anxiously to sounds from belowstairs, lest she hear the sounds of Mr. Corydon's abrupt departure.

But she heard nothing, and all the buttons finally were slipped through the narrow holes in the pearly kid, and after smoothing down her hair one last time and wondering whether to powder cheeks that were distinctly flushed, Jane slipped down the stairs, hoping that her apprehensiveness would seem the bloom of health.

She came upon Priddy sitting calmly on a small chair conversing with Mr. Corydon, who leaned gracefully against the arm of the sofa across from her. As he rose to greet her, Jane felt a catch in her throat at his appearance. He was attired in shades of blue, a beautiful bright greenish blue that in his waistcoat glowed as iridescent quicksilver that changed with every movement. She lifted a glowing face to him, wishing she could tell him just how handsome he looked, but managing heroically simply to greet him.

He bowed charmingly over her hand and told her that he had enjoyed his opportunity to talk with her mother, that she had condescended to show the most intelligent interest in the plans for the resort. Priddy smiled but said nothing, and Jane could see from her face that she was biding her time before she said the words that would make the excursion impossible. But before she had the chance, an extraordinary thing happened.

Livvy appeared. Jane and Priddy both gaped, forgetting the presence of Mr. Corydon. Livvy was wearing a gown of Priddy's, a heavy drab gown of brown stuff that had been one of Priddy's work gowns. She had made it over to fit herself, but so hastily and clumsily that the effect was arresting. One huge dart had been sewn seemingly haphazardly to the left of her stomach and another tuck, running horizontally, had shortened the bodice and achieved the effect of a rather oddly shaped bosom. The skirt had been hemmed in bits and pieces, it seemed, resulting in a trainlike effect of greater length, unfortunately in the front of the gown, which hobbled her as she walked the few steps from the hallway to the saloon. On her head she wore an old hat that Jane had never seen before, of close-cut beaver that was singularly out of style, out of season, and out of porportion to Livvy's small, delicate head. Over her shoulders she had draped a woolen shawl of hideous taupe, and on her hands wore yellow Bath gloves whose fingers were at least an inch longer than Livvy's own, and which, as she adjusted her shawl, wobbled back and forth at the ends of her hands like odd and floppy claws.

While Jane and Priddy, and perhaps even Mr. Corydon—although Jane hadn't taken her eyes from Livvy to see—stood openmouthed, Livvy, behaving with the most regal and rigid formality, said, "I am ready."

Priddy rose and moved near Livvy, as though to block her from Mr. Corydon's view. Obviously, it seemed to Jane, she had decided simply to ignore her. "You must forgive us, Mr. Corydon, for causing you a false start this morning. I am sorry but Ariadne cannot accompany you today. We had forgotten that I had a previous engagement and the footman is away on business. So you see, there is no one to escort her. I am so very sorry."

Mr. Corydon lifted his hand to Livvy and said, "But your maid . . ."

"Our maid has other duties, I'm afraid."

Jane found herself in the unenviable position of having to argue that this ragbag assemblage of a servant she found standing before her would do perfectly well as a chaperone. She took a deep breath and addressing the space over Priddy's head, since even in her determination to have her excursion she could not look Priddy in the eye, said as cheerfully as she could, "Mr. Corydon is quite right, Mother. Lizzy will suit admirably."

"Indeed, Ariadne, in the normal course of things, you would be correct, but today I think it would be a better use of her time to prepare a crust for tonight's dinner."

This sounded so positively rude that even Priddy comprehended and had to retract. "No, of course it is better for her to go with you, I do apologize, but she is so young, you see . . ."

"Sixteen is not so young, ma'am," Livvy said in a deep, sepulchral voice that Jane assumed she had adopted to convey great age and maturity.

Priddy was silenced; it was, after all, the age they had agreed to pretend Livvy had attained. She looked away in defeat and Jane felt a sudden lift of spirits.

"Well," she said, plumping the bow of her bonnet, "shall we go then?"

"Delighted." Turning to follow her out of the door, Mr. Corydon made a final bow to Priddy and cast one last glance around the room, taking in, once again, the splendid and surprising vase on the mantelpiece. Observing him from beneath her lashes, Livvy took a few stumbling steps forward, lifted her skirts, and followed them from the room.

On the pavement, Mr. Corydon extended his arm to

Jane who tucked her hand in it happily. A sudden nudge forced them apart and Livvy inserted herself between them. "I'm here to chaperone you," she said in her new, deep voice.

"Yes, Lizzy, and glad I am that you could come," Jane said pleasantly. "But you may walk behind us."

"May but won't." Livvy spoke as though the dignity of a maid rested entirely on brevity. She stood stolidly next to Mr. Corydon, and when Jane tried to slip in between them, was immovable.

"Lizzy, please walk behind us," she said as pleasantly as she could.

"No."

"Oh, dear." Jane tried to sound humorously frustrated. "Mr. Corydon, do you think you could persuade my maid that it is right and proper for her to walk behind us?"

Mr. Corydon rose to the occasion and, smiling warmly at Jane to show her that he was choosing to be as amused as she, spoke quite slowly and distinctly to Livvy. "Your mistress has asked you to follow behind her, and I can assure you, if you have any scruples on the subject, that it is considered fine form in London, and in the country as well, to walk behind her at a respectful distance."

Livvy looked quickly up at him and then at Jane. After a long pause she flushed and said, "No."

"Excuse me, Mr. Corydon," and Jane turned her back on him to face Livvy. "Livvy, whatever is the matter with you? Why are you doing this? Stop it at once!"

"If I'm going to chaperone you, I have to keep you from private conversation."

100

"Private conversation? What on earth are you talking about?"

"Chaperoning."

"Is this something you have read?"

"Yes," she said eagerly, sounding like herself. "In *The Bride of Sevilla* the chaperone was put to death because she allowed the Duke of Alba to speak with Ana!"

Jane glanced quickly up at Mr. Corydon who was politely gazing at a point far distant behind them. "Livvy, that is nonsense. This is England, this is not a novel. Now I must insist that you let us walk side by side and follow at a distance."

Livvy looked mulish.

"Please," Jane added desperately. "it is good of you to escort me, Livvy, and I do appreciate it, but you mustn't make it impossible for me to talk to Mr. Corydon."

"Very well," Livvy answered in her deep, gravelly tones.

Jane essayed a laugh, "All settled, Mr. Corydon. It is the price of having such a young maid. One never quite knows what to expect."

Mr. Corydon bowed and again offered his arm. This time Jane took it with a firm grip and was pleased to find that they were not forced apart. She turned to smile at Livvy and bumped heads with her instead. For although Livvy condescended to allow them to walk abreast, she was hovering immediately behind them, leaning her head in between theirs. "A little further back, Lizzy, will do just as well."

"Can't."

"Can," Jane said as lightly as possible.

"Have to tell mistress."

Jane tried to ignore her. "What a lovely day for a walk, Mr. Corydon!"

"Indeed, it is, Miss Montcrief. Excuse me . . . is it . . . Lizzy . . . could you step back just a bit?"

"If you'll talk louder."

"What?" Mr. Corydon asked.

"I have to report to my mistress what you talk about. It is one of the duties of the chaperone. If you talk louder, than I can walk a bit further behind." Livvy sounded more plaintive than husky.

"Report?" Mr. Corydon looked blankly at Jane.

Jane laughed again. She would have to practice this gay unconcerned laugh. It wasn't convincing even to her ears. "Mr. Corydon, let us just pretend there is no one here but we two. I think it is the only way to go on."

"Well, yes. It is a lovely day."

"Indeed . . ." Jane said weakly. Real conversation was impossible. Nonetheless she tried again. "What wonderful chance it was that brought us to Wixton just as such a wonderful transformation was about to be begun . . . Lizzy, please move back!"

"What did you say about Wixton?" Livvy asked from behind, panting now in her efforts to control gait, skirt, and hat.

"I was saying . . ."

"Ah, there are the others!" Mr. Corydon spoke quickly and Jane had the awful fear that it was relief she heard in his voice. She looked up. So absorbed had she been in the contretemps Livvy had served up, Jane had not bestowed so much as a glance at her surroundings. Her smile dimmed as she realized that there was a cluster of people standing before the Dancing Tides, and that they were made up of most of

102

their shared acquaintance. Mr. Corydon turned toward them, and Jane became painfully aware that they were meant to be part of the afternoon's excursion. Her heart sank. She had recognized the Fotheringays, as well as Mr. Rankin and Lady Arabella, her housekeeper, and her father.

"Shall we be making a party, then?" she asked, trying to keep her voice light.

Turning back, Mr. Corydon covered her hand with his. "Oh, yes, my dear Miss Montcrief. I am so sorry, for I would have enjoyed a *tête-à-tête* with you, and your charming . . . maid, but there is such interest in this enterprise that as soon as it became known that I planned to walk out with you today, it happened that everyone wished to accompany us. It is Lady Arabella who arranged things." He looked knowingly down at her.

She smiled bravely back, "I understand, Mr. Corydon."

"I am sure you can understand my disappointment, Miss Montcrief."

Jane looked down modestly. A sudden happy thought occurred to her. "Oh, and Lizzy, you may return now. With Georgianna and Mrs. Fotheringay present, I shall be quite satisfactorily chaperoned. Thank you so much."

"Oh, no, ma'am," Livvy said in her grave tones. "I must not."

"Do go on, Mr. Corydon," Jane said as gaily as she could. "I'll join you presently."

Mr. Corydon, his gaze fixed on the assemblage across the road, gave her a polite nod and took his leave.

"Livvy, you are completely ruining things. Look

how he crosses to Lady Arabella. How could he not prefer her company to mine given your behavior?"

"It's not my fault, Jenny, it's yours. You aren't trying hard enough. If you are going to succeed in prying him loose from her clutches, you will need to be a lot more aggressive than you have been."

"Livvy, leave this instant or I will not be answerable."

"I can't let you down, Jenny; it would be the easy thing for me to turn my back on you."

Jane stared at her sister. Had she always been this awful?

She glanced behind her and found that the party was breaking up, seemingly headed for carriages, and that Lady Arabella had appropriated Mr. Corydon to her side.

"Very well. I can't force you to leave, but if you stay, I shall be furious with you, and if you speak one word, just one, Livia Marlingforthe, I shall see that you are put on bread and water for twenty-seven years and never once let out of your room. Do you hear?"

"That's nothing. Gabriella Sabatini lived for thirty-five years on bread . . ."

Jane turned on her heel, leaving Livvy to trail along after her, and warmly greeted Sylvie and her mother who both regretted Priddy's absence and warmly congratulated her on the presence of her maid. "It is so kind of you to allow your maid an outing," Sylvie said warmly, smiling at Livvy, who tried to look abashed and grateful and ended by looking—in Jane's estimation—only sly.

Sylvie explained that Lady Arabella had just disposed of the company. She herself along with Mr.

Fotheringay, Mr. Rankin, Mr. Corydon, and her father were to ride in one carriage, and the housekeeper, Miss Bingley, herself, her mother, and now apparently Ariadne and her maid, would ride in the other.

Jane felt Livvy's assessment of her ability to stand up against Lady Arabella to be painfully accurate. Not only was she losing her opportunity for a private afternoon with Mr. Corydon, but she felt eclipsed by Lady Arabella. Up to that moment, Jane had been content with her pale aquamarine gown, but standing near Lady Arabella, she felt like a shadow without color. That lady wore a vivid daffodil walking gown trimmed with cerise bands, and her blazing hair was crowned with a raffish bonnet trimmed with heaps of cherries and loops of cerise ribbons.

The only consolation to be found was that Sylvie looked exquisite in a new apple green gown which enhanced her lively coloring. Jane resisted bestowing an approving glance at Sylvia's brother—who anyway was caught up in Lady Arabella's orbit, and listening in apparent fascination to something Mr. Rankin was saying.

Livvy sidled up to Jane. "They're going to put you in a different carriage. If you don't *do* something, the whole day will be in vain."

Jane rounded on her. "Hush! I warned you."

Livvy hissed at her. "Go up to Mr. Corydon, tell him what a wonderful omen it is to have such a lovely day to walk to the site of the resort, that the propitious weather promises propitious beginnings, and that a slow walk to savor the beauty is something everyone must gratefully anticipate."

Jane stared hard at Livvy, thinking that she must be nine-parts goose to listen to her at all. But with nothing else occurring to her, she nodded curtly.

Taking Georgianna's arm for moral support, Jane strolled as casually as she was able to the group of men around Lady Arabella. "What a fortuitous day for our expedition," she began rather loudly, praying she didn't sound too foolish, "All the propitious weather and propitious beginnings . . . We must walk to appreciate just how wonderful a day this is."

Lady Arabella did not even turn in her direction, but answered dismissively, "We are riding; you're in the other carriage."

"Riding?" asked Jane, stung to courage by Lady Arabella's attitude. "Ah, of course, Lady Arabella, it is such a great distance. I had not thought how wearying you might find it. Forgive me."

Lady Arabella's face worked. Sylvie squeezed Jane's arm in alarm. Jane struggled on. "I am sure the gentlemen would enjoy the chance to stretch their legs, but it is of no matter when a lady feels indisposed, is it?" she asked, not daring to look any of them in the eye.

Mr. Corydon attempted diplomacy. "It is not faintheartedness that suggested the carriages, but its obverse, an eagerness to arrive immediately at the site, so as to enjoy its pleasures."

"Ah, I see," Jane said with the appearance of wisdom. "But what a shame to lose the chance to walk the route to see the landscape unfold, to understand its relationship to the village, the distances involved, the approaching scents and signs of the seaside."

"Much better!" cried an unexpected ally, Sir William. "Let's have done with this talk of carriages

106

and set out. I for one am happy for an excuse for a brisk walk."

"You may well be right, Papa," said Lady Arabella measuringly, not taking her eyes from Jane and managing to convey both challenge and victory in her scrutiny. Her capitulation meant that she relinquished control in one direction only to seize it from another. "Miss Fotheringay, Mrs. Fotheringay, you may proceed, then Mr. Rankin, will you be so kind as to accompany my father? Mr. Fotheringay, Mr. Corydon, I shall have need of your opinions as we walk and you," she nodded to Jane, "will find suitable escort in Miss Bingley and your friend . . . or is it maid?"

Jane caught Livvy's welling gaze which said too clearly, "Do something!"

But Jane could think of nothing to do, short of putting herself forward in a very obvious way. Livvy was not without resources, however. Speaking quite loudly despite the hoarseness she still affected, and looking directly at Mr. Corydon, she announced, "My lady is too gently bred to speak of this herself, but she is quite prone to fainting and will require a gentleman's arm."

Chapter Seven

Lady Arabella disposed of this insignificant challenge to her authority by the simple expedient of taking Mr. Corydon's arm and leading him away. Mr. Fotheringay, looking amused, strolled toward Jane and Livvy. "Might my arm do as well?"

Jane managed a creditable smile and said, "I am afraid my maid much exaggerates matters. I haven't fainted in my life."

Livvy burst forth. "Oh, she would never admit it, but she has a most decided tendency to swoon. She swoons at sad stories, Mr. Fotheringay, and when she sees an injured animal. Why just yesterday . . ."

"Lizzy, that will do." The party had set out, Sylvie and her mother in the company of Sir William, and Mr. Fotheringay, Jane, and Livvy were left behind to make up their own group. Trying to smother disappointment and irritation at having her greatly anticipated excursion take place in the laughable company of Mr. Fotheringay on one hand and a sister distinctly drifting off into heaven-only-knew-what freaks on the other, Jane resigned herself to biding her time until the opportunity arose once again to be private with Mr. Corydon. She would give herself over to what were left of the pleasures of the countryside.

Livvy set herself between Lord Charles and Jane. As she walked, she wrestled with her skirt and hat, until she abruptly tore the latter from her head. The action seemed to free her tongue. At first Jane thought to stop her conversation, but thought what did *she* care for Mr. Fotheringay's opinion, and decided to give Livvy her head. As though she had any choice, she thought ruefully.

"Mr. Fotheringay," Livvy began, gushingly, "you are so tall. You are quite one of the tallest men I have ever met. I am sure you must be very strong."

Lord Charles looked affronted. In a cold voice he replied, "I am tall."

"Oh, that is the way with these tall, strong men, ma'am, they are so very modest. You will find that the really good-looking men—the truly handsome specimens of their kind—are loath to have others dwell on their superiority."

There was a silence.

Livvy was undeterred. "And may I say, what a fine figure you cut on the dance floor. I know I should not be referring to this, but I would like you to know that I find your dancing unequalled, unparalleled, unmatched in grace and liveliness. Why the way you hold yourself is almost *heroic!*"

"Lizzy!" Jane's voice came out in a croak, so hard was she trying not to laugh. She didn't dare look at Mr. Fotheringay.

"I should love to see you on horseback, Mr.

109

Fotheringay. I know that you could control a steed to within an inch of its life. I see you on a great white charger, your manly form encased in the steel of the Middle Ages. Yes, your eyes on a distant battle, invincible and unafraid. You would move forward, at one with the animal beneath you, hurling yourself into the fray, charging, wheeling, feinting, attacking . . ."

Lord Charles cocked an eye at Livvy, suddenly comprehending. "You read novels."

Livvy was genuinely startled. "Yes."

"That's where you're getting all of this!"

"And what's wrong with that?" she asked. "I think more people should read novels. Conversations would improve if people read them more. Especially the conversations between men and women."

"Ah, so that is your point, to improve the courting behavior of men and women?"

"Well, in a manner of speaking," Livvy said, struggling not to refer to Jane's manifest deficiencies when it came to the pursuit of men.

"Is it—Lizzy?"

"Yes, sir."

"Lizzy, your presence here at my side is like the freshest zephyr wafted down from the wooded hills to linger against my person like a fragrant whisper."

"Oh, that is nice, Mr. Fotheringay!"

"Your eyes are like the blue of the sky seen after a year's most foul storms. Your teeth are like the first drop from an icicle after winter's most foul cold. Your lips are like the petals of a rose, unfurling before the sun after a season of the most foul drought."

"Oh, Mr. Fotheringay!"

"Your form," continued Lord Charles, speaking

110

theatrically, employing his hands with great energy, "is like that of Aphrodite, your wisdom like that of Athena, your smile is like that of La Gioconda. In short, my dear, you are the very measure of women."

"Really?"

"Well, I was trying to give you a sample of . . ."

"Are you trifling with me?"

Jane finally laughed. "Please don't trifle with the affections of my maid, Mr. Fotheringay."

"Indeed, I meant to do no such thing. I was only trying to show her the versatility of my compliments, one of the first requirements of any well-spoken suitor. How would you judge me, Lizzy?"

"Better on form than sincerity," she sniffed. "Why don't *you* try, ma'am?" she goaded, paying Jane back for her laughter.

"Oh, no, I fail at compliments completely."

"So I had observed," agreed Lord Charles.

"Consider this a chance to practice," Livvy said with patronizing kindness.

"Very well, then. Whom shall I compliment?"

"Mr. Fotheringay, of course."

"Yes, try to address some courtly phrases to me. It should challenge you sufficiently."

"Indeed, I shall take up your challenge. Mr. Fotheringay, your eyes are like the black coals that I place in the stove to start my tea water boiling. Your teeth are similar to the uncooked white of an egg. Your hair is like . . ."

"Oh, stop!" Livvy's face screwed up in disgust.

"Oh, no, don't stop. My hair—lank seaweed, perhaps? A well-used mop? Pray, enlighten me," Lord Charles urged.

Jane permitted a smile.

The road they had been following had led them through woods and an occasional field, but now it opened up into the last few hundred yards of the wide, low expanse that embraced the sea. Jane looked about at the great, bright reach of the sky, the glimmer and sheen of the water, and involuntarily stretched out her arms as though to embrace its loveliness.

Livvy saw her expression change and suddenly burst into a madcap run, issuing over her shoulder the challenge of their childhoods, "Can't catch me!"

Jane looked longingly after her, then laughed deep in her throat and spun around, sweeping a huge turn, her skirts lifting out from her body, and then threw herself down the road after Livvy, catching her with her hand and together they ran pell-mell for the shore, laughing and shrieking, their skirts alight, feet flying.

Lord Charles was sure he would never forget the transformation he had seen in Jane's face, and wondered what it would be like to be the cause of such a joyous change.

The sisters stopped at the water's edge, out of breath and doubled up in laughter. Jane spun around, wishing passionately to throw herself into something huge and exhilarating—to abandon herself. Inchoate feelings of longing almost overcame her. It must be the day, she thought, it must be Mr. Corydon. Oh, perhaps, she thought, it might be love.

There was one other who was as pleased with her heedless romp as was Jane. Not Sylvie who thought it merely delightful, not Mr. Corydon whose eyes lit up at the fine figure she cut. It was Lady Arabella who found the greatest satisfaction in Jane's display. As soon as the remainder of the group had caught up and could hear her, she spoke. "I would not credit what I have seen were it not for the fact that everyone has seen it as well. That you were such a hoyden, Miss Montcrief, I had no knowledge. That you should be forced upon my notice and into my acquaintance is something I shall remedy. It is only fortunate that your mother is not here to be disgraced by your behavior."

"Now, now," Mrs. Fotheringay put in. "What is youth if not impetuous?"

"I'm sure that I fully understand the nature of youth, being of an age with Miss Montcrief," Lady Arabella said haughtily if somewhat untruthfully, "yet I hope that no one would call me impetuous."

"No, I'm sure no one would call you impetuous," Mrs. Fotheringay said equably.

Jane hid a smile in bending to straighten her skirts. Mr. Corydon came to her side and spoke low but sincerely. "I thought your gallop was most charming, Miss Montcrief. You are a woman after my own heart."

"Oh, Mr. Corydon! I was afraid that the behavior of my maid might have given you a dislike of my company."

"Miss Montcrief, it would take more than the starts of a rather unusual maid to drive me from your company, if indeed anything could."

"Mr. Corydon, you quite take my breath away."

"And so I hope will the description of the improvements I plan for this exquisite and beautiful shoreline."

Jane nodded in beaming delight. Mr. Corydon smiled and bowed himself away.

Livvy hissed from behind her, "That was good, Jenny, you got him to speak of his attachment to you. Believe me, he will propose today, I'm sure. You did well to run like that; it was my idea, of course, but you did look pretty, and now he's said that nothing will ever separate you. Oh! You are going to capture him, I know it!"

"Livvy, you must be quiet. Promise, not another word from you or I will publicly insist on your leaving."

"No you won't, you're too happy."

Jane had to laugh. She turned away, in charity with Livvy for the first time that day, to listen with rapt attention to Mr. Corydon.

"Over there," he was saying, indicating with a sweep of his hand a broad, flat stretch of ground to the south, "shall stand the great hotel. I envision a structure large enough to house one hundred separate parties with the elegant, spacious public rooms which Wixton so regrettably lacks. Behind it will be extensive shrubberies, a bowling green, and gardens to rival those of Sydney Gardens and Vauxhall.

"And over there," he continued, indicating the north, "below where the larks dip and sway in the sea breezes, will stand the . . ."

"Rooks."

"I beg your pardon?" Mr. Corydon said impatiently to Livvy.

"They're rooks, not larks."

"Lizzy!" Jane nudged her sharply.

"Well, ma'am, look for yourself. They're rooks!"

"Please excuse my maid. Lizzy, will you please take yourself away until you can govern your tongue."

Livvy, perhaps reconsidering the wisdom of displeasing the only-too-recently ensnared Mr. Corydon, allowed herself to be shunted aside as though in disgrace, and humbly kept her eyes lowered.

Jane, not quite trusting her, moved closer to Sylvie, as though to deny acquaintance.

"As I was saying, over there will stand the promenade. We will build it far into the water, so that one can stroll out as though into the sea itself, and at the end have a grand prospect of the sea on all sides. It will form one side of the cove for the harboring of pleasure boats. And there will be all the other improvements one would wish, walks, gazebos, benches . . . yes, what is it?"

There was a stir emanating from the direction of Livvy. Jane steeled herself. It was Lord Charles who spoke. "Yes, the water does seem shallow. Is it deep enough, do you think, for the kind of harbor and use you anticipate?"

"Of course it is, what a foolish question," Mr. Corydon scowled at both Lord Charles and Livvy, the obvious source of the disruption.

"Well, uh, um," Sir William Sneed tried to speak, habitual apology and his daughter's fierce expression acting as restraints. "Well, in truth, the sea here is very shallow, not more than four or five feet for almost a mile. It would be hard to construct a harbor just here."

"Harbor! Sir William, you jest. We haven't been talking about ocean-going vessels, have we? Ha-ha." Mr. Corydon's expression was kindly, Jane thought, and took away any sting his words might contain.

"Papa, how foolish of you. As though Mr. Corydon's plans are not perfectly fitted to the conditions that pertain."

"No, Lady Arabella," Mr. Corydon said tactfully, "your father's knowledge of the land must be seriously considered. If it is as shallow as he says, then we must take into account the extra difficulties and expense of the enterprise. But I want you all to know that Mr. Rankin and I are determined to see it through, no matter what the obstacles!"

Jane wanted to shout, "Hurrah!" and expected that everyone else would join her in applauding the wonderfully handsome and heroic man before her. Oh, that he should waste such smiles on others. Did he not know the effect of his smile on her? She would soon be able to tell him.

"How exactly do you plan to finance this undertaking?" Lord Charles asked.

Jane rolled her eyes. Leave it to him to miss the grandeur of the scheme and see in it only the boring aspects of business. A faulty imagination—she could almost pity him—he knew so little of great emotions beyond the silly phrases he culled from books. She attended to Mr. Rankin with only half an ear, but froze when Livvy's voice burst out.

"But you can't build a resort here!"

"Lizzy!" Jane cried, vexed to the marrow at last.

"Come, Miss Montcrief," Lord Charles interposed, "your maid has made some very sensible observations today. Pray, Lizzy, why not?"

"I beg your pardon, Mr. Corydon, for you are the last person I would wish to fault, for I admire you tremendously and approve of what you are planning with all my heart, but I cannot help but think this site is just not right."

"Please, will you silence this creature!" Lady Arabella said sharply.

"Lizzy," Jane said helplessly.

"No, let her speak."

"Thank you, Mr. Fotheringay. What do you think of when you think of a resort? You think of the vistas, the seas, the bracing air. You think of cliffs and crags and eyries and bleak prospects and high promontories from which to look out at the farthest reaches of the sea. You can't build a resort here. There are no heights. This is paltry, Mr. Corydon, paltry, tame, and flat."

Lord Charles burst into laughter. It was the only sound on the beach as everyone grew silent and cast stealthy assessing looks over the beach. Sylvie especially seemed to find something in Livvy's comment, for she nodded and whispered something to her mother.

Jane forced herself to speech. "Thus speaks a young and impressionable maid, whose notions of what constitutes a resort come from the most vivid and highly rendered scribblings. She doesn't understand the nature of a more domestic, cozy seaside."

"Can you deny, ma'am, that it is flat?"

Mr. Rankin was outraged. "Allow your betters to speak and be silent."

Lord Charles said quietly, "I don't think we need to intimidate a young maid."

"It is not a question of intimidation," Jane said firmly. "Mr. Rankin is quite correct. Lizzy has spoken out of turn and must apologize."

Livvy had the grace to quail. Backing away, she announced with a catch in her voice, "Forgive me, it is the curse of a maid to have imagination. It is a curse, yes, a curse." And on that she wheeled away and went

117

running back up the road towards town and away from the group which looked after her with mixed amusement, bafflement, and relief.

Jane's relief bordered on delirium. She turned back and forced herself to utter yet another apology. It was not supposed to have been a day of apologies, she sighed. Really, it was unfair. Nonetheless, she began. "Mr. Corydon, I humbly beg your pardon for my maid's behavior. But more I beg your pardon for any questions that have been raised about your plan which I consider the most wonderful plan I have ever been privileged to hear of. I want you to know that I think that this is a perfect location, the perfect prospect, the perfect harbor, the perfect shoreline, the perfect height, indeed the very best height of a shore I have ever seen. In fact it is so perfect that . . . words fail me."

Had she sounded as foolish as she feared? No, for Mr. Corydon approached her, beaming. He took a step toward her and said graciously, "We owe your maid a debt of gratitude that her behavior here today brought forth from her mistress such glowing praise of our paltry—I mean simple—efforts."

Jane gazed into his eyes and only at the last moment let them fall. She felt positively silly with joy. She might have been betrayed into even more foolish speech had not Mr. Corydon been called to answer a question put to him by Sir William, and had not Sylvie joined her.

"That was a most spirited defense, Ariadne. Is it true that you have no doubts about this scheme?"

"None at all. What is there to doubt?"

Sylvie hesitated. "I don't wish to sound like a naysayer, but altering this lovely village and the tranquil countryside . . ."

118

"Oh," Jane said dismissively, "that is nothing, Georgianna. Countryside is changing all the time; this is a time of growth. The manufactories in the north, are they not changing the landscape?"

"It is hard to equate those ugly structures with what should be a place of calm beauty."

"I was just trying to point out that as a general rule the country changes, and that to stand against change is to stand against the very nature of life."

Sylvie looked consideringly at Jane. "You have great faith in Mr. Corydon's plans, have you not?"

Jane was pleased that she didn't blush. "I think his plan is a fine one, yes."

Sylvie said quietly, "Then we disagree."

They were joined by Lord Charles. "I am sorry your maid has gone. We will be much duller for her absence."

Jane inclined her head. She would not say one more word about Livvy.

"It is surprising that she should have a more critical eye than her mistress, given her lack of years and education."

"There's no accounting for tastes, Mr. Fotheringay."

"No. I, for one, find this plan laughable, as well as entirely impracticable."

"I am not surprised. It takes a man of spirit to embrace such a plan."

"Do you fancy yourself a woman of spirit, Miss Montcrief?"

"Well, yes, since you ask me, I will admit I do. Which is why, I am afraid, we shall never see eye to eye."

Jane was sorry for the dismay she saw on Georgianna's face, but the irritation in Mr. Fotheringay's quite made up for it. She mustered an apologetic smile for her friend, but the look on her face as she nodded to Mr. Fotheringay and walked away displayed the frankest contempt.

Mr. Corydon broke off instantly to come to her side. Loudly enough for all to hear, he said, "I think the best recommendation for building a resort on this spot is the lovely roses that bloom in the cheeks of the ladies who stand here."

Jane was content. The day had not been lost; the signs were accumulating.

Chapter Eight

Jane twirled her parasol, watching the color it shed on her arms and white gown. She had known that a purple parasol would be dramatic. As she walked along the road to visit Georgianna at the Oaks, she felt beautiful and delighted with the world, and especially at the way the parasol turned her dress lavender. How clever she was! How beautiful she was! How Mr. Corydon admired her!

As well as she was dressed now—in case that handsome man should just happen to be out at this time of day—no one would have guessed that a mere half hour before she had been up to her elbows in the makings of sausage. She had had to scrub at her hands to banish the smells. It was not that her kitchen labors were new—indeed, she and Priddy had prepared all the food eaten by the family for years—but it was the necessity of having to conceal it, to do it in the morning, so that by ten she might be able to walk out looking as though she had just risen and taken her morning chocolate in leisurely indolence.

She lifted her hand and frowned at what seemed to be a telltale redness, then remembered the parasol and held it beyond the lavender circle and smiled at its reassuring pallor.

The lane from the road to the Oaks was all but concealed in the hedgerow and Jane, often preoccupied, had missed it more than once. But she was paying attention to her surroundings, noting the white hawthorn in bloom, and shortly was walking up the drive.

The Oaks was an undistinguished house; her own hired home was far more graceful and imposing. This was little more than a cottage, really, with a half-story concealed, windowless, under the eaves, built thus to avoid the window tax, she assumed, requiring the servants to sleep in unventilated rooms. It was also densely grown up with trees. Jane remembered Mrs. Penworthy saying that the owner was an elderly widower who had recently removed to Bath for his health. The grounds showed neglect, although they were presently smoothed and the shrubs near the house had been neatly trimmed.

If they had money for gardeners' attentions, Jane thought disapprovingly, then they could afford to spend more than they did. Than Mrs. Fotheringay and Georgianna spent, she amended. What a waste, she thought, for Mr. Fotheringay to spend such large quantities of money on his clothes only to appear so drab; he had nothing of Mr. Corydon's fashionableness. He was one of those men whose purse was open only to himself; he would make a terrible husband.

Jane hoped that she would not see him this morning. She and Georgianna were in the habit of meeting in the mornings, and most mornings Jane saw nothing of him. Surely he would not wish to see her either, unless he should wish to do so simply to vex her. Odd that she had ever thought him handsome, when he had nothing of the brilliance of Mr. Corydon's fair hair, light blue eyes, his air of mystery and charm.

She laughed aloud. How wonderful a charming man was! She had never really known one before. Her father, in his last years, had been so weary and despairing, as a result of his financial problems and his worry over their future, that all his native liveliness was suppressed. Ned was just a brother. Mr. Fotheringay a posing bore. But Mr. Corydon!

She was smiling and playful when Sylvie ran out the front path toward her and caught her up in a spontaneous hug.

"Oh, Ariadne, isn't this a beautiful day! Would you like to sit outside? I have discovered a lovely hidden place, quite out of the wind, where I sometimes sit in the mornings. Would you like to have tea served out-of-doors?"

Jane smiled at her friend's blooming enthusiasm. She caught her hand and laughed. "Of all things I should like to sit outside today."

Sylvie led her around the house to a charming secret garden, created by an overgrown hedge which showed signs of recently having been tamed by the gardener's shears. Within it was a wrought iron bench set near the house, facing south and the warm rays of the sun.

Jane looked around her and said, "Oh, Georgianna, this is exquisite. What a lovely spot! I see why you sit here. It seems quite the place for passing a spring morning. Look at the daffodils!"

123

"Yes, I think it must have been made so on purpose."

The two women looked about them with pleasure.

Lord Charles, whose window gave onto the enclosed shrubbery, regarded the two women. They made an attractive picture, two slim women silhouetted against the morning sun, their white gowns bright against the soft spring green. He knew that Sylvie often passed the morning hours there reading, but because she had always been alone he had not realized that through the open window he could hear distinctly every word spoken.

He should, of course, draw their attention to this fact, or at least greet the interfering Miss Montcrief as politeness required, but he was deep in his work and decided to continue on until luncheon interrupted him, assuming that his powers of concentration were equal to the distraction of their voices.

Sylvie excused herself and ran into the house to order tea and cakes. Jane amused herself by bending to smell the daffodils, by lifting her face to the sun, unaware that she had caught the attention of a man who found that his powers of concentration were, perhaps, not up to the temptation of the sight of a lovely woman amidst a profusion of spring flowers.

Sylvie rejoined her and they sat on the bench and arranged their skirts.

"I'm thinking of going into Colchester sometime soon to get a length of lavender muslin," Jane said. "I was just admiring . . . wait!" She leapt up and got her parasol and showed Georgianna the effect of the light on her white dress. "Don't you think lavender would be wonderful?"

"Oh, yes. And with the parasol, some parts would be

124

darker than others—it would shimmer."

"What a good idea! You must come with me and you could get a parasol and muslin, too, but yours should be green. You look wonderful in green. It would resemble moving water or the shimmer of wind on grass."

Sylvie laughed. "I have all the gowns I need, now."

"How can any woman have all the gowns she needs? Gowns aren't for needing, but for looking beautiful in."

"Ariadne, you sound like a vain woman, when I know you aren't."

"But how do you know I'm not a vain woman?" Jane asked, lifting an eyebrow. "I happen to know that I am one of the vainest women of my acquaintance."

"I should think Lady Arabella would cast you into the shade, no matter which vice you tried to take on as your own exclusive property."

"Well, it is true, I could not compete against *her*. But I do love beautiful clothes. I . . ." Jane broke off, just as she was about to say how little she had known of them and how her present lust was only a barely satisfied—in fact barely piqued—devotion.

"I love clothes, too, but not half so much as I love my books. I am afraid that if I went into Colchester with you, I should spend all my money on books and come home with no cloth at all."

"Well, that would be no crime. Why don't we plan to go? I'm sure our mothers would welcome an outing."

"Well, yes, we must sometime."

"What about next week—let's choose a day."

Sylvie grew uncomfortable. She was reluctant to venture into such a populated town as Colchester, and she knew there was no money for the kind of shopping expedition her friend had in mind. "But I am well fixed for books, dear Ariadne, and I have no interest in shopping for more frivolous items."

Jane found herself arguing against the very economy she was herself forced to practice, and although aware of the hypocrisy of her words, nonetheless pursued. "Oh, dear Georgianna, how I would love to outfit you in the kinds of gowns that would most become you. You should wear all yellows and greens, I can see it now. It wouldn't be a great deal of money, I'm sure. With our mothers along we should be able to find some bargain that would challenge their dressmaking talents. Oh, do say you'll come."

"I'm sure nothing would be more pleasant, but to be honest, Ariadne, our circumstances require that we not . . . that whatever beautiful gowns I can envision not be instantly purchased."

Jane knew she should smile at such a gracious admission and drop the subject, but instead she pursued it.

"But your brother would surely not begrudge the expense, for his own clothes are of the first stare, a bit dull, perhaps, compared to someone with the London polish of Mr. Corydon, but they *are* expensive, I don't doubt."

Sylvie looked down at her hands. "He is the most generous of brothers. He has shown my mother and me the greatest kindness."

"Well, as he surely should!" Jane looked at the downcast face of her friend with the most outraged indignation. "To be grateful for what is only rightly yours!"

What more she might have said on this subject, Lord

Charles was not to discover, for the maid brought the tea and cakes and the interruption was sufficient to still Miss Montcrief's tongue on that matter. He wondered just how much money he would be obliged to surrender to the two women to keep the charade they were enacting within credible bounds. He knew Jane could not know that Sylvie had one solitary gown to her name when he came upon her, and that he had bought *all* the others, and all the undergarments and shoes she had worn since, and that moreover he had urged even more on her since Miss Montcrief's harangue. He sighed. He wasn't angry at Sylvie's needs or his own outlay on her behalf, he would have been happy to spend ten times as much. It was being seen as a clenchfisted boor that infuriated him. What an irritating woman she was, in spite of her oval face shaded by a purple parasol which turned her amazing eyes to indigo.

"This is delicious," Jane exclaimed, unaware of being the subject of such bitter ruminations, sinking her teeth into a cake which held the surprise of jelly.

"Yes, it is, isn't it? It is a receipt that my mother has from my father's mother. It's one of my favorite treats."

"Ummm. Oh, this is heavenly. It is such a lovely day."

"Yes, indeed."

The two women were silent for a moment.

"Your mother, is she also Mr. Fotheringay's mother?"

Sylvie laughed, choking on her cake. It took her a moment to overcome her mirth. "Oh, no. My mother is Mr. Fotheringay's stepmother."

"To be sure I hadn't thought so, but I was confused

as to your relationship . . ."

Sylvie plunged into the arranged story. "My mother, after my father died, he was a vicar," she added, grateful for the grain of truth that lay in the story, "married Mr. Fotheringay's father. Then his father died."

Jane frowned. "But why is *your* name Fotheringay?"

Sylvie looked at her absolutely blankly.

Jane stared. Aware of the awkwardness, she offered, "I understand, Mr. Fotheringay's father adopted you, and you took his name."

Sylvie looked at her, hesitant to admit to anything, so unnerved was she by this flaw in their story.

Jane seemed satisfied and leaned against the back of the bench munching on another cake. "But it is so strange to hear you address your brother as Mr. Fotheringay. I can't imagine calling Ne . . . a brother by anything but his first name."

"I do call him Florian, most of the time." Sylvie found the courage to change the subject. "His work is so fascinating, Ariadne, I am sure if you could read what he is writing, you would be so interested."

"What is he writing about? I'm afraid I've forgotten." She swept a hand over her lap to remove some errant crumbs.

"About his experiences in the wars. The volume he is writing now is about his work with Lord Wellington at Waterloo. He was at the Congress of Vienna as well. There is so much history in his memoirs!"

"I daresay. And a lot about his having been a very brave soldier, too, I am sure."

"Well, not really," Sylvie said. "There are some descriptions of the battlefields at Waterloo, the attacks, the bloodshed," she shivered. "It was a terrible battle, Ariadne, it is a miracle that he was not injured."

Jane smiled. "Well, I suppose it is hard to be injured when you're standing on a distant hill watching it all through a spyglass."

Lord Charles threw down his pen, breaking the point he had so carefully shaped preparatory to his day's work. What was it his nanny had said, *if you eavesdrop on conversations about yourself, you will hear no good?*

Sylvie defended him. "No, he did take part in the actual fighting. I'm sure he did."

"Well, surely you remember."

Sylvie, relying on nothing but his manuscript which contained more history of the engagement than his own part in it, was at a loss. She said quite simply that she didn't know what the extent of Florian's war experiences had been.

Jane, finding the weak point she had always known was there to be discovered in Mr. Fotheringay's heroic distortions of an inglorious part in the war, continued, "And in the Peninsula, no doubt, he fought the enemy virtually single-handed, while *of course* recommending every action that Wellesley should take."

"He was with Wellesley then, I think. That is why Lord Wellington asked him to join him in Brussels as well."

"Amazing that he should survive so many battles without a wound."

Sylvie, who knew nothing of a certain long scar on Lord Charles's back, nor of a promotion given to him after the battle of Bussaco, nor of his reputation among his men for fearlessness bordering on foolhardiness,

129

could only reach for the tray with the cakes and offer Jane another one. She felt unhappily that she was letting Mr. Fotheringay down, but then she did not have any knowledge of his experiences, and she did not dare lie.

"You seem to have taken my brother in dislike," she said slowly.

"Oh, no!" cried Jane, stung that this soft, mild-mannered woman had found her own manners lacking. "No, you must forgive me. It is only that now, four years after the war, one does grow tired of war stories, heroic escapades that become more dangerous with every telling. I suppose I am only grown a little wary of these sanguinary and self-congratulatory stories that so many tell." Sylvie could not know that this sweeping generalization was based on a detested nephew of the Alvenleighs whose exploits Livvy, Jane, and Priddy had been regaled with to the point of desperation.

"Yes. Perhaps that is true in the main, but my brother's accounts I think you could not fault. They are little to do with himself; I think you would find them modest."

Jane contained a snort of derision—modest because nonexistent. But she said placatingly, "I'm sure I should. It is in his favor, this modesty. I shall congratulate him on it next time I see him."

Sylvie looked up in alarm.

"Oh, I am just funning you, Georgianna. I don't know why I tease you so on this subject."

Lord Charles did not hear the truce. If he had, he might not have felt it necessary to go for a stroll which ended in the shrubbery, where in surprise he discovered its occupants. He would never for a moment have admitted that he found it necessary to confront the intolerable woman who seemed so determined to find fault with him. And so undeserved, he thought with some heat. It was also necessary to protect Sylvie from the necessity of having to defend him when her ignorance and reluctance to lie made such a course difficult.

"Ladies," he said, bowing deeply. "I intrude upon your privacy, I'm afraid."

Sylvie looked up at him with a welcoming smile and Jane found herself eyeing them, trying to understand just what kind of brother Mr. Fotheringay was to his charming sister.

"Oh, no, Mr. Fotheringay, there are so many cakes we should have required your help eventually. How is your mother? I hope to see her this morning before I leave."

"She is well, Miss Montcrief, she is enjoying the spinet which we have just hired. Perhaps you can hear her play?"

Jane was silent but could hear nothing. So, he was generous enough to allow his stepmother this pleasure.

"No, I cannot hear her, but I envy her the pleasure. We have no pianoforte in our home and I miss having one." Jane could not play, for she had never owned a pianoforte, it having been sold soon after the tightening purse of her father had forbidden the hiring of music masters. She was hardly aware of the lie.

"I have been telling Miss Montcrief about your book . . . F . . . Florian." Sylvie put in warningly, "She is most interested in your personal experiences of the war."

"Are you, Miss Montcrief?"

"It is always a pleasure to be in the presence of a war hero," she said. "Your sister has painted such a very formidable picture of your modesty, however, that I fear we shall never hear just how glorious your service for his Majesty truly was."

Lord Charles sat down on the ground and looked up at Miss Montcrief whose large, deep blue eyes studied him from beneath the brim of her close bonnet.

He was wise enough to know that if he said anything that reflected credit on himself, she would dismiss him as a braggart, but that if he said nothing of his exploits, she would simply assume there were none.

"Those of us who were selected for Lord Wellington's staff usually were chosen on the basis of reputation of achievement in the field."

"I am pleased with your honesty, Mr. Fotheringay. For I know few heroes who would admit that their positions were due more to reputation than actual service."

"That is not . . ." Lord Charles flushed and stopped. "Just so, Miss Montcrief. I happen to have a gift for puffing up my reputation quite outrageously. You can see the effect of that ability in your own estimation of me, I think."

"Oh, Mr. Fotheringay, I do believe you do yourself and me a disservice. I am sure that my opinion of you is quite in keeping with your own merits."

Sylvie frowned at this exchange, wishing she could dispel the frostiness which had grown up between these two kind people by telling Ariadne just how good a man Mr. Fotheringay really was. She was feeling all the more guilty because she believed that her own awkwardness in the situation was the chief cause of

Jane's poor opinion of him.

Lord Charles went on the offensive. He didn't know why he felt such pique at the demure but empty-headed woman sitting above him on the bench. If he had been present, his brother Stephen might have put his finger on it instantly. Since he had come down from Oxford, Charles de la Marre, Earl of Leith, had been considered the most eligible man in England, from an impeccable family and wealthy to the point of grandeur. Added to that were his adventures and considerable reputation on the battlefield and in the corridors of diplomacy. He had excited the most intense admiration in the breasts of the mamas and daughters who sought to attract his notice. He had met with no young woman who had not fallen into tremors of shyness or silliness or affected sophistication at his mere appearance. A woman who was contemptuous of him, who doubted his honor and his heroism, who had the audacity to mock him, was a new experience for him, and as infuriating as it was unanticipated.

"Miss Montcrief, I hope your deep appreciation for architecture and learning is being satisfied here in Wixton."

"Oh, indeed, Mr. Fotheringay. I was just saying to Georgianna that we are fortunate indeed to have the services of the devoted Mrs. Penworthy to keep us all from getting quite dull."

"And what are you reading now?"

"Human nature, Mr. Fotheringay."

"Always a challenging study. But I meant, what book are you reading now?"

Jane forgot the title of the most recent book Ned had asked her to secure for him—some tedious essays.

133

"Locke," she said, with a yawn.

"Locke!" Lord Charles said, startled.

Jane raised her eyebrows. "Do you think I should restrict myself to novels, Mr. Fotheringay, as do so many of your sex?"

"No, indeed, with a sister such as mine," he said, smiling to Sylvie, "one who reads four languages and can speak them as well, the last thing I should do is speak slightingly of women's tastes in reading."

Sylvie blushed. She had studied with her father and had not given a thought to its meaning out in the world of polite society, but she was afraid it was a handicap. She was embarrassed to think that Ariadne might think her a bluestocking.

"Yes, Georgianna's intelligence shines through," said Jane fondly, "it is the secret of her sparkle."

Sylvie blushed touchingly and Jane couldn't help but put a hand on her arm.

Lord Charles was glad for Miss Montcrief's kindness. He thought for a moment that perhaps her intolerable manners and arrogance sprang from circumstances of her life and not from her character, for certainly her kindness toward Sylvie was genuine. She could easily patronize or ignore her.

"Sylvie has the kind of intelligence that does not need to advertise itself," she continued, "but which exists for those who are fortunate enough to know her to discover at their pleasure."

Lord Charles fumed at the barely disguised insult. Well, so be it. This woman would never find in him anything to admire, and what difference did it make? He got up and stretched his tall, muscular frame above them. "Pray excuse me for I must get back to my self-advertisements." He bowed and left.

Alone with Sylvie, Jane said contritely, "Oh, I am sorry, Georgianna, I can't seem to hold my tongue around him."

Sylvie laughed but she was truly uncomfortable. "Well, I think of all men he would be the least offended. But I am surprised that he finds your playfulness provoking. But it does distress me, Ariadne, that you do not find anything to admire in him."

Jane looked at her friend and smiled contritely. "Forgive me, Georgianna, for I would do nothing to cause you pain. I am afraid that your brother and I have gotten off on the wrong footing, that is all. I'm sure it is nothing that further acquaintance won't rectify."

"I do hope so, for he has been very good to my mother and me."

Well, thought Jane to herself, maybe that is it, maybe it is in Georgianna's attitude that I find the source of my unease. It might be her way, to be grateful and not put herself forward. Perhaps it is the sister's character that has in some convoluted way made me think ill of her brother's. Jane vowed never to speak ill of Mr. Fotheringay again in Georgianna's presence. But she made no vow to think well of him.

Presently the young women went into the house so that Jane could pay her respects to Mrs. Fotheringay, and after politely refusing the opportunity to demonstrate that she knew nothing, not even the scales, of the pianoforte, she took her leave and returned home thinking as she walked along how lucky it was that the

135

Fotheringays, in spite of their hailing from Northumberland, were never inclined to speak of it.

Mary Churchill looked at Sylvie after Miss Montcrief had gone, and marveled at the difference these weeks in Wixton had made in her daughter. She was far more at ease than she had been even before the dreadful entry of Mr. Flood into their lives.

She smiled and invited her to sit on the bench with her.

Sylvie put her arm around her mother's waist. "Have you decided yet, mother?"

"Yes, dear. I am afraid that as congenial as it is to live here, we must return home and cease being a burden to Mr. Fotheringay. It is kind of him to pretend that our services merit his expenditures on our behalf, but it is not true. I will write to our solicitor tomorrow, describing what has happened and seeking his advice about prosecution."

Sylvie played chords on the pianoforte. She seemed to be concentrating on them fiercely. Then she lifted her head and said quietly, "Yes, mother. I was afraid at first of the notoriety it would cause, but I am no longer."

Mrs. Churchill squeezed her daughter warmly. "I'm glad, Sylvie, for we must begin to set our life to rights."

Sylvie smiled in answer, but knew that it would be difficult to leave Wixton, the Montcrief family . . . and their servants.

Chapter Nine

On a warm but overcast day a few days later, Jane was in the kitchen with Priddy and Ned, taking turns churning butter. It was an economy like all the rest they had decided to make—the kind that could be concealed. The standard of their table, the carriage, their clothes, were chosen to suggest that they had unlimited funds. Their contrivances required work and imagination. Jane had decided to try to dye an old and faded muslin dress lavender, hoping that she might achieve the success she hoped for without having to go to the expense of a new gown. She and Priddy were going to begin refashioning the gown as soon as the butter set, which, in the warmth of the kitchen—they had no dairy—seemed to be never.

They were bickering, as they always seemed to do when they were alone. Ned, particularly—who had lost the most in this enterprise, for he had, after all, been away from home for three years at Cambridge and had been on the receiving end of the family's many sacrifices—was now restricted to a single set of livery, to the house, and to the public deportment of a faithful servant. The great adventure had become dull.

He was forever chafing. "Jane, he lives just by Norwich. It is twenty miles from here. No one would see me, and it would just be for a few days. I would take him into my confidence; he would say nothing. Please!"

"No! I said no, Ned. It's just too risky. Whitaker might seem like a perfectly reliable friend, but you have no idea what he might do if he were to get wind of what we are up to. He might feel it was too good a joke not to share with his friends. It is just too chancy."

"But, Jenny, you don't really expect me to sit here docile and tame churning butter for the rest of my life."

"Ned, you are in no fit shape for civil conversation today. Take yourself off. Take the carriage or one of the horses and get some of the dust blown off you. Go on. Priddy and I can manage."

Ned was off before she could reconsider. Livvy wandered in, her maid's uniform immaculate but her hair tied in loveknots which she had been practicing in her efforts to persuade Jane to try something more *à la mode* than her severe bun.

"Where's Ned going?"

"He's going to take the carriage out. He needs to get out of here or he will drive us to distraction with his complaints."

"Oh, may I go!" Livvy whipped around and threw herself down the hall and out the front door before Jane had a chance to catch her.

"Oh well," she said, returning to Priddy. "I know I've kept her on a very tight rein since that day at the beach. I just hope nobody sees her in that coiffure."

138

Priddy groaned, straightening up.

"Oh, dear Priddy. Here, let me have a turn, your back isn't up to this. Sit. Pour yourself a glass of malmsey and keep me company."

"I'm fine, but my back does ache." She sighed and sat down gingerly on one of the wooden chairs. She glanced at the fireplace and turned the mutton on the spit and sat back down, her feet on the rungs of another chair, and leaned back, closing her eyes.

Jane looked at her with remorse. Priddy was tired. Although she had part of the day to rest and to play the lady in leisure and comfort, the jobs that fell to them were especially hard on her. Jane made a vow to carry more of the work herself. After all, she was young and strong and could work at night if need be, after Priddy had gone to bed.

"Priddy, why don't you rest? Yes, yes, I know it is a crime, not even mid-morning, an absolutely immoral time to be abed, but do, just this once, for I warrant that what your back needs is a rest and, if you don't lie down, then you might make it worse."

"You might be right, but I have in mind a nice long walk. I think I might just go into the woods and turn off toward the sea. I am so glad that we have the sea here, too, for I have grown used to it. I cannot think what it would be like to be away from the bounding of the waves, the rhythms of the sea."

"Yes," Jane said, pausing again, "I have thought about that, too. Can you believe that I even miss Cornwall? This sea is so tame!"

Priddy laughed. "Well, those who live here say it can be very wild and are offended by any suggestion that it is placid. But I will go for a walk. Are you sure you can manage?"

"Oh, it's bound to turn soon," said Jane with her cheeriest smile. "Now go, before someone comes to call and you won't be able to escape."

It was not five minutes after Priddy had gone that there was a peremptory knock at the front door. Jane decided to pretend no one was home and wait for the person to go away. The knocker sounded again.

She looked down at herself. She did look a sight. It was quite unusual for anyone to call on them in the morning except for Georgianna, who she knew was not planning to call today. Mrs. Woods and Mrs. Penworthy always paid their calls in the afternoon. Well, she was not dressed to maintain the charade, so she ignored the summons and continued churning.

It was with shock, then, that she looked up at the window to see the tall form of Mr. Fotheringay striding across the back of the house, and to hear a knock at the back door.

She froze. Through the glass in the door Mr. Fotheringay was looking straight at her. Their eyes held.

There was nothing to do but face this embarrassment with as much equanimity as she could muster and brazen it out.

"Mr. Fotheringay," she said without ceremony, opening the door.

That gentleman's eyes raked her from her hair, which instead of the habitual severe bun was tied simply behind her neck, tendrils escaping to lie against her cheeks, her gown so old and well washed as to be almost colorless, and the drab apron which covered but did not conceal her exquisite figure, to her feet which

140

even within the house were shod in pattens.

"You wished to see me or my mother?" she asked, blushing under this scrutiny but feeling more angry than embarrassed.

"I came to see you," Mr. Fotheringay replied. In fact he had come merely to pass from Sylvie to Miss Montcrief a book which the former had rushed through so that the latter might read it at the first opportunity, but he was so intrigued by her deshabille that he promptly decided to extend his visit.

"Come in then," Jane said with dignity. "As you can see, I was churning butter. If you don't mind, I shall proceed to do so."

Jane sat firmly on the tall stool, straddled the churn, and resumed pumping the handle, up and down. She was unaware of the extraordinary picture she presented to Lord Charles. Her cheeks were flushed both from his scrutiny and her exertions. Her hair, slipping from its ribbon, fell along her face and made a frame for the delicacy of her cheek. The lifting and falling of her arms displayed the beauty of her figure as well as what he suddenly discovered was the engrossing beauty of the action itself. He had never seen butter churned before.

Jane was aware that he was watching her without bothering to make conversation, but she was too vexed to think of a topic herself. She figured that such a conventional man as he would be scandalized, and she was rehearsing excuses and reasons to explain why she was churning butter, not for his benefit but for the benefit of those in the village who might hear of it from him.

He grew aware of her silence and realized with

astonishment that she was not at all intimidated by his presence. This was the most remarkable thing he had discovered in all his experience with women. Susan would never have allowed herself to engage in, much less be caught out in, such drudgery, and if she had, would certainly have broken off with the most charming if false excuses to devote herself to his pleasure.

But the woman before him doggedly continued to work and did not trouble to speak.

Suddenly he found himself saying, "Here, please, if you can show me what to do, allow me to help you. It seems to be quite a strenuous job."

Jane looked up with humor. "I'm afraid it is not something that one can just *do*. I know it looks easy, but in fact there is a feel to it, a rhythm . . ."

"My dear Miss Montcrief. I hope you are not telling me that I am so stupid that I am not able to churn butter."

"Not stupid, precisely," she said with a smile, "it requires a knack."

"Then would you allow me to see if I might have the knack?"

Jane gazed up at him and saw in his eyes the twinkle that had first attracted her to him, before he had revealed the dull, posturing, autocratic traits which had turned her interest to disinterest. "Mr. Fotheringay," she said. "Perhaps I have underestimated you. Perhaps you can indeed churn butter."

He laughed, and as she rose from the stool, she passed near him, where they both stood between the table and cupboard. She realized they were alone. Surely it could not matter. It couldn't matter when churning butter. Suddenly she laughed.

"Surely there is nothing to laugh at yet. I haven't even begun," he said in mock petulance. He had got himself into position and was grasping the pole and heaving it up and down in a reckless display of muscle.

"No, not like that. I can see that you have no talent. You are going at it as though you wish to slay it. It requires only enough effort to make it go up and down, gently, like this," and she leaned forward and demonstrated the tempo.

"I see, like this," and as she released her hands, he continued.

"Yes, that is more like it."

She studied him as he continued.

"Well, how am I faring?" He raised laughing brown eyes to hers. Their eyes were almost level, he sitting on the tall stool, she standing across the churn from him. Their eyes caught, his brown ones full of laughter, her deep blue ones of wary interest.

"You do surprisingly well."

"I knew it," he said in a swaggering way, "I knew I could master it. I figured I would probably excel at making butter."

"Indeed, Mr. Fotheringay, you are to be congratulated on the quickness with which you have picked up the art."

"Perhaps I shall take to churning my own."

"You might. We do ours because we find it superior. It is one of our small vanities, to have better butter than anyone else."

"Ah, then that explains why you should be at such a tedious domestic chore."

"But, of course, does not your mother pride herself

143

on some domestic activity that she performs better than any maid, cook, or housekeeper?"

Lord Charles thought of his mother, the Countess of Leith, and had to smile. The idea that she would ever toil was quite fantastic.

"Ah, I can see she does, but that you are not going to tell me what it is, lest I should set myself up in competition with her."

"That is quite right. You women, I can see, jealously guard your housekeeping secrets."

Jane watched his hands on the pole and thought them strong. They were not a writer's hands, but rather those of someone used to outdoor life. As she watched him, she realized that the rhythm had changed, that the churning was becoming difficult.

"Stop!" she cried. She lifted off the lid and showed him what lay inside. *"Voilà,* butter!"

"Ah, as simple as that!"

"Simple! You had the last ten minutes of it, while I have been at it the better part of an hour."

"Yes, but under my efforts it became butter, did it not?"

Jane laughed. "Would you like to taste it? A reward for your labor?"

"Yes," he said, feeling quite pleased with himself for reasons he did not examine.

Jane sliced a piece of bread from the morning's baking and covered it lavishly with butter scraped out from under the buttermilk. Mr. Fotheringay took it gravely, sank his teeth into it, chewed consideringly, gazing into space while he judged it.

Jane grew aware that he was deliberately keeping her in suspense, dragging out his weighty judgment. She found herself pushing against his arm, laughing up at him, and saying, "Mr. Fotheringay, it is not all that difficult a judgment. What do you—"

She broke off because suddenly she realized she was in a room alone and quite close to a very handsome man, and although her head told her that he was beneath her notice, her body told her that he was inches away and that he had butter smeared adorably on his upper lip and that she might wipe it off. She turned away and walked to the furthest reaches of the kitchen and said in her coolest voice, "You never did mention what you came to see us about, Mr. Fotheringay."

Lord Charles laid down the unfinished bread, wiped his mouth with the back of his hand, all the while watching the beautiful woman who had surprisingly and disturbingly stirred his senses, and thought that he must go immediately. He said curtly, "A book, there." He nodded toward a shelf. "My sister asked me to bring it to you on my way to the village."

"I see, thank you."

"Not at all," he said, bowing.

They did not look at each other as he made his way to the door and she busied herself with crocks for the butter.

When she heard the door close, she knew she would tell no one about this episode. And she would put it out of her mind as well.

Lord Charles, striding home along an unseen road, thought to himself, I shall not tell anyone what happened. And if I have any sense, I'll forget about it as well.

*　　*　　*

145

A few hours later Jane, groomed and dressed as befitting her station in life, walked along the High Street on her way to make purchases at Mr. Gregg's shop. She had not meant to go to the shops today, but she wished to face down anyone, including Mr. Fotheringay, who might dare to tease her about her early morning chores.

But her heart leapt up when just beyond the church she saw Mr. Corydon, who saw her as well and walked towards her across the road.

"Mr. Corydon," she said, extending her hand.

"Miss Montcrief, how fortunate I am to discover you abroad this morning. Your mother, is she well?"

"Yes, thank you."

"I am glad."

Jane knew she was foolishly staring at him and dropped her gaze to stare at the roadway.

"Miss Montcrief, I cannot tell you how happy I am that chance has brought us together here in Wixton."

"Yes, it is such a coincidence."

"I am surprised that we have never met before, perhaps in London."

"I have spent little time in London," Jane said, "we have been obliged to travel little from Northumberland due to my mother's health."

"Where is your home in Northumberland?"

"Oh, it is quite set apart, a little village unto itself, you know how it is with a large estate. It is one of the problems, the more land one owns, the farther one is from one's neighbors." Jane wished Ned could hear her.

"Yes, I know exactly what you mean. It is that way at my estate in Wiltshire. That is probably why I appreciate so much my smaller homes in Yorkshire and Kent, and my London house which puts me quite in the middle of things."

"Ah!" Jane managed, her eyes glowing at this proof of his wealth.

"Miss Montcrief, I hope that we may have a longer time to talk soon, but there is Lady Arabella coming from Mr. Gregg's shop and I must escort her home. We cannot all choose our duties, you know."

"I know, Mr. Corydon," she replied, looking fatuous.

He bowed and took her hand, his back to Lady Arabella who was glaring impatiently at them from across the road. He lifted her hand and Jane knew that he would have kissed it had Lady Arabella not been there.

She stood rooted to the spot and watched him take Lady Arabella's arm and walk down the road.

Jane spun on her heel and returned home. She required the privacy of her chamber to relive this moment: to go over it again and again.

"Oh bliss, oh joy!" Livvy stretched her arms over her head and dropped them to run her hands along the delicate sprigged muslin of her gown, inspecting it in the light of the carriage lanterns. "Has there ever been such a beautiful dress, and this bonnet! Do you think it makes me look eighteen? Sixteen? Fourteen? Oh well," she said, assessing her family's glances, "I adore it. Do you think the flowers on it are all the crack? I had thought of grapes, but there weren't any grapes in the trunks. Flowers, flowers, flowers. Grapes would have gone with the pink. Well, it's more lavender, isn't it? Pink and lavender. Oh, has there ever been such a beautiful gown?"

Priddy, Jane and Ned forbore to halt Livvy's runaway raptures. For a twelve-year-old to be dressed as she was with her hair up and a gown appropriate for someone of Jane's twenty years was outrageous. But Jane and Priddy knew that it was unfair to ask Livvy to pose as a mature if young servant and not allow her the same privilege when it came to their clandestine, delicious outing to Colchester.

It was night. The coachman they had hired to drive them was curious why Ned wasn't driving the carriage himself, but no explanation had been offered and under the protection of the dark they had the carriage drawn up to the house and settled into it before anyone could see them.

All Jane's doubts faded away with the miles put behind them. It would be a pleasure to be herself for a change, even if only for a day, to be free from making up fires, preparing meals—the myriad tasks of house-keeping.

A gibbous moon cast sufficient light for night travel. The land was flat, but the roads dipped in and out of stretches so overgrown with hedges that it seemed as though they traversed tunnels.

They were planning to stay at the King's Head Inn and Jane looked forward to a luxurious respite, to the excitement of waking in a new bed, to the chance to look into shops with more to offer than Wixton. But especially she anticipated the opportunity the trip would afford the family to review strategy and assess their progress.

It was a subject that now afforded her the greatest pleasure to discuss.

"He is handsome, isn't he? And very distinguished-looking. Mrs. Penworthy told me that he was disappointed in love. How tragic. There is something about his face, about his expression, that proclaims a suffering man, one who has tasted sadness and is now ready . . . more appreciative . . . well, of a nice pleasant wife."

"Ugh," Ned snorted. "Between you and Livvy, I can see that this ride will be interminable."

Jane ignored him. "It is more than a matter of handsomeness. His bearing is so elegant, his manners so pleasing. But I think what recommends him, what must recommend him to anyone," she said with a pointed look at Ned, "is his boldness in the field of enterprise. Many men might just sit on their income and waste it away, like that boring Mr. Fotheringay does with whatever mean sufficiency it is that he lives by. But not Mr. Corydon. You can see at once just by looking at him that he is the kind of man who asks what can I do to enrich . . ."

". . . myself," Ned put in.

"Yes. Myself. And what is wrong with that, Edgar Marlingforthe? Are we not embarked on an enterprise to enrich ourselves? We can hardly dare to judge him, going about his own affairs with the openness and candor which are so great a part of his character."

Priddy gave a sigh.

"Ah, Priddy, you have been able to talk to him about the plan for Wixton. Ned, if you'd been there and heard him, you would not be censorious. Priddy was there and she knows just how excellent it is."

Priddy sighed again. "I do wish you weren't so set on Mr. Corydon, Jane."

"Whyever not, Priddy? What could you possibly have to say against him?"

"Against him? Only the fact that we know nothing about him."

"Well, that can be remedied. We could write Hasbrook and ask him to look into his background. But then, what does he know of us? Is it not behavior, one's demeanor and conversation, by which one is most correctly judged? Have you anything to say against him there?"

"I have nothing to say against him, as I said. It is his plan I am dubious about, and that in turn throws his character into question."

"Oh, Priddy! You are hopeless there, there is nothing that would convince you that his plan had any merit unless the Regent himself subscribed to it."

"I'm not sure that the Regent's commendation would carry any weight with me," Priddy said with a sniff.

"No, I'm sure not," Jane said grinning, remembering the full dislike Priddy felt for the Regent, due to his mistreatment of Princess Caroline.

"It is not just that the plan seems hardly to make any sense, since the land itself seems to offer nothing in the way of the amenities required for a successful watering place. It is the idea of inviting other people to give you their money for your ideas, without any guarantees at all."

"But that is the nature of enterprise, Priddy. It is called investing!"

"It is also called speculating," Priddy said sternly.

"Oh, piffle," Jane said, enthusiasm overriding

her manners.

"It is usually the case in these affairs that it is the speculator who becomes enriched at the expense of the investors."

"Priddy, where did you get these ideas? You know nothing about it at all."

"Anyone may form an opinion, but as it happens, my opinion has been buttressed by Mr. Fotheringay who knows much more of these matters than I would ever pretend to."

"Oh, Mr. Fotheringay," Jane said dismissively. "No wonder you are fainthearted, nourished on that milk-and-water man's opinion."

"He is not the fool you take him for, Jane."

"Very well then, he is a genius. But he is wrong on this count."

"I am not so sure of that."

"Oh, Priddy, can you not be grateful that Mr. Corydon is a man of wealth and vision? Any doubts you may entertain about this project must be dispelled by the fact that so wealthy and well-placed a man as Sir William is investing in it. He is willing to part with both land and funds to further its success."

"I wonder if Sir William has much choice in the matter," Priddy muttered darkly.

"I suppose you think he is being led by Lady Arabella."

"Is there any doubt of that?"

"No, I suppose not, but surely his man of business has looked into it and given it his approval."

"That may be, but with such a daughter he might have gone against his advice."

"Yes, Jenny," said Ned, "what of Lady Arabella? How are you planning to fix the interest of Mr.

Corydon when he has someone as determined as Lady Arabella blocking your path? She certainly is a formidable competitor. She is wealthy and well born as well."

"Jane is just as beautiful and well born. After all, she is Lady Jane Marlingforthe," Livvy stuck in hotly. "And Lady Arabella is a hussy."

"Livvy!"

"Livvy!"

"Young lady!"

"Well, isn't she?"

There was a small silence in honor of this truth.

Jane broke the silence. "The problem, as Ned said, is how to fix his interest—how to let him think we are rich. I told him we owned a huge estate in Northumberland, but if we invested in his project we should certainly convince him, and we would earn money into the bargain."

"Moonshine, young lady, and we certainly haven't so great a supply of funds that we could throw any away on a scheme as foolish as Mr. Corydon's."

"Priddy, I will not have you speak against him. And while I grant there isn't money, there is the vase."

"Grandfather's vase?" Ned asked incredulously. "Are you thinking of selling Grandfather's vase for money, which you would then give to Mr. Corydon, so that he might think you rich and offer for you?"

"He's seen the vase, Jenny, he'd notice if it were missing," Livvy put in, remembering his visit.

"We could tell him . . . oh well." Jane admitted to herself that it was not her best plan. "But the question still remains how am I to get him to offer for me?"

Chapter Ten

Breakfast at the King's Head was a wonderful repast, chiefly because it was served to the Marlingforthes who reposed indolently, consuming as much as they wished without lifting a finger, replete with the pleasures of food and laziness.

But Livvy was eager to explore the town. It was market day and although still too early for the quantity of stalls that would be in place later in the summer, there was all the bustle of a Saturday morning with peddlers and traders who had come from outlying farms and villages to buy and sell, meet acquaintances, and lift a pint in one of the taverns. The excitement stirred them all.

They stepped from the inn into Head Street and were greeted with bright sunshine and a sprightly breeze which quickened their steps. They passed St. Peter's and came to the broad High Street which poured as a cataract down a long hill crowded with carts and carriages, where pedestrians jostled to cross without stepping in the paths of horses and vehicles.

Livvy's eyes were wide and she pulled on Jane's arm to point out the bonnet the woman in front of them was sporting, the shop with slippers just the shade of berry she had always loved, the horse which looked like their father's old Thunderer, and the carriage which displayed bright yellow trim which they must copy.

As they walked, they sought out shops to return to: Ned, a bookseller's; Priddy, a shop with a wider supply of silks than Wixton offered; and Jane, a place she might purchase the dye with which to transform her old gown. Livvy wanted to go everywhere.

They wound through narrow side streets and came out into a charming road called Eld Lane which contained centuries-old buildings propping each other up, dark and secret, the kind of shops which made Jane think one might happen upon the most wonderful surprises. They slowed their pace and peered into the darkened doorways and through small panes to view the goods within.

Livvy was impatient to spend the coins Jane had given her and was clutching them in her hand like a small child. At every shop she saw something she desperately needed, a stick of anise candy, a bit of lace, an engraving of a fashionable man who she fancied resembled the hero of *Castle Rackrent*.

Suddenly she gripped Jane's arm. "Look, Jenny, just there. Don't turn," she added, pointing with her elbow in a futile attempt to be discreet.

"Where?"

"Over there. Don't let him see you. There, can't you see? It is Mr. Corydon, with a woman."

Jane narrowed her eyes. About ten doors down stood Mr. Corydon and with him was a woman about

154

his age, judging from her plump chins and matron's cap. But what was most astonishing was that they seemed to be engaged in a fierce argument.

Jane nudged Ned and Livvy who were gawking with open mouths, and watched out of the corner of her eye. The four of them backed into a narrow door that gave onto a chandler's shop, all the while continuing to monitor the astounding spectacle in the adjoining road.

Suddenly Mr. Corydon, who had been haranguing the woman—although from their distance they could not make out the words—grabbed her by the arm. Instead of shrinking away or struggling, she allowed him to propel her into a doorway, all the while shouting back at him in equally fierce and strident tones.

When the door closed with a slam behind the couple, Jane and the others turned toward each other. No one spoke. Priddy pursed her lips and studied Jane.

Riled, Jane blurted out, "I am sure it can be explained."

Priddy continued to watch Jane, who grew red with frustration. She was never able to hide her feelings from Priddy, and it was all she could do to appear calm, as though she had all the confidence in the world in Mr. Corydon. Escape was the best solution. "I'm returning to the High Street," she said, pulling away, "Livvy, you stay with Priddy and Ned."

She spun away from that too-noticing regard of Priddy to be alone to ponder the frightful scene she had witnessed and try to find a benign explanation. Ned caught up with her, putting his hand on her arm. "Slow down, Jenny, you need an escort."

Jane stared stubbornly at the pavement before her,

155

illogically furious with Priddy and Ned who had seen what she had seen. Ned veered into a bookseller's and pulled her along with him. She stood, numb, and watched him lose himself among the dusty heaps of books. Unnoticed she slipped away and ducked into a milliner's shop.

Her heart was heavy. She had to admit that what she had seen reflected no credit on Mr. Corydon. How could he be involved with such a common woman, and on such a level of intimacy or intimidation that he could shout at her? Perhaps it was a sister. She frowned; he hadn't mentioned a sister—it hadn't *looked* like a sister.

There was only one explanation: His mistress. But what an unlikely mistress! No, certainly not, she decided firmly, fingering a bonnet which the shop-keeper was itching to snatch from her. No, it was much more likely that it was a tiresome dependent, someone he supported out of the goodness of his heart who was now importuning him for more and more until, driven to be stern, he had been forced to enact the scene she had happened upon. Yes, that was it. She gazed at the bonnets, seeing Mr. Corydon's angry face in every one. It was not a sight she wished to dwell on.

She wandered out and returned to the bookseller's where Ned continued on, unaware of her arrival as he had been of her departure. She found herself drifting into a haberdashery and staring at a length of kersymere with such a thoroughly abstracted air that the shopkeeper did not even bother to entice her to consider more costly fabrics.

When she emerged she was so lost in thought that she

was jostled by more than one passerby before she came to herself. Then, in front of her, she saw a triumphant Ned, beaming at her, a smudge of dust on his forehead.

She laughed and reached with her thumb to wipe away the dirt. "You look like a cat in a cream pot."

"I found the volume I wanted. Essays by Pope."

"Pope. I had no idea you were interested in him. Ugh. Dull."

"I don't find him dull. But the book isn't for me, it's a gift. I want you to give it to . . ."

Ned broke off and lifted his hand to wipe his face as though to banish embarrassment.

"Edgar, what are you up to?"

"I want you to give it as a gift to Miss Fotheringay."

"Oh, Ned!" Jane smiled, but felt dismay. She looked into her brother's love-stricken face and felt a wave of pity that he might never be able to win Georgianna's hand. She reached up and kissed him.

Ned, touchingly awkward, allowed her to kiss him and gave her a quick kiss in return, and they exchanged a brief embrace for an instant in the midst of the busy traffic that swirled around them.

Charles de la Marre had concluded his business with an agent whom he employed in Colchester as a means of keeping track of his affairs, many of which still required his direction even though Stephen had taken over the bulk of them. The day was balmy and bright and as he stepped into the busy High Street he was met with a river of people, wagons, horses. He was in a particularly good mood.

He had completed the first draft of the second volume of his memoirs and would be able to send it to John Murray, his publisher, within a few weeks. He was elated as well by the weather and by a feeling of well-being whose source he hadn't bothered to track down.

His most pressing business was to determine how long to extend his stay in Wixton. Once the book was finished he should return to Windmere, but he no longer felt that would satisfy him. He was beginning to enjoy Wixton, especially the freedom from the burdens of his rank, a freedom he had not enjoyed since the brotherhood of the battlefield.

He stood in the street holding his hat in his arm, adjusting his gloves and taking in the scene, when suddenly he beheld a certain pair of unforgettable blue eyes.

It was Miss Montcrief herself coming up the road, gazing into the face of a young man with curls almost as dark as her own sleek, black hair, a young man he didn't recognize, dressed quietly but well. Something about him looked familiar, however.

Lord Charles stepped forward to greet her when all at once she rose to her toes and kissed the young man, who returned the kiss. Lord Charles was treated to the spectacle of the couple embracing in public, in the High Street!

He stared as they walked away, arm in arm, Miss Montcrief leaning in a posture of complete intimacy. They were silent, as though in the grip of deep emotion.

Love, he thought, and was shocked. For in the

moment they turned away, he had recognized the young man she had so publicly, scandalously, and eagerly embraced. It was none other than her footman!

What compelled Jane to turn back at that moment, she was never to understand, but as she walked away on Ned's arm, she glanced back over her shoulder and met the riveting gaze of Mr. Fotheringay.

She pulled away from Ned and whispered, "Oh, there's Mr. Fotheringay. He looks furious."

Ned, his idyllic thoughts of Georgianna Fotheringay interrupted, looked back and discovered Mr. Fotheringay towering above the crowd with a face like thunder.

At the moment of Ned's seeing him, however, without so much as a nod in their direction, Lord Charles turned sharply on his heel and marched away up the steep road.

Ned and Jane looked after him.

"I hadn't thought him rude—why didn't he greet us? What on earth is amiss?"

Ned said nothing.

Jane looked up at him and saw a tight, grim face. "Ned, whatever's the matter?"

"What did he see, Jenny?"

"He saw us, here, he saw me kissing my brother, what . . . ?"

"Not your brother," Ned said fiercely. "Your footman."

"Oh, no!" Jane gasped, realizing he was correct. "Oh, Ned!"

"We'd better return to the inn."

They walked in silence, each busy with the implications of having been seen, and trying to decide what, if anything, they might do to repair the situation.

Back at the inn, they ordered lemonade to be served in one of the private parlors.

"To have come a cropper over such an innocent thing," Jane moaned.

"Well, so you kissed your footman. We'll just have to concoct a story about my being a cousin you have taken in as the last wish of a dying uncle."

"We've used that story already."

"Then think of a better one."

"I wish I might. Oh, that such a clodpole could undo us!"

Ned looked stricken. "Oh, Jen. He'll tell Georgianna. What will she think!"

Jane considered. "She has a soft heart, Ned. She wouldn't believe such a thing didn't have a suitable cause. She's fond of me, and not a little afraid of him, I think. I'm sure I can convince her it was all in innocence."

"But what if she believes I have a tendre for you?"

"She won't, I promise."

"Oh, Jenny, she is so sweet. She knows Latin and Greek."

"That's not her fault!"

"I couldn't bear to lose her."

"Ned, what do you mean lose her? You don't *have* her. There is no way you can offer for her. You're a footman."

"I know," he said bitterly, looking at her accusingly.

Jane breathed a heavy sigh. "I am sorry, Ned. I had no idea that this complication would occur."

"Complication! My loving Georgianna is not a complication, Jenny."

"I didn't mean it that way."

They fell silent. Ned pushed himself heavily from the table, went to the door, and shouted for ale. When it came he swallowed it down and wiped his mouth with his sleeve. Jane watched him warily, knowing that he held her responsible for the frustration of loving an unattainable woman, but unable to point out to him, no matter how tactfully, the stark truth that it was his poverty that made him ineligible.

Oh, she thought, to have our efforts undone by Mr. Fotheringay, that stupid lummox! That he should be the one to stand in their way! Her anger restored her sense of humor.

She laughed. "Oh, Ned, it really is funny."

Ned did not laugh.

"Oh, don't take it so to heart, Ned. It will come out all right, I'm sure. But think! You have compromised me! If you were not my brother, you would have to marry me!"

Ned was too wrapped up in his misery to smile. He stared out through the diamond-shaped panes at the back of the room, his shoulders slumped.

Suddenly Jane sat up straight, her eyes alight with a brilliant thought. Compromise! She had it! A plan began to take shape in her mind.

For a week Lord Charles had been able to hold

161

himself aloof from Wixton society, furiously editing the volume he had just completed. He had posted it, and he would have left for Windmere immediately— resigned to burying himself in his duties—if it were not for the Churchill women. They were millstones about his neck, holding him to a place he was sick of.

He was standing in his room at the Oaks, trying to valet himself into the proper form for an intimate dinner with dancing at the home of the vicar. Cheever had proved singularly useless at valeting, and Lord Charles had dismissed him for the evening. He and the Churchill ladies had agreed to attend the party too long ago for him to back out of it, or he would never have found himself facing such an evening. He was hot with annoyance as he tried to tie his neckcloth into something presentable.

A week had passed since Miss Montcrief's stunning display of vulgarity. He studied the results of his clumsy, impatient efforts in the looking glass, called under his breath for patience, ripped the neckcloth off, and began again. He was furious with her and furious with himself for being furious. She had shown him nothing but the greatest contempt—even if she had been kind to Sylvie. It was because of that that he had not told the Churchill ladies what he had seen. He wondered if they would be as distressed as he had been.

She was shameless, wanton, depraved, unworthy of his notice. Not that he had noticed her particularly.

He sighed heavily. He would have to tell Mrs. Churchill and Sylvie that they must make plans to leave. He knew they had written their solicitor, but whatever the answer, they must still leave. He could not abide this provincial backwater one minute longer. He resigned himself to the prospect of supporting them until they could recover their home and funds.

In disgust he turned away from the looking glass and shrugged himself into his coat. He had to admit that living with them was becoming daily more comfortable and pleasant. Mrs. Churchill no longer feared the imminent arrival of Reginald Flood and Sylvie had recovered her spirits, and no longer felt overcome by shame but was instead feeling a healthy outrage. She had not the high spirits and confidence of Miss Montcrief, but then, he reminded himself, Miss Montcrief's spirits were not under the governance that decent society required of a young lady.

It was galling to see Sylvie continue their friendship unabated, not knowing what kind of trollop Miss Montcrief was. Daily Lord Charles had to witness the spectacle of Sylvie laughing more frequently, speaking more spontaneously, and growing altogether more easy in her manner, knowing it was the work of Miss Montcrief.

And himself, of course. It was for her sake that he was now brushing his locks forward into suitable disarray to satisfy fashion and anticipating an evening of intolerable boredom. He reminded himself that as long as he remained in Wixton, he owed the Churchill ladies his ungrudging escort, and it was that noble thought which propelled him down the stairs, into the drawing room, where he gathered them up and walked through the soft evening air to the vicarage.

The Woodses were not accustomed to giving entertainments such as the one they were now preparing for. Aside from the Sneeds—whom they avoided as much as they could, despite a certain sympathy for the hapless Sir William—Mrs. Penworthy, and the octogenarian who had just removed from the Oaks to take up residence in Bath, there were few people in the village whom they wished to entertain beyond an occasional tea or supper. But the addition of so many people, particularly so many lively young people, had challenged their interest.

Childless, they had longed for the vitality of young people and were excited about the prospects for their little party tonight. Mrs. Woods was particularly attracted to Miss Montcrief, but she was deeply sympathetic to young Georgianna whom she had taken under her wing, and, with Mrs. Penworthy, had invited for conversations about books which seemed to gratify her. Mrs. Woods had decided on first meeting her that discussions about literature would not interest Miss Montcrief, but they were just the thing to animate Georgianna.

Mrs. Woods, in a rustling blue dress that she had not worn above twice in the last three years, spoke with her cook, and then came abovestairs to look over the reception rooms. The vicarage was large but its rooms were small. She and Mr. Woods had decided to move the furniture from the back parlor, which had doors to the garden and would lend itself best to dancing. In the bookroom they set up tables for Sir William, Mrs. Fotheringay, and Mrs. Montcrief if they wished to play cards. She passed through the dining room and assured herself that all was in order, that the daffodils she had picked in great profusion were all charmingly displayed.

She was satisfied and turned to await her guests, pleased with the prospect of a diverting evening, and not just a little bit guilty because she knew that the best part of the diversion would be the sparks which would fly between Miss Montcrief and Lady Arabella.

There had been another small mutiny before Priddy and Jane had gotten away. Livvy had begged and pleaded to go with them, and although Jane never for a moment considered allowing her, she still felt like a cruel sister for denying her. Ned, who knew he could not attend, had caused her pain, for although he was perfectly silent, she knew he dreamed of spending an evening in the company of Miss Georgianna Fotheringay and dancing with her in his arms.

Jane dreaded the evening. She had not seen Mr. Fotheringay since that awful moment in Colchester, except for the back of his head at services and chilly bows in the churchyard. But from Georgianna's continued visits to the house, and her increasingly warm and intimate manner, she knew he had not given her away. That would have been more of a comfort had she been able to rest assured that he would never do so.

Of Mr. Corydon she had seen little. The proposal Livvy had prophesied had not come about, but worse, Jane had not even been able to meet with him alone. She had only chatted with him after services, where he had at least sought her out. And once in the village—when she had been on one of the many urgent trips she had felt it necessary to make in the past week in hopes of encountering him—she had succeeded only in exchanging pleasantries about the weather. She had, of course, said nothing about that awful woman she had seen him with, and he had said nothing about having heard that she had kept a secret rendezvous in Colchester with her footman.

Tonight she anticipated a chance to dance with him, a chance for a stolen word, and a chance to put into effect a certain plan.

Chapter Eleven

At dinner Lord Charles found himself seated between Lady Arabella and Miss Montcrief. It could not have been worse. He had avoided the famous Lady Arabella since he had discovered her in Wixton, well aware of the spectacular failures of her Seasons in London, which all her father's wealth had not rescued from her vindictive tongue. Miss Montcrief was a more recent object of avoidance, and a much more disturbing one.

Lady Arabella was typically voluble. She had, by the time the turbot had been served, held forth on the glories of Wixton and the improvements that the resort—which, did everyone realize, had been named Belleview in her honor—would bring to the country, the tedium of London compared to the advantages of a fine place in the country, although, mind you, she did not mean *any* place in the country, but only the superior kinds of places that might be found within a two-mile radius—to the southeast over the Bourne Mill road, to be exact—of their present location, and on the manners of the majority of women who had never availed themselves of a Season to acquire town bronze. "And wasn't that true, Mr. Corydon?"

Mr. Corydon was seated at mid-table and made to cry amen to her statements so often that he was unable to pay attention to anyone else. Arabella's unflagging conversation might have amused Lord Charles, had it not fallen to him to make conversation with Miss Montcrief.

That woman he found as disposed to silence as Lady Arabella was not, and monosyllables were all he was able to prise from her. He suspected that her silence stemmed from his knowledge of her guilty secret, and considered how to make use of his power over her. After comments about the weather, the nature of this year's crops, the condition of the sea following a surprising mid-week storm, and the presence of nightingales in the fields near the Oaks had been met with nothing more than Yes, Oh, Ah, and Hmmm, he decided he'd earned the right to enjoy himself.

"Tell me, Miss Montcrief, what it was that drew you to Colchester last week? I was sure I saw you, although I might have been mistaken, of course."

Jane shot him a hopeful look. Could it be that he would let her off the hook by pretending he had not seen her?

Her hope was short-lived for he immediately said, "I was there to look over some horses, for although I have my own mount, I've been remiss in securing one for Georgianna whom I am assured would benefit from riding. Her comfort, as you are well aware, is my first goal in life. But then if I expand my stable I will require more servants—chiefly a groom. Already we make do

168

with only one man-of-all-work and some women from the village. Tell me, how do you manage with one young maid and one—although quite satisfactory, I am sure—young man?"

"I do very well," Jane said, giving him a look she hoped was quelling.

Lord Charles was taken aback by her poise and persisted. "I am sure that you do. He seems a versatile young man, capable of a wide variety of undertakings."

"He is everything I wish for in a footman," she said, staring him straight in the eyes. There, she thought, let him deal with that.

Lord Charles almost choked on his wine. Of all the reactions he had anticipated, brazenness was not one of them. He returned her stare and found himself checkmated. He could hardly credit that such a young woman could be so bold.

He gave a slight bow of his head, acknowledging that she had won that round, and she turned her face away, anxious that he not see the blush which stained her face. She had read his thoughts as directly as if he had spoken them. He thought she was a jade. Well, as long as he kept his opinion to himself. She thought of the adage about deceit's tangled web with a new respect for the force of its truth.

But their silence, their absorption in the food reposing on their plates—untouched but minutely inspected—their faces working with emotion would be noted, and, in fact, already had been by Mrs. Woods, who was quite curious to know what had passed between them.

Lord Charles's vanity would not allow him to sit in silence at table. Besides, he had a score to settle with

Miss Montcrief. "Tell me, Miss Montcrief, from your wide reading and learned pursuits, you must be intimately conversant with the poems of Byron. I am sure you have read "Beppo," his Venetian story which has newly appeared. I wonder if you would explain it to me, for I find it quite difficult to comprehend."

"Oh, Mr. Fotheringay, how can you ask such a thing of me? Is he not a dissolute and libertine? Would *I* read the works of such a one? Oh . . ." Jane managed a fine imitation of trembling outrage that threatened to spill over into tears. She had, of course, read everything Byron had written, and although he was not one of her favorites, he was certainly one of Livvy's.

"Surely you exaggerate, Miss Montcrief. I have known many young ladies who have read Byron."

"Young ladies of your acquaintance, perhaps, but . . . oh, dear, Mrs. Woods, please," Jane called softly across the table. "I am sore beset. Please explain to Mr. Fotheringay that young ladies who are of good character and gently bred, do not read Lord Byron."

Lord Charles ground his teeth while he listened to Mrs. Woods who, puzzled, responded as though the question were serious, not trusting her sense of humor, which told her that something was not quite right with Miss Montcrief's appeal.

"Mr. Fotheringay, perhaps you are unaware of the nature of his personal life, and the way that rather scandalous personal life has intruded into his poetry. Many young women and their mamas do not approve of him or his work, although in my experience," she was unable to resist, "those same young women and their mamas are often amazingly familiar with both."

Lord Charles was required to listen to this with

straight-faced interest and managed a polite nod when she had finished.

"So you see," Jane added in die-away tones, "to ask a young woman such as I, if she has read him, is to suggest that she . . ."

"But I am sure Mr. Fotheringay meant nothing by his question," Mrs. Woods said reassuringly.

Jane turned huge, liquid eyes upon him.

"Indeed not, Miss Montcrief. I must beg your pardon for having caused you distress with my question."

"Thank you, Mr. Fotheringay. You are forgiven."

Jane turned back to her food and Mrs. Woods saw an astounding transformation wherein distress became a most mischievous smile. On the other hand, Mr. Fotheringay's earnest expression changed to one of thunder while he averted his face to drink from his wineglass.

After a pause Lord Charles cleared his throat, noting that Mrs. Woods was agog with interest, and succeeded in asking, "What poet do you enjoy reading then, Miss Montcrief?"

"Cowper."

"Of course, Cowper. And what is your favorite poem?"

"Oh, you do press me hard this evening, Mr. Fotheringay. Is this a test, are you making an attempt to catch me out? I will readily admit to being no bluestocking, you need not work to make that discovery, I hand it to you."

"Miss Montcrief, I am doing no such thing; I am merely attempting to make conversation. I have not meant to wound or embarrass you."

171

"Oh, Mr. Fotheringay?" Jane asked, looking directly into his eyes.

He had the grace to blush.

Jane smiled openly in her triumph. "'Jack Gilpin.'"

"Jack Gilpin?"

"My favorite Cowper poem."

"Well, that is wonderful." Lord Charles said, unable to think of any other response, torn between wanting to overturn the table and spill his wine down the lovely white bosom of his exasperating companion.

Jane feigned sadness. "I knew I would disappoint you: you are not troubling to mask your irony. I have never been able to hold my own in serious discussions. Used to Georgianna as you are, you must think me terribly stupid. It is so daunting to discover that one is thought stupid."

"I do not find you stupid," he said, between clenched teeth.

"Oh, how wonderful! Oh, Mrs. Woods, Mr. Fotheringay has given me the most marvellous compliment. He has just told me that he does not find me stupid!"

Lord Charles tore at the slice of mutton before him, sank his teeth into it, and chewed as though it were the flesh of a certain very awful young woman.

Sylvie, seated next to Mrs. Woods, diagonally from Ariadne, marvelled that her friend whom she admired so for her poise, seemed to be having such an awkward time. But then, she knew that her friend and Mr. Fotheringay did not find each other congenial, a circumstance that continued to sadden her.

For herself, she expected to be awkward in social settings, and this evening was proving no exception. She was thoroughly intimidated by Lady Arabella across from whom she was seated, and even though she was not required to respond to her, she found the torrent of opinions and criticisms quite daunting. She was seated between Mr. Rankin and Mrs. Woods, and although she knew she could fall into easy conversation with that lady, she felt it her duty to find the courage to address the London gentleman.

"Are you satisfied with the progress you are making on Belleview?"

Mr. Rankin turned to Sylvie and noted the contrast between her beauty and her intense shyness. He was bored. Corydon had summoned him to Wixton to make the appeal to Sir William, and just last night they had signed the papers wherein Sir William had agreed to put land and cash into their hands. It was a considerable coup and Rankin knew it had not been his blandishments which had brought it off, that indeed they owed their success to Lady Arabella's determination. He eyed Corydon appreciatively across the table and hid his smile. He had to hand it to him, he certainly had known how to play her. He did not bother to acknowledge Sylvie's question.

Sylvie received the snub with a furious blush and looked down at her plate. She had looked forward to this evening, for she was comfortable with most of the guests and had few anxieties about appearing in this company. It was discouraging to have her old sense of inadequacy overcome her. She worked at the mutton diligently although she had no appetite. It was more than her discomfort with the company which stole her small appetite away. It was a sense of guilt and unease which she knew arose from the fact that she had a secret from her mother, a secret so shameful that even thinking about it brought a scarlet blush to her cheek.

Miss Montcrief's footman, Nettles, had given Ariadne a book to give her. Ariadne said it had been chosen for her by her footman, and that he had wished it given to Sylvie as though from Ariadne herself, but she said she could not stoop to such subterfuge and that her friend must know its true origin. Ariadne had not seemed to think it at all out of the way that her footman should be giving books to a young lady, nor that the young lady should accept with pleasure.

Sylvie hardly knew what to think, but she thought of it all the time. It was discomfort with these thoughts that impelled her to turn to Mrs. Woods and ask whether she had seen the kites the children had raised on the green this morning, trying all the while not to think of Nettles's warm, green eyes as she listened to Mrs. Woods's amusing account of the exertions some of the local lads had expended disentangling a kite from one of the trees in the churchyard.

When the last remove had been cleared, Mrs. Woods led the ladies to the front saloon where they walked about the room, having been confined to the table for nearly two hours. Sylvie and Jane gravitated toward each other although they had met earlier in the afternoon.

"I have started the book your footman, Nettles, gave me," Sylvie began, blushing furiously.

"Oh, yes," Jane said pleasantly as though it were an

everyday occurrence. "Have you enjoyed it?"

"Oh, yes, very much." Sylvie's eyes shone.

"I'm glad."

"What are you talking about?" Lady Arabella came up to them, having no male to better direct her energies toward.

"Pope."

"I am Church of England and do not hold with Rome. I am surprised to hear you do."

Jane studied Lady Arabella with an air of gratified discovery. "Oh, did you hear that, Georgianna? Lady Arabella is Church of England. How kind of you to vouchsafe that information. Georgianna, did you hear?"

Sylvie's eyes twinkled but she found it difficult to participate in Ariadne's nonsense.

Lady Arabella continued. "I don't hold with Quakers, either. I do hope that neither of you has Quaker tendencies."

Jane hung her head in mock shame. "Oh, but I do. Just the other day I found myself donning a grey gown with neither lace nor ribbons, and I thought, how wonderful to be wearing such a plain gown, but then it suddenly sprang into my mind that it might be thought a Quakerish tendency, and I tore the dress off and threw it from me in abhorrence."

"How very extraordinary," Lady Arabella said.

Jane remained silent, studying the beautiful woman whose whole interest seemed now to be focused on a bow on her sleeve which threatened to come undone. She was lovely; her auburn hair lent her distinction enough to draw all eyes, even without her commanding height and proud carriage. She was not really all that much older than Jane, perhaps three or four years at the most, much too young for such mean-spiritedness. She behaved like an old woman with a lifetime of disillusionment behind her, and a future where pleasure was to be derived only from the submission of those she could command. Jane could find nothing in Arabella that suggested warmth, joy, or delight. She would like to think that this was due to her having been so very spoiled, but perhaps it sprang from great loneliness. But clearly, arrogance and pride had alienated her from the pleasures of friendship.

Nonetheless Jane felt no pity, and when Lady Arabella asked her whether she felt daunted by her present company—meaning, Jane assumed, herself— Jane pointedly looked at Mrs. Penworthy and replied, "Yes, her knowledge of literature does intimidate me, as does Georgianna's knowledge of languages and history, but I try to remind myself that knowledge is something that can be acquired by diligent application and that, if I were to undertake it, I might have some hope of attaining, to some degree, their superiority."

Lady Arabella stared at her in disbelief. "My dear Miss Montcrief, that was not at all what I was referring to."

"Oh, but of course," Jane said, catching sight of Mrs. Woods who was perched on the arm of the sofa listening to the exchange with amusement. "I comprehend you now, you mean the piety of our host and hostess." Turning toward Mrs. Woods, she curtseyed with a wink and said, "Ma'am, I hope that you will forgive me if I have failed to show signs of having been awestruck by your presence, as I ought to have done."

Mrs. Woods laughed and Sylvie joined her.

Lady Arabella looked wrathful but puzzled. She knew she had been insulted, but she also knew she was unassailable and so she deigned to say to Jane only that she found her gown completely out of fashion. She then took herself to the doors of the dining room, threw them open, and said in stentorian tones, "Gentlemen, it grows quite boring without your company. Have done with your cigars and port and join us!"

The shock with which this command was greeted resulted in a silence which was terminated by a group of bemused men stubbing out their cigars, swallowing the remaining wine from their glasses, and scraping back their chairs, and in the room behind her, by a group of women hastily smoothing gowns and thinking not only how insufferably rude Lady Arabella had been but also how many times *they* had wished to have the courage to draw the men from their masculine fastness in such a peremptory way.

The gentlemen entered the small saloon and Sir William found a place by an open window near where Jane was standing with Sylvie. Jane had never spoken to the man, who always seemed to have little to say, at least around his forceful daughter.

With elaborate courtesy, he greeted both ladies by name.

"I have been wishing to tell you, Sir William," Jane responded, "how much I admire the audacity and vision of using your land for the splendid spa Mr. Corydon has conceived."

"Ah, so you are an enthusiast, too, are you?" he asked, looking over his wire spectacles at her.

"I suppose I must be, but I would have thought you the most enthusiastic of all."

177

"Now that is hard to say. I confess myself to be a stick-in-the-mud. It is you young people who keep me on my toes."

"It is a good plan, don't you think?" Jane pursued.

"I don't know. I sometimes wonder what Dora would think of it. I'm not sure that Dora would like it at all."

"Dora?"

"My wife, my wife. Died when Bella was born. She would have known whether this was a good scheme or not, she had a good head on her shoulders."

"Ah." Both Jane and Sylvie looked at him with sympathy.

"But then," Sir William continued in a brighter voice, "it is all settled, so it is too late for doubts, no?"

"It is settled? What do you mean?"

"Why, don't you know? The transactions were completed last night, and building will begin as soon as Mr. Corydon and Mr. Rankin go to London to see to the remaining details."

Jane clapped her hands. "Oh, Sir William, I am so glad. So, it is to be accomplished after all. Oh, Georgianna," she said, seizing her hand, "aren't you excited to have been in on something like this from the very beginning?"

Jane gazed at Mr. Corydon who was deep in conversation with Lady Arabella. "Mr. Corydon is an exceptional man, is he not?" she asked Sir William. "To think it was all his idea. It must be wonderful to be able to do things like that."

"Well, from what I understand, it was not entirely his idea, but that of a Mr. Coggelshall, some London man, not," Sir William hastened to add, "that I have anything against London men, but apparently the three of them, Corydon, Rankin, and Coggelshall, have been in partnership for some time. They purchased property in Cornwall at a ridiculously low price on speculation for the resort, but it was Wixton that met with their approval. I was happy to sign over my land and give them an advance against all the costs they are so generously willing to take on, but of course, it will be a while before they can repay me from the profits. If it sounds as if all this is a little over my head, it is. But if Arabella says it's right and tight, it's right and tight to me. Of course, I always thought Wixton quite pleasant myself, never saw the need for all this change, but I am a man of quieter ways than many, I think."

Jane found herself smiling fondly at him while some terrible thought was taking shape in her mind. Her gaze grew blank. Coggelshall . . . the Cornish coast . . . speculation . . .

She stepped away as though to look out the window and thought with horror—*their* Coggelshall? The man who had bought Thrate House? What had Sir William said?

Mrs. Woods stood in the center of the room and called to everyone; when she had their attention, she announced that there would be cards and dancing if the young people didn't mind her quite indifferent playing.

Sir William Sneed bowed to Sylvie and Jane and said that although he hoped to be charmed by their presence at the piquet table, that he must assume they would prefer to dance, so he would take his leave.

There were a thousand questions, but Jane settled on one and asked it offhandedly, so that he could not know the turbulence he had created in her mind. "Sir William, do you know what part of the Cornish coast this Mr. Coggelshall was interested in?"

"Oh, my dear, I'm afraid I have no head for details like that. I'll have to ask my man of business, or you can ask Mr. Coggelshall himself when he comes. He should be here sometime this week, but then, I'm not sure. Arabella would know, do ask her."

Jane felt dizzy but managed a shaky smile and thanked him.

Sylvie, who had no heart for dancing, took Jane's arm and asked her if she would like to stroll in the garden. Jane seized the offer eagerly and the two young women escaped to the back garden where they discovered a small shrubbery which afforded them refuge. Jane's head was whirling. Sylvie, unaware of her friend's turmoil, was silent, glad for the solitude. They strolled in silence until a halloo from a cheerful Mr. Woods summoned them to the dancing.

Jane hesitated a moment and took a deep breath. She had many goals for the evening, all related to Mr. Corydon, but now she had another: to discover whether this Mr. Coggelshall was the very man who had taken their home from them.

Chapter Twelve

Jane's first dance was claimed by the vicar who led her through a lively reel. Despite her distraction she found his enthusiasm and energy contagious, and it was all she could do to keep up with him. She laughed and her cheeks were bright and she found as usual that the gaiety of dancing—an activity often dreamed of— was so delightful, that there was no room in her head for anything but its lively pleasures.

Mr. Corydon was making his way to claim the next dance when he was intercepted by Lady Arabella who had resented his dancing with Sylvie rather than herself and was not about to allow him to insult her further by ignoring her again.

Jane was abandoned to Mr. Fotheringay, standing a short distance from her. He was dressed as soberly as he had been at the Sneeds', affecting an all black costume relieved only by a figured grey silk waistcoat. Jane, in one of her prettiest gowns, a pale blue silk embroidered with dark blue and purple butterflies, felt infinitely more stylish. Not only did his clothes proclaim that he had no intention of enjoying the evening, his stiffness told her that he was as little eager to lead her into a dance as she was to be led. She essayed an escape, but Mrs. Woods, banging away with more energy than finesse, cried out to Mr. Fotheringay, while nodding towards Jane, not to let her slip through his fingers. There was no choice but that he should turn to Jane and ask her for the dance.

They stood opposite each other with eyes averted, looks of resignation on their faces as they bowed and curtseyed. Jane traced the steps with duty and restraint, forcefully refusing by smile or word to show any pleasure in the exercise.

Mr. Fotheringay was all that was grave. It would seem he was attending a rite of sacrifice rather than dancing with a woman he found exquisitely lovely, especially now when her perfect features, unleavened by a smile, were soothing and peaceful. He thought anew how at odds with her character her appearance was. What seemed modest was coarse; what seemed serene was crude.

Jane's thoughts were far away and she would have been surprised to know the extent to which she occupied Mr. Fotheringay's. That he considered her person unattractive and her character beneath contempt was now established, and she surmised that under those circumstances the dance was a socially necessary test of endurance for both of them.

They were standing apart with their hands joined above their heads, making an arch for a couple coming down the line, when Mr. Rankin—no very excellent dancer—who was supposed to twirl his partner after passing beneath their hands, lost his timing and his

182

footing and began to swing around before he had cleared the arching couple. His foot, lifted in pirouette, caught Jane's ankle as she was about to execute a dainty skip and she found herself suddenly with no feet on the ground and nothing to clutch at but the large and massive body of Mr. Fotheringay.

Lord Charles, surprised by the instant collapse of his dancing partner, had no choice but to reach out and clasp her in his arms to prevent her from crashing to the floor.

And that is how it came about that he was crushing Miss Montcrief to his broad chest, feeling her soft body against his, and how it happened that Miss Montcrief's arms were encircling his neck and that they were regarding each other closely, discovering interesting things about each other's eyes and lips, and studying each other's faces so minutely that it seemed as though there would never be enough time for the study to be completed but they must stand all night in this posture, when Mr. Rankin suddenly broke into their small and private world.

"I say, Miss Montcrief, I am dashed sorry. Never was a gallant on the dance floor, I'm afraid. I didn't hurt you, did I?"

Jane pulled away from Mr. Fotheringay in a trance of bemusement, and stared at Mr. Rankin as though she had never seen him before.

"I knocked you down, I think," he said, puzzled that she should not know what he was talking about. "I'm the one who bowled you over."

"Oh, yes," Jane said, gathering herself together. "It was nothing, Mr. Rankin. I'm afraid I lost my footing."

Others who had been dancing and who had stopped

when the accident occurred were gathered around the unfortunate Jane who wished fervently not to be examined at this moment. She forced herself to laugh and say, "Perhaps we should abandon this dance, it seems ordained to be catastrophic."

But Mrs. Woods recommenced playing and there was nothing for it but that Jane must extend her arms to her partner and manage to complete the dance, which she did without once looking at any other part of Mr. Fotheringay but his shirtfront.

They did not bother to curtesy or bow after the dance but turned instantly away to find distraction and relief. Jane dazedly stood next to Sylvie as though for protection and nodded, without hearing, at whatever Sylvie said. She was quite lost to what was going on around her. All she knew was that there remained her plan for the evening—no matter how many shocks there might be along the way—and that to carry it out required more composure than she currently could claim. She must therefore shelter in Sylvie's company until it returned.

It was only a few moments, however, before Mr. Corydon requested the dance she had been awaiting all evening. His invitation marked the commencement of her campaign, which began with her bestowing upon him her hand and her most dazzling smile.

"I would be delighted, Mr. Corydon. I hoped you might not neglect me."

Mr. Corydon raised his eyebrows at such direct flirtation and smiled widely. "I was hoping for a waltz, Miss Montcrief, however, I am persuaded there will be no waltzing tonight."

"A waltz would have been . . ." Jane broke off,

smiling archly.

"Divine, Miss Montcrief?"

"Divine, Mr. Corydon."

"But to dance with you at all, Miss Montcrief . . ."

"Is the greatest pleasure, Mr. Corydon."

They exchanged gleaming smiles and parted as required by the figures of the dance.

"You have brought so much pleasure to Wixton," she said when they came together again, "but I think it is as nothing to the pleasures you will bring in the future."

He looked at her with open admiration and said, "But Miss Montcrief, imagine the pleasures I have discovered here. So many more than I had ever hoped for."

"Mr. Corydon, you flatter our poor company."

"Miss Montcrief, I was not referring to our company but to one charming part of it."

Jane smiled and turned away to execute skips and jumps that matched the rhythms of her heart. How she loved to flirt! The pleasure of it made everything inexplicable and worrying—Mr. Corydon's questionable female acquaintances, Mr. Coggelshall's fell hand in her destiny, the odious pomposity of Mr. Fotheringay—all fade into the background. But, she admitted to herself, in the midst of even such delicious flirting as she was presently engaged in, her campaign ruled out any direct inquiries tonight. There would be ample time to get to the bottom of those mysteries, tonight it was enough to be held in the arms of Mr. Corydon.

"You dance so well, Mr. Corydon, with such effortlessness and grace."

"And you, Miss Montcrief, dance as though a

feather on the wind."

Jane caught herself glancing at him doubtingly. The man was a practiced flirt, no gainsaying it. She looked at his face as he turned from her and saw that to some the lines she found so attractive—the lines of sorrow as she had imagined—might be mistaken for the marks of a dissolute life. What an odd thought! She banished it from her mind and met him, when he turned toward her again, with a demure smile from a bowed head. Her glance through her thick lashes made him catch his breath.

"We have all come to dote on you, Mr. Corydon, it will be such a loss to us all should you ever leave Wixton."

"But what makes you think I will be leaving, Miss Montcrief?"

"Oh, I don't know, perhaps it is such an unpleasant prospect that I fear none of us could survive it."

"Then it would seem I must not leave at all, does it not, Miss Montcrief, rather than cause such wholesale loss of life?"

Jane smiled a roguish smile and gave him a merry look out of the corner of her eye as she sank in a deep curtsey.

Mr. Corydon glanced over her head and saw Lady Arabella glowering at him from where she was curtseying to Mr. Fotheringay.

"Miss Montcrief, would you care to take a turn in the garden?"

"Mr. Corydon, I would like it above all things; it is so warm in here that I was about to suggest it myself." Indeed, she thought, my whole plan depends on it!

As they strolled toward the door, Jane whispered to

Sylvie who was standing with Mr. Fotheringay and Mr. Rankin, "Georgianna, would you do me a favor— it is most urgent. Would you send Mrs. Woods to me in the garden in about five minutes?"

Sylvie looked confused. "Have Mrs. Woods go to the garden to get you, you mean?"

"Shhh. Yes, five minutes. Do you understand?"

"Of course, I suppose. Yes."

Jane returned to Mr. Corydon and took his arm with a melting smile.

He put his hand over hers and looked down on her with what Lord Charles judged a wolfish smile. The spectacle of their behavior during the dance had put him in a filthy mood. That she should wear her heart on her sleeve for such as Corydon showed her true character. And what did she want Mrs. Woods to follow her into the garden for? He found himself ruminating.

In her earlier perambulation of the shrubbery, Jane had noted an arbor enclosing a rustic bench in the far corner of the garden. While seeming to stroll along with Mr. Corydon without thought or purpose, it was to that corner she meant to lead him by the gentlest of inducements.

"Do you not love violets, Mr. Corydon? Look what a veritable carpet of them Mrs. Woods has contrived to grow here."

"They are like your eyes, Miss Montcrief. Would you be offended if I told you that you have the loveliest eyes of any woman I have ever known?"

"Oh, Mr. Corydon, how could you think I would be offended by what every woman would dream of hearing, that she was in some way, by some special

187

man, singled out for approbation?"

"Ah, Miss Montcrief, if I have not been able to convey to you my approbation before this, then many of the things I have said have been in vain."

"Perhaps not in vain, Mr. Corydon, for I do think I hoped I might have detected that perhaps you do not abhor me."

"Abhor you, Miss Montcrief? Of all the things I feel for you, I cannot imagine admitting to an instant of abhorrence, and yet, I can and must confess that at times my feelings toward you have reached the intensity of violence."

"You alarm me, Mr. Corydon, I am sure I do not understand you."

"Oh, Miss Montcrief, I had hoped you understood me."

"Oh, what can you mean?"

Jane turned from him in mock distress, aware that they were only about ten feet from the seat she had in mind. She slipped from his side to pretend to discover it and stood looking about, allowing her figure to show to advantage, and noting that Mr. Corydon was availing himself of the opportunity.

"Look, Mr. Corydon, at this lovely seat. Isn't this a charming garden, such a lovely secluded space; consider the person who created it; what an appreciation for the beautiful, for all that is natural, for all that is lovely in the world . . ."

"Miss Montcrief, you are all that is lovely in the world."

"Oh, Mr. Corydon." Suddenly, barely within the protection of the arbor, but in fact in full view of whoever might walk down the garden path at that

188

moment, Jane rose to her full height, wrapped her arms shamelessly around Mr. Corydon's neck and kissed him full on the mouth.

Mr. Corydon started, drawing back at this astonishing development. He himself might have hoped for a stolen kiss but to be so directly attacked! Almost immediately thoughts such as those were driven from his mind as he slowly took in the sensation of a woman's body against his and the tender lips offered his own.

Jane found her neck becoming stiff from the uncomfortable angle at which she was required to hold her head and found that Mr. Corydon's lips were hard and that when he opened his mouth she was repelled and yet she hung on to the kiss and wondered when Mrs. Woods would come. She found the kiss drawing out and Mr. Corydon's hand, once firmly on her back, beginning to trail around to her front perilously close to her breast, which was not at all what she had in mind. Everything was getting out of control and *where was Mrs. Woods!* Suddenly a voice she had certainly not wished to hear cut through her panicking thoughts.

"Ah, Miss Montcrief, I believe you wished to speak to Mrs. Woods. She is occupied, but then, I can see that you are as well."

Jane slowly lowered herself to her heels and unconsciously wiped her mouth as she turned to face Mr. Fotheringay who loomed nearby, his great size blocking the dying light of evening.

Mr. Corydon stepped away from her and began, "I say, Fotheringay. This is completely . . . I should say that . . ."

"Please do not trouble yourself with an explanation,

189

Corydon. I fully understand how it is with Miss Montcrief."

And with a glint in his eye, he made them a very deep, mocking bow and walked rapidly back to the house.

Jane felt an infinite weariness steal over her. It was supposed to have been the proper vicar's wife who was to have seen her compromised into the necessity of a proposal of marriage from Mr. Corydon. But Fotheringay! He was at once too stupid and too cynical about her to raise the necessary alarm among their acquaintances.

She took a deep breath and started for the house, but Mr. Corydon caught her arm.

She turned back, startled, and found him gazing down at her with warmth and intensity. Her hopes rekindled.

"Miss Montcrief. If you will permit me, I have been wishing to ask you this for some time, but until this moment I have not had the opportunity. That which has passed between us has given me reason to hope."

Jane lifted a glowing countenance to him, triumph and delight barely contained. Mr. Corydon retained her hand in a gentle clasp and continued. "Now I have the courage to dare ask you, Miss Montcrief. How much do *you* wish to invest in the building of Belleview?"

"Invest?"

"Yes, your enthusiasm for the project, your understanding and vision . . . I have known from the beginning, Miss Montcrief, that our hearts beat as one, that we are united by something greater than us both— the building of Belleview. Can you deny it?"

"No. Yes. I . . ."

"Think, Miss Montcrief, your investment, say five hundred, a thousand pounds, at five percent over twenty or thirty years. Oh, Miss Montcrief, do you not thrill to think of the return you will see, but more, of the pleasure of knowing that your small contribution helped build so great a project?"

"It is very sobering, Mr. Corydon."

"Yes, I understand," he said, lifting her hand to his chest. "I know it is one of those moments in a lifetime which we shall look back upon and realize was a turning point."

"Indeed, that is so."

"Then will you say yes, Miss Montcrief, and make me a happy man?"

"I . . . I must think about it, Mr. Corydon. I am honored, but it is so sudden."

"Of course, I understand. These things must not be rushed. Take your time, Miss Montcrief, but remember that I ardently await your answer."

"Yes, Mr. Corydon."

Jane turned and walked back up the path to the house, where through the windows she could see the flying, laughing figures of Mr. Woods's guests. She was not thinking, she was simply forcing the concentration required to put one foot in front of the other, to mount the steps and to pass through the open doors with a look on her face that might be indicative of the presence of intelligent life within.

A dance was completed as she entered and another was about to begin. Mr. Corydon, who had entered on her heels, his eyes alight with satisfaction, thought it politic to play a hand or two of cards with Sir William. Jane stood motionless within the door while people came and went, unseen.

Mr. Fotheringay, noting her dazed look and the smugness on Mr. Corydon's face, could guess only one cause, and he felt such a rush of rage that he propelled himself to the front room and out the door with only the briefest explanations about forgotten business and promises of returning later to fetch his womenfolk.

It seemed to Jane that the evening had ended, but in fact she drank lemonade, stood for another dance, spoke to Sylvie about flower pressing, allowed herself to be snubbed by Miss Bingley, took her leave, walked home, and fell into bed. She suddenly found herself shuddering, wanting to scream and throw things, and then all at once breaking into a torrent of tears.

It was a spring morning of the freshest beauty. The
woods were still damp, but grass had sprung up, leaves
had unfurled, and the breeze that wafted them gently
about was warm with the promise of summer. Beneath
the tall oaks, elms, and larches that made up the
canopy, bluebells were tossed by gently stirring air
heavy with the scent of newly warmed earth and the
burgeoning of life.

Chapter Thirteen

It was a spring morning of the freshest beauty. The
woods were still damp, but grass had sprung up, leaves
had unfurled, and the breeze that wafted them gently
about was warm with the promise of summer. Beneath
the tall oaks, elms, and larches that made up the
canopy, bluebells were tossed by gently stirring air
heavy with the scent of newly warmed earth and the
burgeoning of life.

It was still and quiet but for the birds overhead, and
the squirrels which scurried across paths and up and
down the trunks of trees in the ritual spring restlessness
of all animals. Above, a thrush called. And then a
squirrel suddenly froze on a limb and began a harsh
scolding for the disruption below.

Jane stood, catching a ray of the sun through the
trees and letting it fall on her face. She looked up at the
squirrel and wrinkled her nose at its indignation. She
bent to pick a bluebell but drew back, remembering
how swiftly they faded when picked. Instead she lifted
her arms high and then wrapped them around herself

tightly. A tear came in spite of herself. She would have thought she had cried herself out last night, but ever since she had sneaked away from the house to find some time alone this morning, she had found that she could not stop the tears that seemed determined to leak of their own volition.

What is wrong with me? she wondered. It frightened her to find that she could not control her tears, that her emotions seemed to have a life of their own, in spite of her decisions and wishes. She willed herself not to cry anymore.

Reaching for a stout stick, she slashed at some brambles and felt better. Increasing her meandering pace to a brisk walk, she clomped the stick down in rhythm to her steps and marched along for about ten more feet. A trick of light distracted her and she found herself peering into a tiny clearing, where the sun in a golden stream of light pooled about a rock which she felt must have been placed there by human hands. She considered, poised at the edge of the clearing, venturing forward and sitting on the rock in the sun, but she felt too restless, and giving another halfhearted whack at a tree, she continued down the path.

The woods began near the village and ran for about six miles diagonally down to the sea. They passed behind the Oaks where the Fotheringays lived and were in fact the origin of the name for their hired estate. She and Sylvie had taken walks together in the past weeks and she knew many of the paths that branched off to nearby farms, to a neighboring village, to the sea.

She stopped and listened for birdsong that she might recognize and then her mind veered off again. There was so much to think about, and she could barely think at all for she just wanted to cry.

There had been a terrible scene in the house this morning. She told them that instead of proposing marriage to her, Mr. Corydon had proposed that she make a sizeable investment. This had caused explosion enough, with Priddy finally saying outright how much she detested the man, and with Ned fuming that he had just been sniffing around after money all the time and that Jane was a goose. Priddy said she was certainly misled, and they were both astounded when Jane had burst into tears and fled from the room.

They had caught up with her in the hall and cajoled her back into the front saloon, where only Livvy seemed genuinely to grieve for her as she, too, had found Mr. Corydon the most elegant man alive—except that he was far too old and looked like a grandfather—but she still thought that made him romantic, and anyway he was rich, and why were Ned and Priddy yelling at Jane when she had done so much to help them and all they could do was stand there and make her cry.

Jane tried to rally at this misguided consolation but had to impart another piece of news which raised the level of consternation even higher. That was that there was a man named Coggelshall involved in the whole terrible mess, and that he might be the one to have bought Thrate House, but he might have sold it again. The worst was that he was coming here to Wixton, and they must try to keep out of his way, and maybe they should get in touch with Mr. Hasbrook. It was at this point that Ned had shouted and stood up and turned red and slammed his fist down on a dainty sidetable which had immediately cracked in two, pitching onto the floor an indifferent porcelain figurine which they had bought in London. It was a measure of their distraction that no one noticed or cared and didn't even bother to reprimand Ned for his violence. They were all talking at once, but he overrode them and said that this is exactly what happened when you let hysterical, foolish women run affairs that are beyond them, and that he should have taken charge long ago. He doubted that anything but ruin and the worst possible social scandal lay ahead of them, which just possibly he might be able to avert if he were only allowed to think, and if they didn't all stop talking this instant he would thrash them all. Priddy told him to mind his manners if he didn't want to spend the day in his room, and he was so incredulous at what she said that he started laughing, Jane started crying again, and Livvy began jumping up and down because at last life had achieved the high drama she had always wanted from it.

Ned stormed out of the house toward the inn for the carriage and who knew what destination. Livvy started begging Priddy to let her change into a gown to go into the village. Priddy marched into the kitchen and began punching at dough as though her life depended on it. And Jane fled to the woods.

But far from soothing her, the woods were simply offering her the quiet to feel just how confused and miserable she was. She came to a small path she had never taken before that ran down toward the sea, and set her feet upon it, because of all things she wanted to be alone, and this path showed no signs of having been trod since last autumn's shedding of leaves.

Here the woods grew thick and Jane found herself hurrying through as though they were oppressive, shutting her in too closely with her thoughts. Her gown caught on a low protruding branch and she didn't stop to untangle it but simply gave her skirt a jerk which tore the fabric free. It was an old gown, the flowers on the muslin had faded years ago, but it had been one of her best until the refurbishing of her wardrobe in London.

She felt the pins holding her hair at her neck loosening with her pell-mell run through the dense, chilly woods, and impatiently reached up and pulled them out before they fell and she would have the task of finding or replacing them. She shook her hair free and felt its silky warmth cascade down her back. Suddenly she was a child in Cornwall, rushing headlong over the cliffs above the sea, feeling the wind lifting her hair in long banners behind her, and feeling its length encircle her when she spun against the wind. She ran as fast as she could, stumbling occasionally over a hidden branch or an unevenness in the ground, gathering to her not only the need for flight from these darkened woods, but also the memories of a childhood which now seemed the freest, least complicated time of her life, a kind of innocent, idyllic interval before the present daunting, humiliating consequences of adult life.

Jane could not remember having felt young. Not young as Livvy felt, wrapped in her own fantasies and hopes for the future. The day her mother died, and the day her father told her the money was lost were the moments she remembered as the two great stepping-stones to adulthood: burdened by adult worries about finding money to feed them all, to keep her brother at Cambridge, to afford Livvy protection for her child-hood. Priddy had been a rock, but she was un-

197

imaginative, and although Jane knew that she loved her deeply and had sacrificed more remunerative positions for the sake of her loyalty and love for the young Marlingforthes, Jane had not been able to throw off her sense of responsibility for the family.

As Jane's pace slowed again, she took her hair in her hands and wrapped it around her like a cape. She thought that unlike Livvy not only had she never been young, she had never dreamed. She had never dreamed of love.

In the novels she read, men and women fell into great loves, passions that drove them to seek the other out across deserts and oceans, against pirates and other villains, but Jane had never felt that she was such a heroine. She was too practical and aware of the necessities of life to be heroic. When Livvy began reading she had become romantic, and Jane had seen romantic fascinations as the preoccupations of little girls. She was a woman and a woman with the responsibility for a family's faltering fortunes.

The most impractical idea she had ever had was devising the scheme to come to Wixton and marry a wealthy man. She had to laugh at herself. Livvy's dreams had never got them into the muddle they were in now. She should have fantasized more about handsome, dashing heroes and less about impractical, deceitful ways to ensnare a husband.

Well, she had failed. Curiously, she wasn't hurt by Mr. Corydon's lack of interest in her as a woman. In fact she had found his kiss quite unappealing. But she was appalled that her plan had gone awry so disastrously. The year would pass, and they would be not only no more advanced, but poorer for the effort.

Losing Mr. Corydon meant losing all hopes for a comfortable future for them all.

But while she had been weeping in her bed she had thought of that kiss and had been disappointed that there had been nothing in it that had pleased her. Kissing was a part of marriage, she knew. It was a part of love.

Love. Jane had prided herself on not thinking about love, on not being a woman who built castles in the air. She knew she must marry for wealth, and she had not had a moment's regret. Love was for Livvy's stories and dreams. A secure future was her business.

But what was love? Was it awful kisses like the one she had endured last night? Surely not. She thought about her father and her beautiful mother, dead when she was ten. She always knew that her father and mother loved each other from the eager way they greeted each other, the special quiet looks that passed between them. Yes, but that wasn't kissing. She had seen them kiss, of course, but not in the way Mr. Corydon had kissed her.

Tears came to her eyes. Thinking of her parents, of the disappointment of Mr. Corydon, she felt sorry for herself. She wanted love, she wanted to be loved; it wasn't enough, suddenly, that she should marry someone only to secure the future of her family. But that was a stupid thought, of course that was what she *must* do. But oh, that she could do it and be loved at the same time!

Jane did not want to cry any more. She broke into a run and ran for what seemed miles and miles. She was sure she should be quite out of the woods by now and coming out onto the shingle or into fields, but the woods continued as oppressive as they had been and on she ran, headlong, feeling almost a panic at being trapped within the impenetrability of these endless ranks of trees. She became breathless, and there appeared before her a huge oak, an oak so broad that its girth seemed to mark it as an ancient of the forest. She slowed, marvelling at the tree, circling it, when all at once she collided with a human form. Suddenly she was teetering, and then as suddenly she was falling toward the ground in tandem with that human being, the only part of whom she could see was a white shirt covering a chest of amazing width, and then she was on the ground, lying beside him, and she lifted her eyes and found that she was gazing into the deep brown eyes of Mr. Fotheringay.

They lay quite still, her skirts and hair entangling him; his arm was around her shoulders, the other under her head, and a great stillness seemed to descend on the forest and all was very quiet. The birds stopped singing and the squirrels held still and all Jane could feel were those arms, the weight of his leg on her own, and the intensity of the gaze that held hers as though they were both under a spell, enchanted.

And then he kissed her, quite slowly, quite intently; he leaned his face toward hers, and with his hand tilted her lovely face just so and brought his mouth against hers and held it there with the gentlest pressure, their lips just touched but nothing more, and then he kissed her. She responded; his hand tightened, and her arm lifted to his face, and his hand plunged into the depths of her hair and he pulled her to him. She found herself wanting to press herself closer to him and she did. Then she wanted to be even more close, and he was kissing

200

her eyes and her neck and she was lifting her face to his kisses and she kissed his eyes and his throat. He murmured something low over and over again which she finally heard; he was saying, "Ariadne, Ariadne."

It was as if someone had poured cold water on her. She disentangled herself from him, pulling her hair out of his hands, and struggling to sit up. He looked dazed, as though he were still in the throes of an ardent embrace and he reached for her shoulder to pull her to him again, but she twisted away and on her hands and knees tried to drag her skirts out from under him and yet he wouldn't let her go but caught first her hair and then her waist and she cried, "No, let me go, let me go."

"No, no, no, I'm not going to let you go," he said hoarsely, and she looked at his face and saw that it was rigid with emotion but that his eyes burned fiercely at her with a fire that she had never seen in a man's eyes. She was almost transfixed, but when he bent his face over her again, she remembered she was not who he thought she was and she turned away and pushed herself to her knees. Hobbled as she was, she nonetheless tried to crawl away, but he caught at her skirts and her hair and she was pinioned, and she cried out again, "Oh, let me go, please, Mr. Fotheringay, please let me go."

And as suddenly as he had been commanded, his hands went slack, and he stared at her with an unfocused gaze. She found that she was no longer held and was able to crawl away unhindered. She stopped and looked back at him, safely out of his reach, and they stared at each other for some time, expressionlessly, unable to read the other's thoughts, unaware exactly of the nature of their own thoughts.

Then he seemed to come to himself and Jane could watch the distortion that sarcasm and disdain worked on his features and he rose, sweeping his large hands over his hard thighs to wipe away the leaves, and he said, "Please excuse me, Miss Montcrief, I have forgotten, of course, that you are a betrothed woman now."

The tone of his voice startled Jane. She rose with what dignity and hauteur she could muster. Shaking herself free of leaves and twigs, unaware of how beguiling she looked in her torn dress with her hair like a woodland nymph's trailing in a black silk cascade over her shoulders, she felt only like a shameless wanton put in her place by a complacent boor.

"I am not betrothed, Mr. Fotheringay. Just because I happened to wish to kiss Mr. Corydon, it does not follow that I am betrothed to him."

"Any more than you are betrothed to your footman for kissing him, I warrant."

"No," she said steadily, "nor any more than I am now, after having kissed you, betrothed to you."

They stood staring at each other. Jane's breast was heaving with the force of her emotions and the desire to bolt. But she would not bolt, she would face this man down.

Lord Charles employed all the will it had ever been his burden to summon up to keep himself from gathering this proud and beautiful woman in his arms. He knew that she had the power to disillusion him since her favors were so lightly given. He also, as the reputed brother of her friend, was not in a position to take her as he would any other common lightskirt, so he distanced himself with an insult that would cool what was left of their ardor.

"Do you know the meaning of the word *putain,* Miss Montcrief?"

Jane did not, but she had no need to. "No, but you are accusing me of selling my favors, aren't you, Mr. Fotheringay? But in this case I have made a double mistake. Yours are not worth submitting to for any price, and moreover it seems that I have failed to gain anything monetary from the encounter."

"Ah, but let me right that sorry lapse on my part, Miss Montcrief. Here," he said, thrusting his hands into his pockets, "I am sure I have about me a groat or two, surely sufficient for such a brief preliminary; let me see . . ."

Jane turned, willing now to bolt as she should have done sooner before he dared offer her such insult, but she was stopped by the distant sound of a human voice. It was calling out a halloo, and something in the timbre of it made her think that there must be a grave emergency.

She saw Mr. Fotheringay grow still as he, too, listened. Neither could make out the name being called for the voice was too far away, but both turned toward it and began to run. A branch nearly sent Jane sprawling but there was a steadying hand immediately under her arm and she thought with an obscure sense of comfort that he might not think well of her, but at least he would not let her fall.

He shouted out, "Who is it? Hello? Hello?"

A voice, now considerably nearer, shouted back, but they still could not make out the words.

Finally Jane heard a name that caused her to become leaden. The voice, a man, was shouting, "Miss Montcrief? Miss Montcrief?" Jane stood, the blood draining from her face.

Lord Charles ran on and she followed slowly. After a turning on the path they came face to face with Mr. Woods, red-faced and breathless. He swept by Lord Charles and went directly to Jane who stood transfixed with fear.

"Now, Miss Ariadne," he said, "it's nothing serious, that is, your mother's quite all right, but the young one, she's fallen from a tree trying to get a kite and she is unconscious. It's your maid, Lizzy, but your mother thought you would want to know and so . . ."

Jane's mouth worked. "Livvy?"

And faster than she had ever run in her life, she spun, and leaving two puzzled men behind, fled down the path to home.

Chapter Fourteen

The three came dashing out of the woods, Jane, Lord Charles at her side, and the huffing vicar considerably further behind. She dashed into the house through the kitchen, unaware of the presence of Lord Charles.

She rushed in calling, "Priddy, where's Livvy? Oh, Priddy. Ned! Priddy!"

"In here, Jane," Priddy looked out from the front saloon and Jane rushed in, only to stop short at the door.

There before her on a sofa lay Livvy, as white as death, as still as death. Jane was vaguely aware of Mrs. Woods in the room and of someone behind her. She felt Priddy take her hand.

"Oh, Priddy," she said in moan, "she's not . . . ?"

"No, but she's had a bad fall."

Jane crept closer, kneeling at the sofa, taking Livvy's cold hands in hers. She laid her hand carefully on the girl's forehead and stroked her hair from her brow. She noticed that Livvy had changed out of her maid's uniform and was wearing one of her own gowns and she wondered what she had been playing at when she fell. But all thoughts fled at the sight of Livvy's deathly stillness.

Priddy squeezed out a compress and laid it on Livvy's forehead and Jane spoke quietly, "Livvy, Livvy. Dear, dear Livvy."

"Here, let me examine her."

Jane looked up at Mr. Fotheringay who was bending over the small girl, his eyes intent on her face.

Jane was about to protest, but something about his assurance caused her to move aside slightly.

"I've done a lot of doctoring . . ." he said by way of explanation before he broke off and gently lifted Livvy's eyelids. Jane assumed that he meant in the wars and hoped he might be able to help. But she said, "Priddy, have you sent for a doctor?"

"There's no doctor in Wixton, Miss Ariadne," Mrs. Woods spoke up. "We sent Jack from Mr. Gregg's to St. Osyth for Mr. Morris. But it will take a while . . ."

Jane watched Livvy, watched Mr. Fotheringay's large hands gently explore her face and then lift her head ever so slightly to feel it as well. His fingers sensitively explored her skull and he said softly under his breath, as though to Jane alone, "Here it is, on the side of the back of her head. Here, feel it."

Jane reached across him feeling his mouth close to her cheek. She felt the lump that had swollen on her sister's head. She raised her eyes to him, "What do you think?"

In answer he took Livvy's wrist and counted her pulse and then lowered his head to listen to her breathing. "I don't think it's serious. I don't believe it's a concussion. I believe that she's just lost consciousness. As soon as she comes around, which shouldn't be too long, I'm sure she will be fine."

"Oh, God, I pray so."

Lord Charles regarded the expression on her face, a mixture of grief and hope but most of all of intense love, and marveled that this woman, whom he had wished to hurt, exhibited more compassion for her maid than many women he had known had shown for their own children.

He moved aside and Jane bent over Livvy, leaning away only when Priddy exchanged compresses, but watching her face, speaking in low tones to her, and clutching at her hands as though trying to drag her back to consciousness.

It was completely quiet in the room but for the ticking of a clock on the mantel. Jane knelt without feeling the strain of her position. She laid her cheek against Livvy's—could it be that it was warmer?—and again softly called her name.

Suddenly, with no preparation, Livvy's eyes flew open and she stared ahead of her for a moment, then her eyes turned and saw Jane—and she breathed, "Oh, Jenny. I fell."

Jane felt her eyes fill with tears and she managed a tremulous smile. "Yes, you certainly did. But you're going to be all right."

"I can't believe I fell," Livvy said, her voice flat but audible enough that everyone in the room could hear her.

"Well, it's nothing to worry about. We're going to have to keep you quiet for a couple of days, that's all."

"But I've got all that rhubarb to chop."

"Shhh. It's all right. The rhubarb will get done."

"What happened?" Jane asked Priddy.

"It was the kites," Mrs. Woods said quietly. "The boys in the village have been mad about them, and suddenly there was this young Lizzy of yours and she was flying one higher than all the others. Mr. Woods and I had stopped to watch them, and then hers got caught in a tree and one of the lads said he'd get it. But your Lizzy wouldn't hear of it, and she said she could get her own kite, she wasn't afraid of any trees. She's a stalwart one, that girl, and she climbed up and when she reached out to untangle it . . ."

"Was she very high up?" Jane asked, feeling sick.

"I'd say about ten feet."

"Oh my God." Jane felt a rush of horror, and at the same time a impulse to laugh and laugh and then to shake Livvy until her teeth fell out.

She felt hands on her shoulders and felt herself lifted up. Lord Charles was saying calmly, "I believe your mother might take over now," and without her being aware of how he did it, he had led her to a chair and made her sit. He squatted before her and stared into her eyes. "You're going to be all right, it's just the shock."

She stared as a child would, hiccuping into his face, and found in his eyes the calm she needed to take a deep, steadying breath. She found her cold hands engulfed in his warm ones, and she nodded and said, "Yes, I'll be all right. It was just the shock."

"You are very attached to your maid."

"She's . . . she's a very special maid," she said lamely.

Lord Charles narrowed his eyes and regarded her. Jane blushed and turned away, then rose and returned to Priddy. She gave the older woman a long hug, aware of how much Priddy must have worried while she was alone with Livvy and Mrs. Woods, and the two clutched each other.

When they separated, both were weeping. Lord Charles exchanged a look with both the vicar and his wife, and the question in all of their minds concerned the odd nature of the attachment of the family to its young maid.

After watching Livvy regain color and struggle to get up, persuading her to remain still, adjusting pillows to make her comfortable, and hearing her account of the fall, Priddy bestirred herself to make tea for her unexpected guests. All declined and said they should go, that this was no time for socializing, but Priddy insisted that it would do them good after the shocks and exertions they had endured. The vicar, who had collapsed onto a chair and was still out of breath, agreed wholeheartedly. Priddy went to the kitchen.

Jane sat on the sofa at Livvy's feet, her hand resting on her leg, unable to be out of reach, needing to touch her to assure herself she was truly recovering. She could see scratches and the beginnings of bruises on Livvy's left arm and cheek and knew that she would soon have to take her abovestairs for a complete examination, but Livvy complained of nothing but her head and Jane could only be astonished and deeply grateful that she hadn't sustained more serious injuries.

But her worries for Livvy's health were banished when the girl, speaking in a very strong voice said, "Oh, Miss Ariadne, will you forgive my wearing your gown. It was something that came over me. I don't know what happened, but I was in your room putting newly washed linens on your bed, and I saw the gown, and suddenly I was wearing it. I am so sorry, I hope you will not dismiss me, for I don't know how I should get on, feeling as I do, wandering through the village seeking employment."

"Please do not concern yourself about it, we are all glad simply that you are safe." Jane's words were at odds with a warning squeeze on Livvy's leg. "You must rest now."

"I only wanted a treat," Livvy said weakly, "for I was so weary—exhausted, I expect. I had been up all night cleaning the grate and polishing the silver and sewing on the gown you wished to wear to church tomorrow. Then I made the bread, I hope you like it, for *I* was too weary to eat any, and then, of course, I had to boil up all the hot water and scrub the floors in the kitchen and pantry, and after that I worked the kitchen gardens and then did the wash, but I grew dizzy from the weight of the heavy garments and the steam from the water, I suspect it was that which made me forget my place and take your gown."

"That will do, Lizzy."

Mrs. Woods was shocked; Jane could read it in her face. Livvy, her face drawn up in noble martyrdom was in seventh heaven. Jane could see that she had barely begun and that she was deep into the fantasy of suffering at the hands of a cruel mistress and there was nothing she could do to stop Livvy short of clamping a hand over her mouth.

Then it occurred to her. "Oh, how terrible!" Jane cried dramatically, "I'm afraid her fall has addled her wits. Oh, my God, you said it wasn't serious," Jane said accusingly, whirling around to face Mr. Fotheringay. "She's gone stark raving mad. Just listen to her!"

"I have not gone mad," said Livvy petulantly, "except from overwork, perhaps. I forgot the coal, carrying the scuttles to the washhouse. I may have injured my back."

Jane squeezed her leg tighter. It was clear that everyone shared Mrs. Woods's horror at the disclosures. She must silence Livvy before they had them up before the assizes. But glowing on Livvy's face was the rapt expression that meant she was deep into one of her romances. She was the center of attention, and if it had to be in the role of abused waif, so be it. Jane knew that Livvy could lose herself in her fictions and be oblivious to how deeply embroiled she was becoming, and how with every word she could undo all that remained of their hopes.

"If it weren't for having to groom the horses . . ."

"The horses! This poor child does all that work and takes care of the horses as well?" Mrs. Woods stared accusingly at Jane.

She heard Mr. Fotheringay add under his breath, "It's no surprise, given how busy the footman is with other duties."

Jane ignored him and addressed Mrs. Woods. "I'm afraid Lizzy has a very vivid imagination . . ."

"But why should she make up anything about this?"

"Because," Jane spread her hands hopelessly, "she just . . ."

"Oh, have I made it uncomfortable for you, ma'am? Oh, do forgive me. I didn't mean to. I mean to do my work willingly, cheerfully even, but I get so weary. Perhaps I shall die."

"Livvy!" Jane started up when Livvy threw her head dramatically to one side and seemed, indeed, to

211

be dead.

Livvy opened her eyes and grinned at Jane.

"Oh, you little wretch. You need a good hiding!"

Mrs. Woods rose. "Stop! Do not lay a hand on her. I can not believe this of you, Miss Montcrief. That you would beat a child, and such a devoted one!"

"I don't beat her, Mrs. Woods," Jane said through clenched teeth.

"No, she doesn't . . . beat me," said Livvy with a pause which allowed them to suspect that the horrors Miss Montcrief inflicted on her poor person were much more terrible.

"What does she do to you, child?"

Mrs. Woods knelt beside Livvy and took her hand. Jane walked off to stare out the window, her back to the appalled group.

"Well, it's not the beatings. It's . . . what I'm given to eat."

"Does she starve you?"

"Oh, no! No, she doesn't starve me. But bread and water . . ."

"Oh, this is outside of enough, Livvy!" said Jane, stamping her foot.

"Yes, I should say it is," said Mr. Woods gravely, rising heavily to his feet. "This child has been cruelly used and whoever is at fault, it is for the magistrates to determine. But I must now insist in removing her to our home where she will be looked after until she recovers from her wounds, all of them."

Livvy was surprised. Suddenly she realized the effect her words were having. She saw Jane's horror-stricken face and the appalled shock on the faces of the vicar and his wife and that handsome brother of Miss

Georgianna's, and blurted out, "I didn't mean any of it. I was just pretending. Honestly, I didn't mean any harm."

"That's all right, my child," said the vicar, going up to her and laying a comforting hand on her shoulder. "It's quite right that you told us. We will see that no harm comes to you; we will protect you."

"But I don't need protection, you must believe me," she said, sitting up, clasping her hands in entreaty.

Jane watched from the window as though it were a play. Livvy's audience was in the palm of her hand, and now that she had their undivided attention she was distressed by the manner in which she had won it. Jane wanted to drop her from another tree.

"You don't understand," said Livvy, truly frightened now. "I was pretending. She wouldn't hurt me. She's my sister!"

"Who's your sister?" said Mr. Woods, taken aback by this new development.

"Jenny. Jenny's my sister."

"But who's Jenny?"

"Ariadne. She's my sister, Jenny."

"You're her *sister* and you abuse her?" asked Mr. Woods in profound shock.

"Oh, dear," said Jane, sinking into a chair.

At that moment Priddy entered the room with the heavy tea tray and saw from the faces around her that something very serious had happened. She looked anxiously at Livvy and saw that she was distressed but not ill. She lowered the tray to the tea table and straightened, surveying the people in the room, waiting for someone to speak.

It was the vicar who took it upon himself to break it

213

to her. "I'm very sorry, ma'am, but it appears that your daughter, and perhaps you yourself, have been mistreating your maid who it now appears is your daughter as well. My wife and I are going to take her—with or without your approval—to our home, where she will not be harmed by anyone again."

Priddy paled; she didn't know what to say that would not make things worse. Finally she looked at Livvy.

The child had the grace to blush.

"Child?"

"I'm sorry, Priddy. I just got started and you know how it is . . ."

Finally Priddy sat down. She looked at Jane and Jane looked at her. They stared at each other for a long moment. Finally Jane shrugged her shoulders and spoke. "I swear to you that I have never mistreated Livvy. She is my sister. I love her more dearly than anyone else in the world. I would never lay a hand on her. But you must understand, she embroiders her stories, she likes to pretend, she has a vivid imagination . . ." Jane hoped to keep the damage to a minimum.

"I really do," said Livvy with a stricken look. "Why I pretended just yesterday that I was Joan of Arc and I tried to tie myself to the tree in the back garden, but I couldn't get the rope tight enough and then Ned . . . Nettles came along and made me untie myself and get back to blacking his boots which I had . . ."

"You act as maid to the footman?" Mrs. Woods spoke in disbelief.

"No, no, I was just doing it as a favor. I happen to be good at blacking boots and at doing the laundry and cooking and scrubbing and . . ." Livvy managed to stop herself before she got too deeply enmeshed again.

"You see," Jane said, entreating Mr. Woods. "It is something she does. She gets an idea and she cannot seem to stop. If you asked her if she would like to be Queen Elizabeth, she would start walking around the room as though she had on one of those ruffed collars and was laden with jewels, wouldn't you, Livvy?"

"I certainly would not, Jane. I can't understand how you could say such a thing," Livvy replied, on her dignity.

"No, of course not," Jane said bitterly, "she imagines only what she chooses, she doesn't do her imagining to order."

"I hate to say this, Miss Montcrief, but the fact that this poor child is your sister, and that you have used her so abominably, speaks more seriously than if she had been a maid in your employ. It shows an even greater degree of callousness and heartlessness than I could credit in two women I had thought such fine people."

Jane fought desperation and held her hands out beseechingly to the vicar and his wife. "Please, Mr. Woods, Mrs. Woods, if you would be seated again and let me explain." She pointedly did not extend the same invitation to Mr. Fotheringay whom she devoutly hoped would take the opportunity to leave, although he showed no indication of doing so. Instead he lifted a roughened boot onto his knee and settled back in the chair with a look that could only be described as deliciously anticipatory. He was about to enjoy the spectacle of watching Miss Montcrief's true nature exposed as he alone understood it. He did not, for the moment, remember the uncertainty he had experienced in this opinion when he had seen that Jane's concern for her injured maid had sprung from depth of real feeling.

"You see, well, we have to begin, actually, perhaps . . . " Jane cast about for a way to tell their story, while trying furiously to go over in her mind whether she would tell the truth or try to invent something that might explain enough without giving away their sordid secret life. She was scowling at her hands and did not hear the sounds of a carriage arriving, nor of footsteps on the stairs, until the crash of the front door being thrown open startled her and she looked up to see Ned distraught, pale, trembling before her.

"Where's Livvy? Oh, I heard you were dead. Oh, Livvy . . ." and Ned buried his head in Livvy's shoulder and did not try to suppress his sobs.

A speechless group watched the affecting scene.

Finally Lord Charles drawled, "I suppose the footman, then, is your brother, Miss Montcrief?"

Jane looked him in the eye. "Exactly, Mr. Fotheringay."

Chapter Fifteen

Ned was not alone. Voices in the hallway rose to shrieking and then there erupted into the saloon the disheveled persons of Mr. Corydon and Lady Arabella Sneed.

Mr. Corydon was limping and oozing blood from a cut in the temple. Lady Arabella, her clothes in disarray and her bonnet hanging by its ribbons, was doing the greater part of the shrieking and the sight of five people staring at her with openmouthed incredulity didn't faze her, if, indeed, she noticed them at all.

Jane came to herself. "Please, I must ask you to lower your voices. My sister . . ." she gestured to Livvy. Mr. Corydon and Lady Arabella stared blankly down at the child and then began their wrangling again in only a slightly lower register. Jane would have interrupted them, but Livvy, far from being overset by this development, was staring with shining eyes, drinking in every word.

"You did. And I will have your head for it," Lady

Arabella was saying, her face working with fury.

"My dear lady, I would do no such thing, I assure you. Look, I have practically broken my leg and may have a concussion for all I know. Do you really think I would risk injury for such an ungentlemanly reason?"

"Ungentlemanly," Lady Arabella scoffed, striding to the mantel where she threw down her gloves, ripped off her bonnet, and tossed it after them. "Is that tea?" she asked, scowling at Priddy. "Give me a cup," she said, holding out her hand.

"Please, if you have some water, perhaps your maid . . ." Mr. Corydon looked doubtfully at Livvy, reclining in a very unmaidlike way on the sofa, wishing that he might tactfully suggest that she vacate the space for himself, so overcome did he feel by his wounds.

"You are injured!" Priddy exclaimed, the first of them to take in his need for attention. She dampened a serviette, asked him to sit, and lightly dabbed the blood from his forehead.

"Oh. Ow. Oh. Mercy. Oh, it hurts so!" Mr. Corydon yelped at every touch. "And my leg, I'm sure it is broken. Oh, please stop. No, don't stop. Please. Oh my God, I didn't realize I was bleeding. I shall bleed to death. Oh, I must lie down. Perhaps your maid . . ."

"She certainly shall not," Mrs. Woods said firmly. "She will rest there until she is well enough to come with us."

"Oh, please don't take me away from Jane and Ned and Priddy," wailed Livvy, beginning to sob quite convincingly, perhaps because quite genuinely.

"And what about me," Lady Arabella cried, storming over to pour her own cup of tea which Priddy had neglected to do. "Has no one a thought for me? Why I might be lying broken and dead on the road this moment, thanks to this notable whip Hector Corydon," she said with a sneer.

"It was not my fault, I've told you. Oh, doesn't anyone care that I might be dying, oh..." and suddenly Mr. Corydon left off what could only be called whining, and laid himself out on the floor of the saloon, crossing his hands over his chest and becoming very still.

"Is he going to die?" asked Livvy through her sniffles, her curiosity getting the better of remorse.

"Die," scoffed Lady Arabella. She walked over to him and it seemed for a moment that she might step on him, but she contented herself with inspecting him as though he were an insect on the public footpath. "He is too much a coward even to die."

"I resent that," said the man, sitting up abruptly and grasping his head as obviously genuine dizziness assailed him. He abandoned his defense and carefully disposed his wounded body again on the floor.

"Mr. Fotheringay," said Jane, although it took an effort to be civil. "Would you be so kind as to see if any of Mr. Corydon's injuries might be fatal?"

She was surprised by a twinkle in his eyes as he bowed and then walked over to the prostrate figure and knelt beside it. They watched as he prodded the lower leg of the moaning man and examined the wound on his head.

"I believe that at most he may have sprained his ankle. Perhaps Nettles, or Montcrief, whatever your name is," he said sarcastically, "if you could help me with the boot?"

Together the two men eased off the boot, but not

219

before Ned had searched the kitchen for a sharp knife to cut it with, the sight of which made Mr. Corydon blanch and nearly pass out.

"Has he fainted, then?" asked the incorrigible Livvy.

"No, he hasn't fainted, and he's not going to," Jane said repressively.

"Fainted! He'd faint at thunder, that worm," said Arabella, storming back to the mantel and beginning to pace the saloon with decidedly long and emphatic strides. Jane suddenly thought what an exhausting woman she must be to live with. She watched her with fascination.

"Ow!" A shriek of pain revealed that, indeed, it was Mr. Corydon's ankle that did bother him. It was slightly puffy and Jane tried to feel some sympathy for him, but had to admit to herself that he looked nothing more than ridiculous in those fancy silk garments lying on her floor and carrying on about injuries that were obviously nothing as serious as those sustained by Livvy. She glanced at Livvy and surprised her with a warm and loving smile.

"Oh, Jenny, I'm so sorry."

Jane went to the girl and put her arms around her and comforted her, willing to forgive her anything, that she was safe and such a gallant child.

"It's ma'am to you, Miss," Ned said in a fury, glad to have some target for his wrath.

"It's all right, Ned, they know you're my brother."

"They do! Then, I'll never wear this again!" he said, stripping off the detested coat.

"Does this mean I can stop being a maid?" Livvy cried.

"Yes," said a defeated Jane.

Lady Arabella, who couldn't believe she was being ignored when she had such deep grievances, spoke in outraged tones. "Is no one going to take me home?"

Ned, restored to his rightful place, turned on her and said, "Do not look to me, ma'am, for I would not drive you to Bedlam, although if you ask me that is where you belong."

Lady Arabella's jaw dropped and she stared at Ned in absolute shock.

Jane saw Mr. Fotheringay turn away to hide sudden laughter and she found it necessary to look at her hands to hide her own.

"Ooooooooooo." Another moan from Mr. Corydon interrupted them and finally Jane spoke the words everyone wished to speak.

"Could someone tell us what happened?"

Ned nearly spit in disgust. "Damn fool overturned his carriage."

"I did not. I told you, something caused the horses to shy," Mr. Corydon cried, sitting up again too suddenly and clutching at his head.

"Yes, *you* did," Lady Arabella exclaimed, nearly leaping on him in wrath. "You did it on purpose, too, you prodded the left horse, the bay, I saw you. You had something metal, and as soon as they bolted, you threw it aside."

"How can you say such a thing?" cried Mr. Corydon. "Do you think me a fool?"

"Yes, that's precisely what I think of you," Lady Arabella said triumphantly.

"Ned, how did *you* get involved?" Jane asked, trying to keep from laughing.

"I was on my way to Colchester. Yes, I was going to

send for Hasbrook to come and get us out of this mess," he said defiantly to Jane and Priddy, "and I came upon their carriage overturned, and a fine hash he made of it, too, crosswise in the road, blocking traffic. It took us over an hour to drag the carriage off the roadside, for two of the wheels were broken."

"Well," Jane said tentatively, "that hardly seems anything to be angry about. Rather, it seems a misfortune. I'm sorry it happened."

"You wouldn't have been sorry if they'd been killed had *you* been the one to drive them back to Wixton," Ned said feelingly. "They fought and screeched the whole way. And when we arrived at the village," he stopped for a moment, gulped a few times and continued, "we were stopped on the green and one of the boys told us Livvy was dead." Ned, his face pale, reached his hand to rest it on his sister's arm, anxious to reassure himself that she was well and that those terrible words had been untrue.

Jane put her hand on Ned's shoulder, and suddenly Lord Charles had the most astonishingly cheerful thought—when Miss Montcrief kissed her footman, she had really kissed her *brother!*

"Surely, it is an upsetting thing, to be overturned, no matter what the cause. It is a miracle neither of you was more injured than you were," Jane said placatingly, trying to dampen the anger of the one and the self-pity of the other. "It's been a day of lucky escapes."

When neither asked what she meant, Jane added hastily, "Of course you have been wishing to ask after Livvy, here, and to share in our joy that she was spared."

Neither Lady Arabella nor Mr. Corydon looked

remotely aware of anything but their own deeply felt grievances.

Lady Arabella again approached Mr. Corydon, now sitting with his head against the arm of a chair, and whispered between clenched teeth. "You are a toad . . . you are a false and devious . . . slug!"

"Don't you two dare start up again," cried Ned, from Livvy's sofa. "I won't have it . . ."

"I, devious, what can you mean? You have pursued me shamelessly throughout these last few weeks, anyone can attest to that," Mr. Corydon said.

"You puling mouse. Eloping—I had not the slightest intention of eloping with you," Lady Arabella exploded.

"That's a lie; you begged me. You made me elope with you," he wailed.

"Oh!" Lady Arabella made a swipe at him with her foot which just missed him as he recoiled behind the chair.

Jane felt it necessary to lay a restraining hand on Lady Arabella's arm and said, as mildly as she could, "Please, we have two persons in this room who are injured and in need of quiet."

"Did you not force attentions on me at every turn? Did you not arrange to meet me in the folly the night before last? Did you not promise to marry me? Do you mean to tell me, you worm, you toad, that you never meant anything you said? You had better think carefully, Mr. Corydon, before I have you taken up for breach of promise."

Mr. Corydon, cowering on the floor, peering up at Lady Arabella who, in her statuesque fury looked for all the world like a modern-day Boadicea, was now shed of whatever glamor he had once held for Jane. It was humiliating that she had ever found him attractive; that he had ever seemed charming was a revelation of the degree of folly she was capable of. She had to admit to some fellow feeling with the abused Lady Arabella. Apparently they were both susceptible to empty charm.

Mr. Corydon scooted further behind the chair, and peering over it, began to whine, "I may have been carried away by your beauty and charm. Yes, I will admit that. But I never did ask you to marry me. Such a fine lady as yourself, how could I ever hope to aspire to your hand, you are the gentry, I am only a London merchant. It never occurred to me that you might take my humble devotion as anything more than the hopeless . . ."

"Oh, stop! Listening to you could drive a woman mad!"

"But, Lady Arabella, I thought when you commanded me to collect you in my coach this morning, I thought we were going to inspect the site for Belleview. I had no idea you thought we were eloping."

"Is that why your portmanteau was stowed on the roof of the carriage?"

Mr. Corydon blushed. "I . . . I . . ."

"Oh," said a soft voice on a long sigh. "You were going to elope. Oh, I think I am the luckiest girl in the world. And you, Lady Arabella, I shall worship until I die." Livvy pulled herself up, reached out, and grasped at Lady Arabella's gown, which the outraged woman snatched back with undisguised revulsion.

"You see, Lady Arabella," Livvy continued in grave accents, "I, too, am going to elope, but I have never known a woman who has done so, and now I shall be able to learn about it from you. May I tell you how much I admire your courage?

"When I elope I plan to go to Gretna Green, is that where you were going? But, of course, for I have read that that is where everyone elopes to, unless you obtain a special license, or voyage to distant lands and are married by the captain. I have always meant to escape at night, though, wearing boy's clothing. Why didn't you think of that, and then Ned would never have recognized you? But how tragic that your carriage overturned. I don't expect my carriage to overturn, but if it does, my lover and I shall simply catch a post coach on the Great North Road, had you not thought of that? Did you really need to come back with Ned?"

Lady Arabella's expression had assumed bemused incredulity. She stared down at the young girl (whose maunderings seemed to have no end) and turned to Priddy suddenly, having caught nothing of the exchanges which identified Livvy as a daughter of the house, and said, "You must get rid of this maid. She's mad as a hatter."

Jane found Mrs. Woods smiling at her. She said, across the confusion Lady Arabella was causing with her stompings and ravings, "I think I am beginning to see what you mean about Lizzy—Livvy."

Jane saw the same gleam of amusement in the eyes of Mr. Woods, and in Mr. Fotheringay's as well. She could not resist.

"But Livvy," she said innocently, "why ever would you have to elope? When Ned and Priddy and I would be ony too happy to see you wed tomorrow, if you wish?"

Livvy opened her eyes wide with delight and then narrowed them. "But I'm only twelve."

"That is a problem," Jane agreed.

"And I don't have a . . ." Livvy blushed.

". . . lover?" Jane added helpfully. "Well, perhaps you could elope and find one along the way."

Mr. Corydon, who had been brooding on his many wrongs, struggled to his feet in spite of a painful ankle and drew himself up to his full dignity, which was just slightly offset by the fact that his clothes were covered with dirt and his expression was childishly petulant.

"I should wish nothing on you as cruel as the fate that has befallen me in coming into the orbit of Lady Arabella. She has pursued me with the contrivance of that woman she keeps, that Bingley, and she has hounded me to marry her by trapping me every time my back was turned, with her kisses and her promises of what she would do for Belleview."

"Ah, poor man," said Lord Charles. "To be so beseiged by a woman. Of course, there was nothing you wanted from the Sneeds, was there, Corydon? Having got Sir William's property and a sizeable sum in addition, you found it unnecessary to continue with your courtship of Lady Arabella as well as the other women who fell across your path," he added, gazing just over Jane's head.

Lady Arabella fumed. "I resent that, Mr. Fotheringay. No man would have the courage to trifle with me. Mr. Corydon's attentions were those of a man in love. My father arrived at his decision to become involved in the building of Belleview *despite* my warnings and doubts."

A silence greeted this dissembling.

Mrs. Woods rose, thinking it her job, no doubt, to try to soothe Lady Arabella's very obviously hurt feelings, even if neither she she nor her reputed lover claimed her sympathy. But Lady Arabella ignored her.

"Do you refuse to admit that we were eloping when you took me up in your carriage?"

"No! Yes! No! Yes, I admit I *pretended* to be eloping. You were driving me mad! I couldn't bear your importunings any longer, you were nagging me to distraction. I thought that if I staged an elopement, and something went wrong with it, and we were discovered, that your father would prevent it!"

"So you *did* goad the horses into running away with the carriage!"

Mr. Corydon looked into her angry face and yelled, "Yes, I did! I did! Can you understand that, Lady Arabella? Rather than elope with you, I risked my life by overturning the carriage so that I wouldn't have to marry you!"

"Good God," said Ned, speaking for all of them, "I can understand not wanting to get leg-shackled, but I can't understand risking your life. Why didn't you just tell her no?"

Corydon looked bitterly at Ned. "You try telling this woman no."

Ned backed away, rubbing his face with the back of his hand. "Oh, ah, well . . ."

"You tried to kill me," Lady Arabella jumped at him and began to pound on his chest with her fists.

"I had to," he cried, backing off and trying to grab her wrists.

"Why, you lily-livered coward, *why?* Weren't you man enough to marry me? Why didn't you just say so,

227

you craven, yellow-bellied . . . You were afraid to marry me, weren't you! Didn't I have enough money for you? You wouldn't dare say I'm not beautiful, and you *did* want to marry me. I know you did, so why did you weasel out of it you dastard, you poltroon, you . . . Why?"

"Because I'm already married!" wailed Mr. Corydon.

Chapter Sixteen

"That woman in Colchester!" Jane gasped.

"What woman?" Mr. Corydon paled, his eyes darted over the faces of those in the room.

Jane advanced on him, pushing Lady Arabella aside. "We saw you, Priddy and Ned and Livvy and I, we all saw you, on a side street with a woman in a cap; you were yelling at her and pushing her. We saw it all! Oh, you were married to her all the time, and she didn't like your pretending you weren't. That is why you were yelling at her, oh, oh, you . . . you . . . you . . ."

"You scum, you knave, you monster, you scurrilous, vile snake, you . . ." Lady Arabella contributed. "Is it true?"

Mr. Corydon looked from Jane to Lady Arabella and beyond them to the others who expressed everything from shock and fascination to incipient hilarity, and drew himself up with dignity. "I am not required to answer."

Lady Arabella, leaning toward him in a rage, said, "You will be hearing from my father! There will be no

Belleview, you . . . you . . . philanderer! Adulterer!"

He tried to escape from the room, but was hampered by his swollen ankle and managed only to shuffle away from the chair, when Jane took pity on him and said, "You must allow my brother to conduct you to the inn. You certainly should not walk."

"No, he won't. I'm not having anything to do with that . . ." Ned eyed Corydon evilly, desirous of settling a score on behalf of his sister.

"Ned, Ned. Then help him to the door and allow him to take our carriage. He can direct that it be stabled at the inn. Please, Ned."

Ned reluctantly, and with visible distaste, took Corydon's arm and began to help him from the room. The vicar took the other and together they were able to arrange him in the carriage. Ned returned alone to the house and the vicar drove Corydon on to the Dancing Tides, feeling human compassion for the man, despite his questionable dealings with the trusting inhabitants of Wixton.

Lady Arabella subsided in hysterics. sobbing and cursing, she was almost an object of pity, although Jane was sure that there was little behind it but the humiliation of pride at being exposed to her neighbors in such a way. Priddy was holding vinegar under her nose and Mrs. Woods wanted to slap her cheeks, but did not dare.

Livvy watched hungrily.

Jane said sternly, "You see this, Livvy? This is what happens when you decide to elope!"

"Oh, feathers! When I elope, I shall do it right. But I have never seen a woman weep like that before! It is prodigiously interesting, isn't it, Jenny?"

230

Jane caught Mr. Fotheringay's eye just as he erupted in the laughter he had been heroically restraining.

Lady Arabella, aware that someone was making more noise than she, looked up and discovered that although she was as usual the center of attention, it was not the kind of attention she most desired, and so did what came naturally. She went on the attack.

"Does it amuse you, Mr. Fotheringay, to mock a deceived woman?"

That gentleman tried to put his face in order. "Forgive me, Lady Arabella, I was amused by something the child said, not by your situation, which engenders quite other feelings in me."

She eyed him warily, then rose. "I require transportation to my home. I do not expect you to offer it, of course, since none of you has my comfort in mind, but would it be beyond the civility of any of you to escort me to the inn?"

Ned stared out the window as though deaf. Mr. Fotheringay sighed deeply and began to rise, when Lady Arabella, red with choler, said, "Don't bestir yourself on my account, please. I would as lief be escorted by a jackass as one of you." At the door she turned back and added, "It will be a relief to be restored to my home, removed from the company of jumped-up servants attempting to pass themselves off as gentry."

She slammed the door. There was a small silence into which Livvy said, "But she got it wrong, Jenny, didn't she? We are jumped-up gentry, trying to pass ourselves off as servants!"

Ned and Jane laughed from relief, the many tensions and absurdities undermining their best intentions. They were joined by the others who had restrained

231

themselves only out of respect for Lady Arabella's lacerated feelings.

Livvy, however, was staring dreamily at the ceiling, and Mr. Fotheringay, noticing the expression on her face, said across the room to Jane, "I wonder where she is now?"

Jane smiled, gratified that he understood, "Well, I suppose on the road to Gretna Green, perhaps fighting off highwaymen or impressment gangs who have roughly seized her would-be husband . . ."

Livvy rolled her head slowly toward Jane and said with contempt, "You are so trite, Jenny, you couldn't fabricate a romance if you tried. I was thinking about Lady Arabella."

"Well, Lady Arabella will have to take care of herself, we have to take care of you. Can you walk upstairs, so I can sponge you off and put you to bed?"

"You can't put me to bed yet. I want to hear all about the elopement from Ned, and I want a cup of tea."

"Well, perhaps we can all do with another." Jane and Priddy repaired to the kitchen, assisted by Mrs. Woods, to replenish the tea pot, and when they returned and all were holding a steaming cup of tea, Jane said, "I know, Mrs. Woods, that we still owe you explanations and apologies for our deceptions." Again, she omitted Mr. Fotheringay, wishing that he would take himself off as she found his presence discomfiting.

Mrs. Woods nodded. "I admit I am curious, but I must tell you that I no longer believe that you mistreated this young lady."

Livvy said, "You can't imagine how sorry I am, ma'am, for saying those things. It's just that sometimes my tongue runs away with me."

232

"Actually her whole brain runs away with her," Ned said.

"Yes, that's true," Livvy admitted, "but I'm getting better."

A small pause ensued. Priddy, Ned, and Jane exchanged a glance.

"Well," Jane began, taking a deep breath and looking meaningfully at Ned and Priddy, "you see, it was all by way of being a joke—a dare."

"Yes," Livvy broke in, "a dare, you see . . ."

"Livvy!" Jane broke in sternly, desperate to restrain Livvy from plunging into the lies Jane was about to tell. One set of lies would surely be enough.

"You see, Ned had just come down from Cambridge where he had taken part in some dramatics. Isn't that so, Ned?"

"Ah, yes. Dramatics. Some friends. Ha-ha. We had a bang-up time. I was telling Jenny about them . . ."

"Your name is Jane, then?" Mrs. Woods asked.

"Yes, not Ariadne. And Nettles is Edgar, that is, Ned, and Lizzy is Livvy . . ."

"And Priddy?"

"Oh, that is a pet name we have for Mother. Isn't it Priddy?"

Priddy, leaving everything to Jane, put on her blandest smile and said, "I'm afraid that is what they have always called me."

"Well, as I was saying," said Ned, "I told Jane I was a dab hand at drama. And she said, well, she bet that I couldn't keep it up for . . ."

"I said well, um, could he do it, I mean act a part for as long as six months . . ."

"Oh, yes," said Livvy, bursting with inspiration,

233

"and I said, I could too, I mean, play a part, and . . ."

"So it just . . . Livvy was dying to try it and so, well, it just happened. I mean their pretending to be servants." Jane ended lamely.

There was a silence while Mrs. Woods stared at one and then the other of the Montcriefs, trying to understand such a frivolous impulse and the wholesale deception of an entire village, wishing she weren't disappointed to find her new friends so lacking in common sense.

Between her lashes Jane found Mr. Fotheringay was apparently more interested in the vase on the mantel then their disclosures. She felt humiliated to be forced to appear such a hen-witted female. She wished she knew what he was thinking, and why he was taking such pains to appear uninterested.

"I can't tell you how sorry I am to have deceived you, dear Mrs. Woods. In truth, none of us realized how hard it would be to carry it out. We had not counted on making friends under false circumstances. When we were planning it, it seemed . . . well, we none of us thought there would be any consequences, I suppose."

"Well," Mrs. Woods said finally to Priddy, "children will be children, won't they?" The underlying question she was posing was, why did you, their mother, allow this freak?

Priddy understood the implied criticism and knew there was nothing she could say.

Jane blurted out, "You mustn't blame Priddy, I mean Mother, for she didn't know about it until it was underway. You see, she was in . . . in . . ."

"She was in Bath, with her invalid sister Camilla Fredericka, who has had the gout most terribly," Livvy

234

began, swinging her legs over the edge of the sofa and leaning earnestly towards Mrs. Woods, "and we were all alone, with our . . . governess, Miss . . . Miss . . ."

"Bridewell," Ned interjected, "and you see, we devised our scheme, and Priddy, Mother, didn't join us until we were already here. No, she joined us in Colchester."

"And, you see," said Jane, desperately, "it was too late, and . . . oh, here is Mr. Woods returned," she said in relief bordering on collapse as she heard footsteps on the front stairs. "You will explain to him, won't you? And tell him how sorry . . ."

But the door to the saloon burst open most unceremoniously on her words, and in addition to the returning vicar were the visibly discomposed and frightened Churchill women.

"Miss Fotheringay!" Ned stood, going to the small woman whose intense distress filled him with alarm.

"Georgianna, Mrs. Fotheringay, what is amiss?"

"Oh, Mr. Fotheringay . . . Florian . . . it's Mr. Flood . . ."

"Flood!" Lord Charles rose swiftly, his face taut with concern.

"Yes", said Mrs. Churchill, "he is here, in Wixton, at the inn. We were just stopping there to arrange for a carter, and we sought you immediately. Mr. Woods told us you were here."

"Did he see you?"

"No," she replied. "No, I'm sure he didn't. We were in the back of the inn and he was on the stairs, he greeted Mr. Corydon. Mr. Woods was assisting him from the carriage and Mr. Flood descended the stairs, took Mr. Corydon's arm, and they went up the stairs again. I am sure he did not see us. But Mr. Corydon called him . . . what, Georgianna?"

"Coggelshall. Wasn't that it?"

"Yes, Coggelshall."

Jane, Priddy, and Ned looked at each other, but aside from growing considerably stiller, they did not betray themselves.

"Please, sit down and have a cup of tea. This has been a day of upsets. I don't know if Mr. Woods told you about Livvy's spill . . ."

"Livvy?" Sylvie asked, allowing Ned to lead her to a seat.

"Yes, her name is Livvy. She fell from a tree but she is well," Jane said, concentrating on putting tea in the women's hands.

"Yes, and I have something to say," Ned spoke, squaring his shoulders before Sylvie.

"Oh, Ned . . ." said Jane, afraid for them all.

"I have to say it, Jenny. Miss Fotheringay, I know you think I am nothing but a footman, but . . ."

"Oh, no," said Sylvie, imploringly. "Please don't say it. It makes no difference to me. You are a fine, intelligent man, and I would not care if you were a tinker. I . . . it would mean nothing to me, for I . . . I . . ."

"Georgianna," cried her mother. "What on earth!"

"I cannot deny it, Mother. Mr. Nettles and I have formed an acquaintance. It was he who gave me that precious volume . . . I know I have deceived you, but I feared that if you knew a footman had dared to form a friendship with me, and I with him, you would ask me to give it up, and I couldn't."

"Georgianna," said Mrs. Churchill wonderingly.

"I . . . I had no idea."

"And, Mother," Sylvie said with her head held high, "you mustn't ask me to break off our friendship, for I wouldn't. It would go against my conscience and my . . . and my inclination."

Jane wanted to both applaud and weep.

Ned threw himself impetuously on one knee before Sylvie. "Oh, my angel, my angel, oh, Miss Fotheringay, you see, there is no hindrance, for I am not a footman."

"Not a footman?"

"No, I am Edgar—Ned—Montcrief. I am Ariadne . . . Jane's brother. And Lizzy is Livvy." He beamed, expecting her to swoon with happiness.

Instead, her adorable face puckered in confusion.

"Ned? Jane? Livvy?"

"Yes, dear heart, it was a joke, a dare, that Livvy and I play servants. We have just explained to Mrs. Woods and your brother. I am pretending to be a footman, you see. I just came down from Cambridge. I'm not a footman. Do you understand? Oh, Miss Fotheringay . . ."

"Oh, please!" cried Sylvie, jumping to her feet and covering her face with her hands, "please do not call me Miss Fotheringay."

"But I cannot call you Georgianna. Oh . . ." he said, rising to his feet, ecstatically taking her hands from her face and holding them in his own, "yes, yes, I will call you Georgianna. Oh, Georgianna!"

He leaned forward as though to kiss her, but Sylvie pulled away.

"No, you cannot call me that either, for I am not Georgianna Fotheringay."

Ned's face screwed up in concentration. "You are not

237

Georgianna Fotheringay?"

"No." She held out her hands imploringly to her mother and Lord Charles.

They exchanged a look. Lord Charles shrugged and said, "With Flood in town, it will come out anyway."

Mrs. Churchill spoke forcefully, "Yes, and we have presumed on your kindness far too long. I must thank you for your protection and for the use of your name." She nodded at Sylvie.

"I am," the young woman said, taking a deep breath, "I am Sylvia Churchill."

"Sylvia? Churchill?"

"Yes."

She broke off because at that moment Ned gripped her hands and, pulling her close to him, kissed her gently on the lips. Jane and Mrs. Churchill both started, but the love between these two was so all-powerful that they subsided, aware that something momentous had just happened and that life for the couple would henceforth never be the same.

There was an awed silence while those in the room took note of the burgeoning love.

Into this silence a very confused Mr. Woods spoke. "Then, if I understand it, you are Jane Montcrief?"

Jane nodded.

"And Mrs. and Edgar and Livvy Montcrief?"

"Actually no," said Livvy, and as her sister braced herself, she merely added, "I am Livia."

"Livia. And this is Mrs. Churchill?"

"Mary Churchill," said that lady.

"And Sylvia, Sylvie Churchill?"

Mrs. Woods, looking bemused, nodding to him. "I think that comprehends it, Mr. Woods."

"Well. I see. I think I should tell you now, Mrs. Woods, I am the Prince Regent."

"No matter, Mr. Woods. For I am the Queen of Sheba."

They laughed and everyone, save for the couple looking foolishly into each other's eyes, laughed with them.

"Well," Lord Charles interrupted, sparing no thought to the fact that he had not thrown off his own false indentity, "if Flood is here, then we must decide what we are going to do."

"Yes," Mrs. Churchill said, emphatically. "Sylvie," she recalled her daughter to reality. "Mr. Fotheringay suggests we decide what to do about the presence of Mr. Flood."

Sylvie extracted her hands from Ned's and went to sit beside her mother, "Yes. We must face him, I believe."

"Wait," said Ned from the window, where he had stood because it gave him such a welcome view of his beloved. "Wait!" He held up his hand. "Fotheringay. Are you Fotheringay or Churchill?" he asked belligerently of Lord Charles.

Unperturbed by his lie, he responded. "I am Fotheringay."

"Then why is Sylvie . . . what are you doing with my Sylvie? Sir, you had better explain yourself."

"Mr. Montcrief, Edgar, Ned," said Sylvie. "Please do not challenge him, he has befriended us at the gravest moment of our lives. Were it not for him, I shudder to think what might have happened to us. It is what we must tell you, about this Mr. Flood. Please, listen."

It was Mrs. Churchill who in the end told the story of their acquaintance with Mr. Flood and his treatment of them, their escape and rescue by Mr. Fotheringay, and the necessary deception in Wixton.

Ned crept closer to Sylvie, ending by standing over her, his hand protectively on her shoulder. Livvy watched with her mouth open and her eyes wide, realizing that at last she was looking upon true love, and that Sylvie was the most romantic and beautiful female she had ever beheld.

At the end of the recital, at hearing that Flood had so much as touched Sylvie, Ned rose to his full height and roared, "I am going there right this minute. I am going to kill him. No man shall live who . . ."

"Oh, Edgar . . . Ned," beseeched Sylvie hanging on his arm.

Jane, too, had leaped up and grabbed him. "Ned, do not be such a loose screw. This Mr. Flood or *Coggelshall*," she said with a nudge, "is obviously a dangerous man who needs to be dealt with by the authorities."

"We were afraid of scandal," Sylvie said, "but now I believe we must confront him and demand our money back. If he does not repay us, then we must make recourse to the law."

"I shall confront him," Ned said through clenched teeth. "There shall be no scandal."

"Oh, Ned," breathed Sylvie, her beauty for once apparent in all its vivid intensity.

"I shall go," said Lord Charles, rising. "I shall bring him back here, and we shall *all* confront him."

"Why you?" Ned asked pugnaciously.

"Because I have already tangled with the man and

have a fair idea of his game. I believe that if I ask him to accompany me here, he will not dare refuse. You, however, he might dismiss, since he could not know that you know him for what he is. We want to get him here peacefully."

"Peacefully!" snorted Ned. "I want to get my hands on him . . ."

"Easy," Lord Charles said, laying a hand on Ned's arm. "If he does not listen to reason, I promise that I will let you land him the first facer."

"Agreed." Ned reached out his hand and the two men shook on it.

Lord Charles left the house, his head spinning. He had to be the first to reach Flood, for a variety of reasons, or his whole life would be in shambles.

Behind him Priddy, Ned, and Jane held a small council of war in the kitchen. They agreed in hushed whispers that no matter what happened, they would not reveal their Marlingforthe identity, which meant that they must be devious in their efforts to discover just what was the status of Thrate House.

In the drawing room Mr. and Mrs. Woods, Mrs. Churchill and Sylvie were the only ones innocent of schemes. That is, unless the happy fantasies of Sylvie could be counted as schemes.

Livvy was scheming how to cut her hair into riotous curls and bleach them somehow to be just like Sylvie's, and to hunch over a little so she could appear smaller and . . . but then she didn't want to marry someone as dull as Ned!

Chapter Seventeen

At the Dancing Tides, Lord Charles directed the innkeeper to go to Mr. Flood's chamber and inform him that Sir William Sneed awaited him in a private parlor. The innkeeper did not question the extraordinary directive, but immediately did as he was bid.

Lord Charles entered the private room and carefully positioned himself behind the door. After a few moments he heard footsteps approaching. Flood entered the room, saying, "Sir William?"

Lord Charles stepped to his side, slamming the door behind him and blocking off the escape of a startled Reginald Flood who spun around and sputtered, "What the . . . Leith!"

"Sit down, Flood. We have some talking to do."

"I have nothing to do with you, let me pass or I'll . . ."

"Or you'll what," Lord Charles drew himself up to his full height and stared down at Flood.

"What's this about then?" Flood asked querulously, backing away.

"Sit down."

"I'll stand. Oh, very well," and scraped back a chair and deposited his considerable bulk onto it.

Lord Charles straddled a chair facing him. "Now, what do you think this is about?"

"How could I know what windmills you have in your head?"

"Does the name Churchill ring a bell?"

"Churchill, no . . ."

A look at Lord Charles's face persuaded Mr. Flood to change his mind. "Yes, now that you mention it."

"They have been under my protection since the day you drove them away," Lord Charles said shortly.

Flood tried to break in but Lord Charles threw up a hand. "You will keep your mouth shut until I have finished."

Flood was the kind of man who felt no fear when preying upon isolated and timid women, but Charles de la Marre, Earl of Leith, was another matter. He chewed his lip.

"They have told me of the fraud you perpetrated on them. It is not the first time, Flood, but it shall be the last. Soon we will go across to where the Churchill women are waiting. You will give them either the amount of money you stole from them plus interest, or a draft on your bank for that amount which you will make out. I will accompany you to London on Monday, if necessary, to see to the transfer of money."

"How dare you presume . . ."

"Or you can rot in Newgate."

Mr. Flood was silent, but his purple face and red eyes testified to impotent rage.

"Next I want to know what you have been doing

under the name Coggelshall."

"So you don't know."

"It is only a matter of persuading Corydon or Rankin to speak. Or," he said, rising from his chair and walking to the shaking man and pressing an iron fist against his face, "I could use other methods."

"You can't do this, I'll call for help, you can't do this!"

"By the time you get a cry out, it will be too late. Tell me, Coggelshall."

Mr. Flood cast his eyes about the barren room and licked his lips. Another look at Lord Charles persuaded him to speak.

"It was under that name that I've been buying property for possible locations for . . ."

"Don't bore me. You have no more idea of building a resort here than you have of building an almshouse. I understand your lay, you swindle fools like Sir William for an initial investment, disappear to hire laborers and materials, and wash up somewhere else with new names. What is Corydon's real name? Oh, don't bother," he said, when Mr. Flood opened his mouth and only a hoarse croak came out. "You can tell all that to Sir William tonight."

He paused and then asked, "What have you bought on the Cornish coast?"

Flood's eyes widened in shock.

"Yes. Cornwall. What have you bought there?"

"Nothing."

"Tell me," he said menacingly.

"Just an old estate, falling apart. A bankruptcy case, for sale for years."

"I said, tell me."

"Thrate House."

"Ah." Lord Charles leaned back with a satisfied smile on his face. His hunch had paid off.

"Where is the deed to this Thrate House?"

"I don't know. Upstairs. In my papers."

Lord Charles threw the door open and shouted to a servant to fetch down this gentleman's papers. Soon there was a tap on the door and the servant came in, buried under a load of documents.

"Find it."

Mr. Flood started to protest, but swallowed and fumbled around until he found what he was looking for. Lord Charles directed the servant to return with his master and with paper and writing materials.

When those came he sat for a moment and wrote. He reached into a pocket of his coat and drew out a purse from which he extracted a sovereign. He placed it on the document and shoved them over to Flood. "Read it," he said.

Flood read, and grew apoplectic. "I won't sign that."

Lord Charles handed him the pen, rising so that Flood could sit before the document he had drawn up. Finally Flood sat down and signed. Then Lord Charles and the innkeeper, having read the document, signed as well. Lord Charles sanded it, rolled it, and put it inside his coat. Mr. Flood reluctantly pocketed the sovereign.

"Have you the money you took from the Churchills? Fifty pounds it was, plus, of course, interest, say—one hundred and fifty, as I figure it. Do you have it?"

"Not with me."

Lord Charles eyed him narrowly, and then dashed off another document, which again Mr. Flood signed and the innkeeper witnessed.

245

"That will do."

The innkeeper retired and Lord Charles stood. "Now we shall go to the Churchills and you will give them that draft. Then I shall turn you over to a young man who will be charged with seeing that you enjoy your stay in Wixton, and give you an opportunity to meet Sir William under slightly different circumstances. Whether or not he will want to notify the magistrates—well?" Lord Charles shrugged. "Tomorrow we will set out for London, unless," he added sarcastically, "you have scruples about Sunday traveling.

"Oh, and one more thing. The people you are about to meet and the Churchill women know me as Mr. Florian Fotheringay. There is no Charles de la Marre, no Earl of Leith."

Flood's eyes opened wide as he saw his opportunity. "What makes you think I'll go along with your little game?"

"You will."

Lord Charles looked menacingly down at him and Mr. Flood assured him that Fotheringay was a perfectly acceptable name to him.

It was with great trepidation that the Churchill women awaited Mr. Flood. They were more astonished than afraid when that gentleman, apparently much cowed by Mr. Fotheringay, approached them and handed over a draft for one hundred and fifty pounds, then retreated to a corner while Lord Charles held a brief, whispered conversation with Ned.

Ned emerged from the conference with bright eyes

246

fixed on Flood and Flood slumped before the obvious relish he read in Ned's face. Nothing could appeal more to Ned than being charged with keeping Sylvie's tormenter under lock and key.

Lord Charles bowed to the group. "I am forced to deprive you of Ned's company, for I wish him to keep watch over Mr. Flood, and I think that the Dancing Tides would be the best place for that." Ned seized Flood by the upper arm and urged him toward the door.

Lord Charles continued, "And I must also, I am afraid, take another away from your company. Miss Montcrief, I should like to have a word with you. Perhaps we could walk out-of-doors?"

"But Mr. Fotheringay, surely . . . I . . . Livvy, she has to be put to bed . . ."

"I am sure that between the Churchill ladies, your mother, and Mrs. Woods, Livvy will be well cared for."

"Yes, but . . . I . . . don't wish to walk with you."

"I beg you, Miss Montcrief."

Jane looked up at Mr. Fotheringay and thought that he did not look like a fool or a poseur or a mere scribbler, or any of those things she had been so sure he was. He was overpoweringly handsome and commanding and there was nothing she wanted more in the world than to have him kiss her again.

Something of that nature must have showed in her face for he grinned and said, "I do think we need some fresh air."

Jane, who both feared and hoped for what might happen if they went out to one of those woodland paths, blushed and said, "No."

"Yes."

247

"No."

"Oh, Jenny, can't you do anything right?" Livvy asked with disgust. "He wants to offer for you, can't you tell?"

"Livvy! This is *not* one of your stories. Now hush!" Jane's scolding did nothing to alleviate her mortification.

"Miss Montcrief," a hugely grinning Lord Charles extended his hand. Jane reluctantly took it and rose to follow him.

"Oh, please, Mr. Fotheringay, please," begged Livvy, "please ask for her hand here where I can see. Oh, I've never seen a man offer for a woman. It would be so wonderful, please."

"Livvy, stop your nonsense. Mr. Fotheringay, I understand we have some business . . ."

"Well, come to think of it," Lord Charles said, stroking his jaw, "It might not be such a bad idea."

Before a nearly swooning Jane could stop him, Lord Charles knelt before her and holding her hand, looked with love and warmth into her eyes and said, "Miss Montcrief, would you do me the honor of becoming my wife?"

"Oh, do get up, you look ridiculous."

"Will you?"

"Mr. Fotheringay, please rise."

"Oh, she will, she will," cried Livvy, jumping from the sofa and rushing to them. She seized Jane's right hand and put it in Mr. Fotheringay's. "There, see, you are hand-fasted now. Oh, thank you. Oh, it was so beautiful."

Jane stood gazing at Lord Charles who stood gazing at her. She shook herself. "Impossible girl. Priddy, get her upstairs. Livvy, you do as you are told. I'm going out and will be back to start supper in about five minutes."

She found that her orders were met with grins from everyone and that no one stirred a muscle in response to her officious demands. "Oh," she groaned, and ran wildly out of the house and down the road, leaving Mr. Fotheringay to catch her if he could.

He could.

"I don't want to walk with you," she said, "you understand that, don't you? It was better than staying in that room, making a spectacle of myself, and watching you make a spectacle of yourself, as well."

"I understand," he said gravely.

"Why you have embarrassed me like this I do not understand; I've done nothing to deserve such a thing. I am not coming willingly, you understand that, don't you?"

"Perfectly."

"This is outrageous, to embarrass me before my own family. And this afternoon, calling me a . . . a . . . and then proposing! You are shameless, Mr. Fotheringay, you are a complete and absolute . . ."

"Blackguard?"

"Yes. Blackguard. Exactly. You had no right to embarrass me before my sister. She is young and impressionable, and she will have a difficult time understanding that it was all a hum. And my mother, what will my mother think? Oh, how could you?"

"Marry me."

"And my brother. You had better be careful there, Mr. Fotheringay, because he would just as soon . . . what did you say?"

"I said, Miss Montcrief, will you do me the honor of becoming my wife?"

Jane stood stock-still and looked around. "There is no one here," she said.

"Would you like an audience? I thought the problem with my first offer was that we had too great an audience."

Jane frowned up at him from under scowling brows. "What are you doing?"

"I am asking you to be my wife. I seem to be making a mull of it, but it is absolutely what I am doing. Perhaps you could suggest to me how to do it in a manner you would find favor with."

As Jane continued to stand rigid, less stony, perhaps, but still infinitely wary, Lord Charles tried again.

"Miss Montcrief—Jane, I love you. I have loved you since the first moment I looked into those bedeviling blue eyes of yours. I have loved you even though you have managed to offer me every kind of insult a woman can give a man and not be thrashed for it. I have loved you when you made a cake of yourself over Corydon."

She gasped in indignation.

"Yes, a cake, a veritable cake, and I have loved you when I thought you were the kind of woman who was available to any man who came along. But I especially loved you in a certain spot in the woods under a certain very large oak tree."

Jane looked less doubting, hope breaking out in her face.

"Yes, I love you, I love you, I love you," he said smiling down at her, amused by the play of feeling on her face. "I would kiss you now and prove it, but heaven knows what would happen to me if I tried. So,

Miss Montcrief, I ask you again, will you marry me?"

Jane looked down at her feet. Suddenly all the fight went out of her and she thought that she had loved this man since his first twinkling look at her, and had fought against herself ever since the first moment of their acquaintance. But how could she marry him? He didn't know her, he didn't know . . .

"Please say yes."

"I cannot."

"Why can't you?"

"I don't, you don't . . ."

"I don't what?"

"You don't know me."

"I know you, Jenny. I have watched you through all this fine spring in all kinds of turmoils, and I know you. I would, of course, like to know you better," he added with a wicked smile.

Jane smiled, blushed, and turned away. "It is something very serious."

"Have done with your scruples. I am impatient. I want you for wife, and I shall have you. Now, is it yes or no?"

"It is most certainly no, put like that," said Jane huffily, her eyes blazing with indignation.

Lord Charles fell to his knees. Seizing her hands, he summoned up every drop of pathetic winsomeness and tried again, "Miss Montcrief, please marry me, or I shall die. I shall never be able to eat again, I shall fade away from hunger . . ."

Jane giggled. "You sound like Livvy."

"Then say yes, damn it, woman."

"Yes."

"Ah."

251

He rose and a very long kiss interrupted the conversation.

"But there is something . . ." Jane said, wiggling out of his embrace. "There's something I must tell you."

"I know."

"You could not possibly know," Jane said, sighing heavily. "You may not wish to marry me after I tell you this, and I shall free you from your promise if you wish."

"But I know already, and I want to marry you."

"Don't be nonsensical. Well, the fact is . . ."

"You are Lady Jane Marlingforthe, granddaughter of Ethelbert Marlingforthe of Thrate House, Cornwall."

Jane's mouth gaped.

"Well, am I right?"

She could only stare and make little noises in her throat.

Lord Charles, pleased with himself, asked, "Well, aren't you going to ask me how I figured it out?"

She shook her head dazedly.

"The vase."

"The vase?"

"The vase. The Marlingforthe vase. It is the twin of one *my* grandfather purchased when he went with *your* grandfather to the Orient. I recognized it because I grew up with the matching one. And there was the fact of your brother's name. I know that Edgars and Ethelberts and Ethelreds abound on your family tree."

"But . . . when did you . . . why didn't you . . . we have no money."

"I know," Lord Charles said gently. "I know about your father's struggles. He was a great friend of my mother's, and she has told me about your financial reversals."

"Yes," Jane said, glad to speak of it at last. "We had to sell Thrate House and move. Priddy—she's not my mother—ah, you had figured that out. Well, we thought by coming here and pretending to have money that I might marry a rich man. Do you mind . . . about our being poor, about our deception?"

"No, how could I mind? I have found my true love, so I could not mind."

"You do not find our masquerade tasteless? You don't think that the entire Marlingforthe clan lacks character, decorum?"

"You lack some sense, maybe," he tousled her hair when she drew away in indignation, "but what you lack in sense, you make up for in sheer bravura."

"Is that a compliment? Is that the kind of compliment I can expect in our married life?"

"Your hair is like lank seaweed . . ."

"Oh, stop," she said, giggling.

"Your eyes are like violets."

"No more," she said laughing.

"I didn't think you'd like conventional compliments, although your eyes *are* like violets, the most beautiful . . ."

They looked at each other, besotted.

After a few more kisses Lord Charles held her at arm's length. "Now," he said, knowing this would not be easy, "I have something to tell you. No, do not say a word, just listen. I am not Florian Fotheringay."

"No!" Jane cried, backing away. "No, I cannot take one more of these disclosures. No, but . . . oh, who *are* you then? Napoleon, the Pasha of Turkey, Lord

253

Byron, the man in the moon, Jack Gilpin—"

"Shhh. Be still. I am Charles de la Marre, Earl of Leith."

Jane stared at him as if he were a snake about to bite.

"It is true. You will have to get used to it."

"This is some kind of jest. Our stay in Wixton has been nothing but an elaborate game. I cannot understand . . ." Jane was torn between laughter and tears, not knowing which would predominate.

"I understand. The Churchills do not know my real identity either. I wanted time away from Windmere to have a chance to complete my memoirs—yes, that's another thing," he said testily. "You're going to have to believe that I was a soldier and a damn good one, too. I didn't tell you sooner, in front of your family, because I hoped you would accept plain Mr. Fotheringay. I didn't want you to marry me because I was an earl."

"Well, I like that! De la Marre—Leith," Jane said suddenly. "Wait, I recall . . ."

"Yes, probably from your grandfather or parents. As I said, our grandfathers were good friends."

"Yes, I remember . . . in Kent?"

"Yes."

"Oh. Are you really an earl?"

"Yes."

"Are you rich?" she asked timidly.

"Yes, very, very rich."

"Oh," she sighed. "How wonderful!"

"You are a most mercenary woman."

"Yes, I am, I am. Do you mind? Oh, do marry me. I did accept thinking you were Mr. Fotheringay, you know, and I do love you and I would make a wonderful wife, really I would. I can churn butter as you know, and I can bake bread . . ."

"Those are not exactly the duties of a countess."

"What does a countess do? Oh, I know, she counts! She counts her jewels, her houses, her gowns, her carriages, her . . ."

"You are impossible," and he quieted her by the effective expedient of covering her lips with his own.

"But," she said sadly, "that still leaves me without a groat, well, without many groats. Poor Ned has no prospects and it would seem he loves Sylvie; he will want to marry. We shall all be burdens to you. And *no* one could be rich enough to see to Livvy's wants."

He laughed. "No, Livvy will need special attention, but I think if we take her with us on our bride trip, to Greece, do you think? Italy? Where would you like to go? Vienna?"

"Are you teasing me? We could go . . . oh!" Jane nearly swooned.

"As for Ned," Lord Charles reached into the pocket of his coat and extracted the deed which, Jane read, showed that Thrate House now belonged to Charles de la Marre, Earl of Leith.

"I will give it to Ned when he comes of age. He is twenty, is he not? And I will help him reestablish the estate. You have tin mines, I remember, and I do, as well. If he is willing, he could manage mine in addition to overseeing the restoration of his own. Do you think he would be willing to do that?"

"Oh, Mr. . . . Charles? Charles. Charles. It is a nicer name than Florian. I am so glad you are not named Florian, although perhaps we could name a child Florian, no," she laughed. "I think Ariadne and Florian are out. Yes, Ned would love it above all things. He loves Thrate House. He would enjoy living quietly there with Sylvie, I think, and having something to do to repay your generosity."

"He need not repay my generosity. I will be grateful to have someone I can trust to take some of my responsibilities from my shoulders, so that I may enjoy my bride."

"Ah," she said.

After a moment, he said, "Perhaps Livvy might come with us another time. Let us have our bride trip to ourselves."

"She could stay with Priddy," said Jane, looking up adoringly at him. "But Priddy has no home, now," she added, drawing back in concern.

"Of course she does. She can live with us or with Ned, wherever she might choose. She will always have a home with us."

"Charles. Charles."

"Jenny."

Jane felt the strength of the man she loved pressing urgently against her and felt herself softening against him as though she were water embracing rock. She lifted her face to his, and they kissed in a long, passionate embrace that was renewed until they broke off, dazed, and stared hungrily into each other's eyes.

"You know," Jane said, reaching up and laying a hand on his cheek, "I think I am meant to be happy."

"I think we both are," he replied.

And joyously they kissed again.